'I had a drea

'Pardon?' she was s

He turned and star
It was a pity to wake
a devilish glint in
wondered.

'Who is this true love of yours?'

'Who?' John smiled. 'We have not met yet, Louis. Have you a sweetheart?'

Louise reddened. 'No, *m'sieur.*' She hesitated before saying, 'But last night you spoke a woman's name in your—sleep.'

'Did I?' His expression froze. 'Of course, there have been women in my life.'

'Many?' she could not resist asking.

'I have travelled much and the world is full of women. But every man dreams of one special one,' he said quietly. 'One who would be all things to him—wife, lover, mistress, companion. Do you reckon it is so with women, Louis?'

June Francis was born in Blackpool during the war, but bred in Liverpool. Her father taught her the alphabet from a signwriters' book of lettering, and told her stories from memory; so passing on a love of storytelling. Although she always wanted to write she did not begin until her youngest son started school—greatly encouraged by her husband. She has had many articles published, as well as short stories broadcast, but her first love has always been the historical novel. History has always been a passion with her—due, she says, to an incurable curiosity about the past. Her other interests are walking, cycling and swimming. She has been happily married for over twenty years, and has three sons. The eldest, who is at Oxford studying Classics, also wants to be a writer.

Previous Titles

FATEFUL ENCOUNTER
MY LADY DECEIVER
BELOVED ABDUCTOR

LOVE'S INTRIGUE

June Francis

First published in Great Britain 1991
by Mills & Boon Limited

© June Francis 1991

Australian copyright 1991
Philippine copyright 1991
This edition 1991

ISBN 0 263 77225 X

Masquerade is a trademark published by
Mills & Boon Limited, Eton House,
18–24 Paradise Road, Richmond, Surrey, TW9 1SR.

Set in Times Roman 10 on 11 pt.
04-9104-78697 C

Made and printed in Great Britain

CHAPTER ONE

THE chill breeze from the Channel whipped Louise Saulnier's copper-coloured hair into a tangled curly cap about her head, and she shivered as the wind found the holes in the youth's tattered hose and tunic she wore. Moving into the lee of the casks piled on the quay, she crouched down. Within inches of her hand was the basket from which issued the smell of roasted fowl. Hunger pangs gnawed at her stomach but she tried to ignore them. Her tanned fingers clawed her shorn hair out of her eyes so that she could see clearly the servant from the inn talking to the Englishman in the black houppelande, who had his back to Louise.

There were many English ships and men in the port of Calais, and·it seemed an answer to her prayer that the vessel near at hand should be the one she was seeking. If only she could get aboard, she felt certain that her search would be at an end. She had no desire to sail on the ship so she would have to act fast, because had she not heard the man confirming that it would be sailing in the morning for Dover?

Her hazel eyes darkened as she heard the Englishman speak again, and she listened carefully. He spoke French well despite the inflexion in his voice that betrayed his origins. Now she was certain that it was the same voice that she had heard in the forest during the skirmish with King Henry's men.

A long weary sigh escaped Louise and hunger suddenly made her feel faint. Her hand reached for the knife at her girdle, and, fumbling inside the napkin-covered basket, she hacked at the fowl there. Placing the knife on the cask, she pulled out a leg of chicken coated in sauce, and began to tear at it with small, sharp teeth.

'Thief! Scoundrel!' A hand descended on her shoulder, dragging her upright. 'Steal my master's supper, would you? Take that!' A stinging blow to the ear brought tears to her eyes and the meat fell to the ground.

She struggled violently. 'English dog!' she spat, as her fingers found her knife. She would have plunged it into the servant's chest if her arm had not been quickly seized from behind. She was swung round to face the man in the black houppelande.

Immediately she recognised the lean, weather-beaten face with the dimpled chin, and eyes as brilliantly blue as a southern sky in summer. 'Ravisher! Abductor!' she cried, fury and fear giving her extra strength as she struggled with him. A couple of years living in the open had toughened her muscles and strengthened her will to survive, but she was no match for the Englishman. The knife went spinning from her grasp and her arm was forced up her back. She closed her lips tightly on the cry of pain that issued from her throat.

'Hold fast, lad,' muttered her captor, gazing into her small, dirty face. 'You're as slippery as an eel, and if you don't keep still we'll be finding out if you can swim like one.'

'Let me go, you son of a whore!' Lowering her head, Louise bit his arm. He swore softly and asserted more pressure. A gasp escaped her and her face paled beneath its veneer of dirt.

He slackened his hold but his eyes had hardened and now flashed blue fire. 'You would be wiser holding your tongue, little thief. Otherwise I'll see that it's cut out and fed to the birds.'

'That is behaviour I would expect from the likes of you,' she cried in a trembling voice. 'If I am a thief then it's because the usurper Henry, and men like you, have made me so.'

His finely arched black brows drew together and the lines about his mouth and nose deepened. 'You seem determined, lad, to insult me. I should teach you a lesson.' His grip tightened on her arm.

'Do what you want with me. I fear you not,' she gasped. 'Just tell me where the maid you abducted is.'

He stared at her. 'Lad, I know not what you talk of. You mistake me for someone else.' His tone was so convincing that Louise had a moment of doubt and her hazel eyes scanned the well-defined features of his face. He was not exactly handsome, but there was that about the structure of the bones, the shape of his mouth and the unbelievable blue of his eyes that made her feel peculiarly weak. 'Well?' he demanded. 'Do you realise your mistake?'

Louise tore her gaze from his face, forcing herself to bring to mind the scene in the forest, and to picture the wounded and dying, as well as her young sister's scream as she was thrown unceremoniously over a horse. 'I make no mistake,' she said firmly. 'You were there in the forest.'

The man shook his head. 'I tire of this.'

'But it is true,' she cried, struggling. 'I recognised you because I saw you at Caen where you English pillaged and raped!'

Disbelief flickered in his face and she knew that she had gone too far. He shook his head. 'Now I know that your eyes deceive you and that I should hand you over to the sheriff as a thief and a liar.'

'No!' she exclaimed fearfully, bringing up her free arm and catching him a blow on the cheek. Instantly he twisted her round, swinging her fast before releasing her. She went flying backwards, lost her footing and tumbled into the sea.

Louise's terror was immediate as the waters closed over her head, but she managed to struggle to the surface, spluttering and gasping with the shock of the icy water.

Her feet sought for the bottom but it was out of her reach. Fear chilled her blood and she screamed in panic before sinking below the surface again.

The Englishman swore as he shrugged himself out of his houppelande and kicked off his shoes, to dive into the water. She did not struggle when his fingers took hold of the back of her tunic to hoist her with bursting lungs to the surface. Her hands scrabbled for a hold on his wet doublet and she clung to him.

A rope hit the water close by and, seizing it swiftly before it could sink, he dragged it with some difficulty beneath her armpits. As he knotted it at her chest, he paused, his fingers exploring the swell of her breasts. He glanced quickly into her wet, frightened face and tightened the knot before shouting to his manservant.

Within minutes Louise was sitting on the quayside, retching and coughing up sea water. She was utterly wretched as she watched her rescuer being hauled from the sea. He stood, staring at her, water forming a pool about his feet. Then he said something in English to his servant, who frowned, and said, 'Are you sure, now, Master John?' He nodded and the man shook his head before taking the basket, and hurrying up the gangplank into the ship.

John spoke rapidly to the Frenchman with whom he had been conversing earlier, and the man nodded and walked away. Then he turned his attention once more to Louise. 'I suggest that you get up and come with me— else you will catch a chill and die in this weather.'

Louise lifted scared eyes to his face; her teeth were chattering so much that she could not speak, so she simply shook her head.

He frowned and hurried over to her. Without any preamble he pulled her upright. She struggled as he lifted her into his arms. 'I don't want to come with you,' she managed to stutter. 'Put me down at once!'

He ignored her request and she was too cold to put up much of a fight as he carried her aboard the *Grace*, not setting her down until he reached his cabin. His servant was there, delving into a chest and bringing out clean, dry garments and towels. At a nod from his master he scuttled out. Louise lunged for the door but John closed it quickly and faced her. She clenched both fists. 'Let me out,' she stammered. 'You have no right to keep me here.'

His eyes passed over her, and he said seriously, 'If you prefer I could still hand you over to the sheriff.' She made no reply, but her fear was a tightness in her chest. He continued to stare at her a moment longer before adding, 'But perhaps it would be better for you if you rid yourself of those rags you wear.' He picked up one of the towels and threw it at her. Automatically she caught it, but she made no move to use it, wondering if he had guessed her secret. For a moment in the water they had been very close, and she had no doubts as to what this man would do to her if he knew her to be a woman. 'Well, boy?' he said, starting to unfasten his doublet. 'Are you so fond of your rags?'

'They are all I have and I prefer to keep them on,' she muttered.

'Don't be a fool,' he murmured. 'We are both wet, cold and hungry, so give me no arguments.' He placed an armful of garments on the bunk behind her. 'For you,' he informed, before starting to strip off his hose.

Louise stood, torn by indecision, shivering uncontrollably as she stared at him, her hatred of his race a flame within her breast. Then as he stood in front of her, almost naked, the dark hairs on his chest matted and wet, she hurriedly averted her gaze. A hot blush darkened her cheeks. In another life she had been the protected, cosseted daughter of a clothier of some substance: that had been before the English had taken Caen by storm. It had been her father who had chopped off her hair and had her dressed in the garments of a prentice. She had departed the city with her virginity intact, unlike many, including her friend Clotilde.

She dared a surreptitious glance in the direction of his feet, noting the strength in the muscles of his calves, but her eyes lifted no further as he spoke. 'Well, lad, what's the delay?' There was the slightest touch of sarcasm in his voice. 'Is it that your hands are cold and you need help with your fastenings?'

His bare feet shifted and Louise's pulses jumped. 'No!' she cried, and, as quickly as she could, she presented her back to him.

The minutes seemed long as she peeled off her sodden clothing and she was fearful of his coming over to her. Her teeth chattered as she rubbed herself scantily with the towel. Then it was on with a fine cream linen shirt, before forcing buttons through holes in a sage-green woollen doublet. It fitted her so snugly that it could have been made for her. She was tall for a woman but the Englishman was large and she wondered fleetingly to whom the doublet belonged. Then with a swiftness that almost proved her undoing—he half turned as she tripped over her feet—she managed to pull on a pair of slops and russet hose. Only when she faced him did she agonise over the shortness of the doublet she wore.

The intentness of his gaze caused her to snatch up the coney-fur-trimmed ochre-coloured cloak that lay on the bed and wrap it about her before she dared to look at him again.

'The clothes belonged to one of my Irish nephews, who uses this ship occasionally to transport horses to Genoa,' he informed. 'He has grown since he last wore those but they fit you well.' There was a gleam in his eyes that caused her fear to surface again, and his next words proved of little comfort. 'Thomas will soon be back with my supper and we can eat.'

'But I don't want to stay here,' she said hurriedly. 'Please—let me go.'

Both his eyebrows rose. 'Why such haste, lad? I thought you hungry.' Her expression stiffened and she pressed her lips tightly together, considering that he was playing some game with her. His voice was soft when he added, 'Perhaps I can draw you on another matter that you seem keen to talk about—me in the role of abductor, thief and rapist. Tell me more about this.'

'Of what use would it be?' she said, just as softly as he. 'You would only deny it again.'

His face stilled. 'You are very sure you have seen me, then. When was it last, lad?'

'At Caen.' She frowned. 'I can't understand how you arrived before me, and why. Because you appeared to be saying goodbye to the man who had my sister in his keeping.'

'Your sister?'

'Marguerite.' Suddenly her control slipped and anxiety showed in her face, and, although she hated pleading with him, she implored, 'Please, sir, surely you must know if she is on this ship? If she is then will you let me see her?'

'There is no Marguerite on this ship.' His keen gaze did not leave her slender face as he pulled on his black houppelande, which reached down to his calves and had a high, rolled neck and long full sleeves. 'But you obviously believe me party to her abduction.'

'You were there in the forest some short distance from Caen,' she repeated positively.

'How long ago?'

She glanced at him and her anger spurted up. 'Why do you ask me when you know how long ago it was?' she said scornfully. 'You English really do like playing japes.'

His eyes narrowed. 'I play no jape,' he said harshly. 'Refresh my memory, lad.'

His tone was so convincing that if she had not seen
him with her own eyes then she would have believed it
was she who was in the wrong. 'You fought with Pierre,
our leader, and slashed him across the hand. I make no
mistake about that, *m'sieur*.' Her eyes smouldered. 'I
had not forgotten you from the storming of Caen, you
see. The memory of what happened then is vivid in my
mind still.' There was a silence and for a moment he just
stared over her shoulder at the wooden wall behind her,
until at last he spoke.

'The siege at Caen and the slaughter afterwards—I do
remember it being said in Bruges——' He broke off as
there came a knock on the door. 'Come in,' he called.

Thomas entered, carrying a tray on which was placed
the chicken minus a leg. There was a loaf and cheese,
and two steaming pewter tankards, as well as two plates,
two napkins, one knife. Such a mouth-watering aroma
filled the cabin that Louise's mind was immediately
emptied of all thought but that of food. Without realising
she did so, she moistened her lips.

John, noticing it, subdued the emotions her words had
caused, and pulled himself together. 'Can you put aside
your dispute with me long enough to sup?' he asked in
a rasping voice. She looked at him but made no reply
and he signalled Thomas, who was collecting the wet
garments, to leave. With a frown still knitting his brows,
John set about cutting two thick slices of bread, placing
one on each plate. Then he dissected the chicken, dividing
it equally on to the bread, before pouring gravy over
both. He then held out a plate to her.

Her hand hovered over the rim and her gaze flew to
his face. 'You are not hungry?' he murmured.

'I have not eaten for two days,' she said stiffly.

'Then eat slowly,' he advised, thrusting the plate into
her outstretched hand. For a moment longer she stared
at him, remembering suddenly how he had dived into
the sea to save her. One of the English methods of getting

rid of unwanted prisoners was to tie them up and throw them into a river. Why had he not left her to drown? Her fingers tightened on the plate. 'Sit down and eat,' he ordered. 'I'm not going to harm you.'

She nodded and looked about her. There was only the chest, which he now seated himself upon, a pail in the corner, or the bunks. She was nervous of sitting on a bed. Yet, mindful that he thought her a boy, she did so. Her fingers reached for a piece of chicken, and she carried it to her trembling mouth. Her tongue savoured the rich wine sauce spiced with ginger and garlic, and her eyes closed in ecstasy as she sucked flesh from the bone. For a while neither of them spoke.

He broke the silence, having decided that he could hardly expect the whole truth from her, just as she would not have the truth from him. 'Tell me what happened to you in Caen. Were you beaten?'

Louise glanced at him quickly, then away. With the back of her hand she wiped gravy from her rounded chin. 'Why do you ask?'

His gaze ran over her. 'When a man is accused of a crime he likes to try and prove his innocence. Is it that you were hurt?'

'A clout on the head,' she said roughly, keeping her eyes on the floor. 'But I counted myself lucky that I escaped with that.'

He felt a certain amount of relief. 'Then why do you hurl accusations at me?' he pressed. 'Did I hurt your sister—or a member of your family?'

She shook her head abruptly. 'I had a friend. We were together. You knocked me senseless but you... took... her. Clotilde was beautiful. I heard you say so.' Her eyes darkened and she sat up wearily. 'Marguerite,' she muttered. 'The man who took her—you must know which ship he sails on?'

'Not so fast,' he said quietly. 'The sum of your accusation is that I am supposed to have clouted you and raped your friend?'

A sharp laugh escaped her. 'You count the loss of a woman's virginity of little importance?' He said nothing and she continued. 'But what I mentioned was of little account compared to the rest of what happened that day. On that dreadful day when the lower town fell, your King Henry had cried "Havoc!" after having slaughtered a great number of the citizens of the new part of the town. And that slaughter was only stopped because he saw a babe still sucking at its murdered mother's breast,' she said in a seething voice. 'Surely you must have had a part in the greater crime of murdering innocents!' She put her plate down abruptly. 'I hope you feel remorse for such acts. But if you do not, then you only add to your sins by lying about the abduction of my sister—she is only twelve, as you must have realised. An orphan who has seen much suffering, as I have.'

He continued to stare at her, his face expressionless, but there was a whiteness about his mouth as he wiped his plate carefully with another slice of bread. 'How came you to be in the forest—you and your sister?'

She was amazed at the lack of emotion in his voice. 'We lived there,' she cried, her tongue stumbling over the words. 'Have you forgotten how many of us were driven out of Caen? My father's house was burnt to the ground during the bombardment from your king's guns. It was set alight by one of the balls filled with flaming tow that came over the walls.'

'And your father, was he killed?' he said quietly.

She shook her head slowly, and her eyelids drooped. For days she had been travelling, cold and hungry. Now warmth and food were working to relax her body, although she sought to keep her wits about her. 'He died last winter, the privation proving too much for his strength,' she murmured. 'We had tried to settle in Vernon but due to the terror your king had caused in the hearts of so many it was filled with refugees. There famine and pestilence broke out so we had to flee.' She closed her eyes. 'I wish you would stop asking me questions and tell me where to find the man who took Marguerite.' Her voice was fretful.

Almost that of a child, thought John. 'I don't know where he is.' The words were barely audible but they caused her eyelids to fly wide.

'But you must,' she cried, forcing herself to sit the straighter.

'I don't,' His eyes were clouded as he picked up one of the tankards. 'But I don't suppose it's beyond my capabilities to find out.' He took a deep draught of the mulled ale. 'How was it that your search for your sister brought you from Caen to Calais?'

'I followed the men at a safe distance.'

'But you lost them?'

She nodded wearily.

He was silent a moment, then he took the other cup and crossed the cabin towards her, only to have her shrink away from him. 'Don't be foolish, lad,' he muttered, seizing one of her hands and pressing her fingers about the handle of the tankard. 'Drink.' A moment she hesitated then obediently she did as ordered, and took a mouthful of the mulled ale. He said pensively, 'I presume that you had no companion on the journey?' She stared at him and he saw the fear in her face. 'There is no need for you to be frightened of me.' His voice was almost a caress.

'You are English—a rapist and abductor, for all you would deny it,' she said dully. 'I have every cause to fear you.'

'Ay, lad. That would be true if I was as black as you've painted every Englishman.'

'They are devils,' she whispered. 'Invincible is how many of my countrymen see them.'

'I am no devil,' he replied. His fingers covered hers as he lifted the cup again. 'Now drink and tell me, afterwards, why you had no friend who would accompany you.'

Her eyes darkened as his gaze held hers above the rim of the pewter vessel. 'Many of our children have been stolen away to be servants in England. Any that would have come with me thought my task hopeless, and tried to persuade me not to follow after her.' She added in a whisper, 'Do you know where Marguerite is to be taken?'

'We will find her,' he said soothingly. 'Drink.'

Louise's throat moved and when she spoke her voice was husky. 'Is it that you wish me to drink because you have put a potion in this ale, *m'sieur*?'

'Such a lack of faith, boy,' he murmured, and took a deep draught from her cup.

She moistened her mouth then drank just as deeply as he, before pushing the tankard away. A long breath issued from between her lips. 'Could we not go and find out about my sister now?'

'No.' He moved away from her to sit on the chest. 'Don't look like that, child. It is far too late in the day to start a search.'

Her lips trembled. 'I am not a child! I am almost nineteen years old. I have taken care of myself and my sister since our father died, and I have been on the road for the last two weeks.'

'All the more reason to rest,' he said roughly. 'I presume that you did not walk all the way?'

'I had a horse.' She struggled against a feeling of lethargy. 'I took it from an English soldier I had to kill.'

His eyebrows rose. 'You killed a man?'

Defiantly she nodded and her eyes suddenly sparkled. 'Will you have me hanged for it? I do not regret killing him. He was a beast and would have——' She stopped abruptly, her heart hammering.

There was a silence and she dared not look at him in case he read the truth in her eyes. She fiddled with one of the buttons on the doublet, half expecting him to punish her for her defiance. So it surprised her when all he said was, 'And where is this horse?'

A nervous laugh tickled her throat. 'He was stolen from me, so that I had to walk.'

'That is why you do not know which ship your sister is on? And when you saw me you believed you had come to the right place?' She nodded. 'You say that you saw me last in Caen?' Again she nodded. 'Your tale is most informative,' he said with a certain amount of grimness about his mouth. 'I believe that it is God who has brought us together.'

She lifted her head and stared at him doubtfully. 'You make a jest of what I say.'

'I make no jest, lad.' He returned her gaze squarely. 'Do you know aught of this man you followed?'

'I presumed he was a wool merchant. Calais is the staple port for the English wool trade and it was obvious that the group he was with was heading for this city.' Her manner was suddenly impatient. 'Why do you ask me? You must have known what he was. I don't doubt that it's possible that my sister is already on her way to England.'

He nodded. 'What were you planning if you did not find her in Calais? Did you plan to smuggle yourself aboard a ship for England?'

'If it was necessary,' she said shortly, folding her arms across her chest.

'And if you were discovered on board ship? What then?'

'I would have worked my passage,' she said confidently. 'I am stronger than I look.'

'Surely.' He smiled, although he wondered how long she thought that she would continue to get away with pretending to be a lad. 'And when you arrived in England, where would you have started your search?'

She hesitated. 'I had not reached that far in my thoughts.'

'No doubt. Do you speak English?'

'A little,' she said reluctantly.

He closed his eyes briefly, expressively. 'You have courage. But England would have proved more dangerous than you realise,' he said softly. 'I see that I am forced to help you.'

Louise's voice contained a note of incredulity. 'But why?'

John returned her stare. 'Let us say that my conscience bothers me—and that I believe God has put you in my way for my reforming,' he said smoothly.

Her look was one of cynicism. 'I wish that I could believe that, *m'sieur.*'

His blue eyes gleamed. 'I will amaze you, lad, by the change in my character. Now finish your drink. It'll help you to sleep.'

'Sleep!' A pulse beat rapidly in her throat as she gazed into his face, and she wondered just how much he saw with eyes of such clarity. 'I cannot sleep here.'

'It's your choice, lad,' he said firmly, draining his drinking vessel. 'How badly do you wish to find your sister?' He put his tankard on the tray. 'I still have business to attend to in Calais, so you might as well take the upper bunk as I'm likely to be out for some time.' Her eyes were uncertain, questioning. 'I won't disturb you when I come in if you are on the top. Be assured, lad, that you are safer in here with me than anywhere else on the ship.'

She spoke without thinking in a low angry voice. 'I don't understand. I had not expected such consideration from an enemy.'

'You should have more faith, lad.' His blue eyes met her hazel ones and his fingers touched the curve of her cheek lightly. Then he had gone.

Louise's hand wandered to her cheek. It seemed such a long time since she had felt such a gentle caress. Pierre had been rather rough when he had discovered that she was not a youth. She shook herself. What should she do? It seemed foolish to trust him. Yet he was the only link to her sister's whereabouts, and he had behaved in a way that hinted at the change in character he had spoken of. Men did repent of their wickedness—sometimes. Still, she would have to be on her guard. She wished that her dagger had not been taken from her. What was she to do?

Her shoulders drooped with weariness and she knew that the chances of finding her sister without help were remote. She drank the rest of the ale, and came to a decision. Placing the tankard on the tray, she climbed on to the top bunk and lay down, pulling the cloak tightly about her. Within minutes she was asleep.

The sound of the door opening woke Louise, and for a moment she lay, instantly alert, wondering where she was. Then the movement of the ship and the sound of waves slapping against the side of the hull caused her eyelids to fly wide.

'God grant you a good morn,' said John, his eyes on a level with hers. For a brief moment their gazes held and she inspected his features carefully, before her defences were erected, and found them attractive. He quirked a dark brow. 'I pray that you have slept well?'

'*Oui, m'sieur.*' Louise's colour was heightened as she sat up, only to bang her head on the beam above. Her head was already aching and her throat sore. She rubbed the spot as realisation hit her and her face paled. 'This ship is moving!'

'Ay. We sailed with the morning tide.'

'Sailed!' She pushed back the cloak, swinging her legs over the bunk, and she would have slid unaided to the floor, but he took hold of her waist between both his hands and helped her down. She pulled away from him, wary of being so close, only to be flung against him as the floor shifted beneath her feet.

'It'll take you a short time to get your sea legs.' Again his arms went round her.

'I have never been to sea before.' Swiftly she wormed herself an arm's length from him.

His hands dropped. 'Not everybody likes it.' He moved away from her. 'Come up on deck and take a look at the sea. It's a fine day, if cold. Don't forget your cloak.'

Louise made no reply, needing to cling to the wooden chest as she stepped unsteadily after him. She was certain that she was not going to like it. As she followed in his wake, the door was torn from her hand by a fresh wind.

A gasp escaped her as she came out on deck to stare up at the billowing yellow sail with the red cross at its centre. Then her gaze moved to reach out over the expanse of sea, restlessly moving as far as the eye could see. Her stomach turned over and she felt the colour drain from her face. 'I'm…not…going…to…like…it,' she said in a faint voice, lurching over to the side, where she was sick. After she had finished retching, the face she presented was so sickly-looking that without saying another word he took her back to his cabin.

His brow was furrowed and his voice concerned when he spoke. 'You're best lying down.' Louise groaned. She felt too ill to argue with him. It seemed unfair to have escaped so many terrors only to die at sea.

The next few days passed in a haze. She was hot and cold by turns, and was barely aware that he kept her well covered. She was conscious of his bringing her drinks, but she ate little. A couple of times she managed to rouse herself and to attempt the passage to the deck, but no sooner was she upright than she wished that she was lying down again. She only prayed that soon they would reach England.

Then one morning Louise woke, feeling better; there was no sound of rushing wind and the ship moved gently as if on calm waters. She looked up at the wooden ceiling, and then carefully sat up. There was no sound of movement from the lower bunk, so she slid awkwardly to the floor.

With slow steps she went towards the door, then, gaining confidence, she hurried to open it, and stepped outside. There was much bustle on deck and she could see a harbour. There were two towers and walls that bore signs of repair. The white cliffs she had thought to see were nowhere in sight. She caught a glimpse of John and moved towards him. 'Is this England?' she asked, her voice sharp with sudden apprehension.

'No,' he said soberly. 'It is Harfleur, and I warn you not to be troublesome.'

Louise, her fear spiralling into fury, flew at him, raining blows on his chest. 'You tricked me! You lied to me,' she cried. 'You said that you would help me find Marguerite!'

'Quiet, you fool. Keep still!' John caught her wrists and swung her up over his shoulder. Then he carried her, cursing him and still struggling, on to English-occupied French territory.

CHAPTER TWO

LOUISE paced the bedchamber floor of the Peacock Inn in Harfleur for the umpteenth time, only pausing when she came to the casement window that overlooked the stable yard below. Tense with angry frustration, she gazed down at John, who was speaking to an ostler. With a great deal of satisfaction she noted the scratches made by her nails on the Englishman's neck. Then she fingered her bruises, and honesty compelled her to admit that she had got off lightly in the circumstances. But it was not over yet. Why had he left her for hours on end, kicking her heels in this room? Where had he been? Why had they come to Harfleur? What was he planning to do with her—this Englishman? Her spirits plummeted and she gazed apprehensively at the large bed that took up most of the chamber. Had he guessed her secret?

Swiftly Louise walked over to the door and tried the latch again but the door did not yield. Her shoulders drooped and she went and sat on the bed, infuriated that her search for her sister should have been brought to such an abrupt halt.

Suddenly she heard footsteps outside and hurriedly she rose from the bed as a key grated in the lock and the door was pushed open.

John entered, smiling. 'Well, we are in luck. I have purchased us a fine horse—although he is not as noble as my Connemara stallion at home in England. Tomorrow we go to Caen.'

'Caen?' She stared at him incredulously. 'But why? I do not wish to go to Caen.' Folding her arms across her breasts, she scowled at him.

His smile faded. 'At the moment your wishes don't count. We go there because it is my will. If that does not please you, then...' He shrugged.

'But what of my sister?' she demanded.

'I have not forgotten her.' A muscle in his cheek tensed and he lowered his gaze so that it did not meet hers. 'I assure you that this journey is absolutely necessary if we are to find your sister.'

'No doubt,' she said tartly, moving away in the direction of the window. She did not believe him. There was something he was not telling her. Perhaps it would be wiser to leave his company. If opportunity came her way then she would climb out of the window. Surely the ground was not as far away as it seemed from up here? There were ships going to England in Harfleur. If he left her alone again then she would take a blanket from the bed and knot it to another blanket, tie that to the bedpost and then climb down. That way the distance to fall would not be so great and she would escape with only a few bruises to add to the ones that he had inflicted.

She was so caught up with the idea that she did not realise that John was behind her until he spoke against her ear. 'If you are considering what I think you are, then I would reconsider.'

'I would not jump out,' she said quickly. Too quickly, she realised as he raised an eyebrow.

'A blanket rope, then?' His voice held an amused note. 'Believe me, there is no need for such ploys. If you wish to quit my company then you are free to do so.'

Louise turned quickly. 'Then why did you push me into this chamber and lock the door?'

'I was angry.' He grimaced as he touched the scratches on his neck. 'There was really no need for such violence.'

A sharp laugh escaped her. 'You—hurt me.'

John shrugged. 'I wouldn't have, if you hadn't attacked me in the way you did. You really must learn to control your temper.'

'*I* need to control *myself*?' She flushed with annoyance. 'How can you speak so after the manner in which you handled me? I could barely believe my eyes when I came out on deck to find the ship here at Harfleur,' she said with some dignity. 'You tricked me and I still don't understand——'

His expression was impatient. 'I would have told you where we were going if you had been in a condition to take it in. But you were ill after your time in the water and were hardly conscious of your surroundings, never mind our destination. But if you do not trust me then you can leave any time you wish. Although I doubt you'll find your sister without my help,' he said silkily. There was a cool glint in his eyes as they ran over her trim figure. 'Now what shall we do to pass the time until the morning?'

The look on his face was such that it caused Louise's heart to beat the swifter, remembering how they had struggled against each other on the ship. Did he have any suspicions at all? 'What do you suggest?' she murmured, slightly breathless.

He smiled unexpectedly. 'Perhaps to promenade would be best.'

'Yes,' she responded quickly as her gaze fluttered quickly over the bed and then about the small chamber. 'Are—are we to spend the night here—in this room?'

He ran a hand through his dark hair, raising it into a crest, and his blue eyes were bland as he murmured, 'I thought you would not object to a comfortable bed, lad, after the bunk.'

'Of course not, but...' She searched for words and found none that would help her out of her predicament.

'There's no need to thank me.' His eyes gleamed with unexpected amusement. 'Maybe later.' He got up and went to the door.

Her thoughts were in turmoil, but after several seconds she hurried after him.

*   *   *

The port of Harfleur was enclosed in polygonal walls, two and a half miles in circumference. It had three gates and the town could only be entered by drawbridges crossing a moat. To the north of the town was the flooded valley of the river Lezarde; to the south and east were marshland. Four years ago, in 1415, the town had surrendered to Henry V and his army. The siege had cost, English and French alike, many lives, but most had died not from feats of arms but from disease and starvation.

All this was in John's thoughts as he walked the busy streets of the port, where English could be heard as often as French. A few years ago he had read a proclamation in York offering houses and cash subsidies to any merchant or artisan who would go and settle in the English-occupied French ports and towns. He had spoken of it to his father, who had shrugged off the information as of little importance, but John had kept it in mind.

Louise was also thinking of the past—of a spring day when she had come to Harfleur with her parents. It had been before Marguerite's birth and her mother's death of childbed fever. Then the banner of St Denis had flown at the town's gate, not the cross of St George.

Patriotic fever heated her blood and she cast a surreptitious glance at the man who walked so close that her shoulder brushed his arm. What was she doing in his company? He was the enemy. How many French people had died here, and at Agincourt, Caen, and more recently at Rouen? What was she thinking of to start to believe that she could trust an Englishman to keep his word? Hadn't he already deceived her? Maybe he did not plan to help her find Marguerite at all for all his fine words. If she took into consideration all that she knew of him, then he was not a man to be trusted at all! Suddenly she was aware of how little attention he seemed to be paying her, and she slowed her pace to see

if he would notice and go on without her. He did not
slacken his stride, and she was away in a flash.

Her sudden swift movement was a mistake because it
drew John's attention. Immediately he was after her. For
several minutes it seemed that she would get away,
because he experienced difficulty forcing his way through
passers-by. Then he shouted, 'Stop, thief!' The ploy
worked beautifully and Louise had a fold of her cloak
seized by a burly citizen and was brought to an abrupt
halt. She whirled and lifted her hand to strike, only to
be sent sprawling by the man's clenched fist.

Louise groaned as she regained consciousness, aware of
an aching jaw. John pressed the folded damp cloth to
her chin, holding it firmly in place. Her eyes flickered
open and she looked up at the shadowy, now familiar
face, so close to her own. 'You really must learn to judge
the strength of your opponent better,' he murmured.

She realised that she was lying on the bed in the inn
and her apprehension surfaced instantly. 'Why did you
chase me? You said I was free to go.' Simultaneously
she tried to sit up and to push his hand away, only to
sway like a drunkard.

'Instinct,' he responded promptly. 'You ran, I gave
chase. There was really no need for any of it. Why did
you run?'

She hesitated, trying to focus on his face. 'I thought
of Harfleur as it was last time I visited it,' she whispered.
'Of Caen, of the defeats that your King Henry has inflicted on us.'

His blue eyes darkened. 'Ah! I understand. I am to
be blamed for King Henry's aspirations—for all the
deaths caused by his ambition to gain the throne of
France,' he rasped. 'Unjust!' He rose from the bed and
moved away.

She forced herself up but her head spun with the effort
and she had to cling to the bedpost. Her gaze followed

him to the shuttered window. 'But you *are* guilty of shedding French blood.'

He turned and looked at her. 'You admitted to killing an Englishman,' he said softly. 'That makes you just as guilty of shedding blood.'

'That was different!' He had startled her and their gazes caught and clashed. 'It was my life or his,' she said forcibly.

His eyes narrowed and when he spoke it was in that silky tone that made her feel uncomfortable. 'I suppose many a soldier would say the same.'

'We do not talk of warfare.' She closed her eyes to shut him out. 'Of equal matched with equal.'

'I'm not attributing blame.' His voice sounded nearer; her eyes opened and she saw that he stood at the foot of the bed. 'I'm sure you did what you had to do. And if every Frenchman did the same then matters would be different in France.'

'What are you implying?'

'Surely France is not without plenty of fighting men?' Again the insidious, silky voice speaking the truth. She was embarrassed and angry.

'You ask me that as if you already know the answer,' she muttered tersely.

'Perhaps I do.' His voice was dispassionate. 'Many of your best men are too busy fighting among themselves. They can't forgive and forget—unite and defeat the common enemy. Your King Charles is mad and his son, the Dauphin, has not the power to bring the two warring factors together.'

She stared at him and her eyes suddenly filled with tears of mortification. 'That must really please you because it makes putting your king on the throne of France easier.' Her voice was taut.

He shrugged. 'Calm yourself, little wildcat. It is of no consequence to me who rules France. All I care about is that Henry's conquests have made the seas safer for

English ships—which is better for trade. I have no
stomach for the crazy dreams of the Plantagenets. For
years they have wasted good money pursuing a war that
in the end they must lose if both countries are to survive.'

There was a silence and her slender face wore a puzzled
frown. 'Then why did you fight in his army? Who are
you? What are you?'

'John Milburn—merchant venturer.' He came and sat
on the bed and she was instantly nervous. His over-
whelmingly male presence seemed a threat when experienced so close. She felt his breath warm her cheek and
out of the corner of her eye watched his mouth form
the words. 'And who are you? What are you? We have
been in each other's company for days and I do not even
know your name.'

She did not blink as the words tumbled from her lips.
'Louis Saulnier.' She inched away from him. 'My father
was a clothier in Caen.'

'A clothier?' He smiled. 'We have much in common—
Louis.' His fingers gently squeezed her shoulders. 'I, too,
sell cloth. Once my father only exported wool to Flanders
but now we have our own weavers, fullers, shearers and
dyers, and King Henry's taxes are not so exorbitant.'

'My father is no longer a clothier in Caen.' Her voice
was barely audible, and she wriggled beneath his hand.

'I know that.' His expression clouded as he released
her and rose from the bed. 'Do you think you could eat
some supper?'

She made no reply, only presenting him with her
profile. Supper, then bed! Apprehension tensed her
stomach and she had an overwhelming desire to burst
into tears. Instantly she was ashamed of such weakness.
'Yes, thank you.' Her voice was firm and she was aware
of his scrutiny.

'The company downstairs is rough.' He moved to the
door. 'I shall have supper brought to us and after that,

if you feel up to it, we shall have a game of draughts. It will help pass the time.'

Louise gave no reply, but her eyes followed him as he left the chamber, noticing that he did not lock her in. For a moment she toyed with the idea of leaving, and she got to her feet and went over to the door, opening it and listening to the babble of voices and singing that came up the stairs. A long breath issued from between her lips. What were the options open to her? To smuggle herself aboard a ship for England with no money and only a few words of the language? To give up her search for her sister and return to the turf and wood hovel in the forest and take up Pierre's offer to be his woman? Or to stay and hope that Master Milburn would eventually do as he had said and take her to England to find Marguerite? It was obvious that she had no choice. She felt certain that there would be a price to pay for staying.

John lowered his goblet as Louise neatly took the last of his crowned counters on the board. 'It seems to me that you have been playing this game much longer than I have.'

Louise grinned. She had felt more at ease since they had begun the game. 'I have played since my mother died,' she said gruffly. 'My father taught me—and he hated being beaten too.'

John raised his eyebrows. 'You are saying that I am a poor loser?' He looked at her, sitting cross-legged on the bed, for all the world as if she were a youth. 'Do you toss dice?'

She shook her head. 'Nor do I play cards. Although I wish I could—but my father refused to teach me, saying they were games of chance. Shall we play again?'

'If you wish.' He drained his goblet, wondering what it had been like for her since her father had died. Had she donned her disguise before or after the storming of

Caen? She must have looked vastly different as a maid. Her mouth, for instance, was much too full and soft for a boy's.

Louise looked at him as she set up the board, and their glances caught. Suddenly she felt unusually self-conscious in her male attire, and she shifted on the bed, sitting back on her heels. 'Why do you return to Caen?' she demanded roughly.

He did not bother with explanations, only saying, 'Do you ever give thought to your own position?'

She gave the board her attention and made her first move. 'Naturally my sister is my greatest concern,' she muttered.

'Naturally,' he said drily. 'What when you find her? Or haven't you thought that far ahead?' He moved his counter to block hers.

Her brows knit as she stared at the board. 'We will return to France.'

'To what? Life under the greenwood? He covered her hand with his. 'Hardly the best kind of life for—a girl.'

She glanced up at him quickly and dragged her fingers free. Her voice went up an octave. 'That is your king's fault!'

'Don't let us start that quarrel again.' He grimaced as he fingered the scratches on his neck. She said nothing, then after several seconds she moved her counter. John determined to beat her and gave the game all his attention.

They played for the next couple of hours, and he won five games and she three. The tallow light flickered low, her eyelids drooped, and she pulled her cloak about her because the room grew more chill. Still she set the board for another game even though her jaw ached, and weariness bowed her shoulders, reluctant to call a halt, knowing then that it would be time for bed.

John stilled her hand 'Enough. The hour grows late and I would have an early start in the morning.'

She watched as he placed the counters neatly in their wooden box. Her heart beat jerkily as board and box were placed on the floor. Then he pulled off his boot. 'You will sleep on the right side.'

'I'll sleep on the floor,' she said hurriedly.

He eased off his other boot and gazed at her from narrowed eyes. 'It is November, lad, and cold. Let us be sensible about this.'

She moistened her lips. 'I have the cloak and I'm accustomed to the ground. This bed is too soft.'

John bounced on the bed. 'Straw,' he murmured. 'Not so soft—but it'll do. You'll sleep on the right and we'll have no nonsense about the floor.' Louise shook her head and backed away from him. For a moment she thought he was going to insist then he shrugged. 'Please yourself. But it is a foolishness on such a frosty night, *boy*, and you are only just recovering from a chill.'

Louise made no answer but took a pillow from the bed and dropped it on the wooden floor. She eased off the boots that had belonged to his nephew, and gave her attention to making herself as comfortable as possible as he got into bed in his hose and shirt. Easing herself down on the floor, she pulled the thick woollen cloak about her.

The tallow light snuffed out suddenly and the darkness was complete. The bed creaked and for a moment she tensed, before curling herself into a ball and dragging a fold of the cloak over her head. She slept.

Louise woke suddenly, aware of pain in her back, frozen feet and a cold nose. She uncurled with some difficulty and sitting up she hunched up her knees and rubbed her feet. It was still black as pitch in the chamber and her spirits plummeted. How long before dawn? Perhaps several hours and likely the cold would keep her awake until then. Lying down again, she wriggled about to find a comfortable position, dragging the pillow this way and that about the floor, until her head came up

against the wooden board of the bed. She stilled and
listened intently, but was relieved to hear the steady
breathing of the man in the bed. After that she had no
idea how long she lay, gradually growing irritable because
he slept and she did not—he was warm and comfortable
and she was not.

Slowly she came to a decision and, creeping on her
belly round the side of the bed opposite to where he lay,
she raised herself up and slid beneath the covers.

Louise did not instantly become warm and fall asleep,
but she lay feeling more snug than on the floor. The bed
was comfortable and some of the pain in her back eased.
She was not relaxed enough to sleep, aware as she was
of John less than a foot away. He filled her mind, his
image stamped upon it as clearly as if he stood before
her, and suddenly she was picturing him not fully clad
but as seen that first time on the ship with a towel
wrapped about his waist. She remembered the broad
chest with its mat of hair, the strong shoulders and the
muscular legs. She had seen men's naked chests and legs
before but now she questioned why the sight of his had
caused unfamiliar sensations to race through her. In truth
she had viewed several men without their clothes,
although she had never looked too long. Instantly she
was ashamed of her thoughts and a prayer rose on her
lips. Automatically she recited all the prayers she had
known since childhood, although she had long questioned why God had allowed such suffering to fall upon
her country. Yet in praying she relaxed and fell asleep.

The second time Louise woke it was to a sense of well-
being, of warmth, but there was a weight on her breasts
and her legs. She froze but the weight did not shift. Did
he still sleep? Unable to bear the suspense of not
knowing, she tentatively reached out a hand, to
encounter his face. Her heart hammered when his nose
twitched beneath her touch and her hand stilled. Then,
though she knew it was foolish, some inner compulsion

caused her fingers to search his features. Still he did not stir and she removed her hand and lay back.

Now her dilemma was whether to chance waking him by removing his hand from her breast and brushing aside his foot. She tried the foot first, only to have him mutter sleepily and to twist his leg about hers in such a way that she could not free herself without a great deal of manipulation. Her movements only served to bring him closer, so that his relaxed body half covered hers and his bristly chin rested against her throat.

She remained motionless a while, only her flurried breathing betraying her inner trepidation. A scream began to build up inside her but she did not give it utterance when, after several counts to ten, he still lay in the same slack position. She allowed more time to pass before trying to free herself by wriggling from beneath him. Indistinctly he murmured a woman's name and his fingers unexpectedly toyed with a button on her doublet; slowly he undid it, and the next button and the next. Then several buttons on her shirt were undone. She held her breath, until she thought that she would burst. She felt powerless to move as his arm went round her beneath the doublet, bringing her closer. His lips brushed her collar-bone, as his fingers stroked the upper curve of her breast, caressed her nipple, and she was amazed at the delightful sensations his touch roused. Her heart beat with heavy strokes as his mouth moved up the line of her throat and lightly kissed her aching jaw. She anticipated his lips covering hers, his body spread over hers, and knew that she should move but seemed paralysed. She began to tremble instead of steeling herself to repulse him. Then suddenly he rolled away from her, freeing a long heavy breath.

Louise shot out of the bed and on to the floor, taking one of the blankets with her. She huddled herself beneath cloak and blanket, conserving the warmth he had created, despising herself for wanting him to continue with his exploration of her body. After all it was likely that he had thought her this Dorothy he had mentioned. Whoever she was. For a moment the thought of him with this woman teased her thoughts, and she hated him, and herself, anew. She only drifted into sleep when a dull grey light filtered into the room.

It was the drip, drip of icy water on her face that caused Louise to gasp and rub at her cheek. She forced her eyes open, only to gaze straight into John's bland blue ones. 'You sleep heavy, lad,' he said. 'Breakfast is here and you must rise.'

She sat up abruptly and was aware of the buttons undone at her throat. Her hand swiftly pulled the edges of the shirt together. 'I'm not hungry!' she said huskily.

'You must still eat.' He put the wet cloth aside, his gaze still on her face. 'I don't want you fainting by the wayside, Louis.'

'I will not faint, *m'sieur*. You insult me,' she said haughtily, assuming as much dignity as she could.

He shrugged. 'Pardon! I thought that after last night we were definitely on friendlier terms.'

Her eyelids flew wide. 'What do you mean, *m'sieur*?' she stammered.

A muscle quivered in his cheek and his eyes were pensive. 'When we played draughts. You forgot to hate me for a while.'

There was a silence as they stared at each other. 'I don't hate you, *m'sieur*. I loathe you, as I do all your race,' she said irritably.

'Ah! We are starting at the beginning again, are we? Foolish boy!' He sauntered over to the window and gazed out. 'I had a dream last night.'

'Pardon?' she was startled into saying.

He turned and stared at her. 'I dreamt of my true love. It was a pity to wake and find my bed empty.' There was a devilish glint in his eyes, and for a moment she wondered. She really did.

'Who is this true love of yours?'

'Who?' He smiled. 'We have not met yet, Louis. Have you a sweetheart?'

Louis reddened. 'No, *m'sieur*.' She hesitated before saying, 'But last night you spoke a woman's name in your—sleep.'

'Did I?' His expression froze. 'Of course, there have been women in my life.'

'Many?' she could not resist asking.

'I have travelled much and the world is full of women. But every man dreams of one special one,' he said quietly. 'One who would be all things to him—wife, lover, mistress, companion. Do you reckon it is so with women, Louis?'

There was a silence; she stared at his upright figure lit by the brightening sky outside, and a peculiar sensation darted through her. She swallowed a sudden tightness in her throat to give a husky chuckle. 'How should I know, M'sieur Milburn? You must have known more women than I have?'

'I thought your having a sister——'

'My sister is too young to be thinking of men,' she said hastily. Then added, with an almost pleading note in her voice, 'You did not despoil her, did you?'

There was a silence and the light in his eyes died. 'I talked of women, lad, not children,' he rasped. 'Perhaps when you know me better your estimation of me will change.' Before she could answer he had moved past her and quit the chamber, leaving Louise feeling as if she was very much in the wrong.

She shook herself, angry that he could make her feel so. Especially after the way he had touched her last night. Did she really believe that he had only been dreaming? Her fingers sought her buttons, quickly fastening them up, then she got out of her makeshift bed.

She washed her face and hands in the basin of cold water on a stand in the corner before pouring herself a cup of ale. She took a sip before cutting a thick slice of bread and cheese. With the food in her hand, she went over to the window and gazed out on frosty roofs turning golden with the sun—to wonder just what this fifth— or was it sixth?—day in the company of the Englishman would bring.

CHAPTER THREE

THE early morning air was noticeably frosty as Louise walked into the stable yard. She pulled the coney-fur-lined hat down over her ears and looked towards where Master Milburn and his servant were talking earnestly at the far end of the yard. She wished that they would hurry and bring their conversation to an end. Now that she had resigned herself to going to Caen she was impatient to be on her way. Perhaps if she was honest then she would have to admit to looking forward to vis-iting the city of her birth. When she had followed after Marguerite there had been little time to take note of any changes made by the English or to see if any of her old neighbours or friends still lived there.

Her hand reached out to the dappled horse already saddled and she stroked its dark mane absently, most of her attention still on the two men. The servant slanted her a glance and then turned back to his master and nodded. Suddenly she was uneasy. A short while ago from the upper window she had seen a boy come into the yard and have a word with Master Milburn. Now she wondered what news he had divulged to cause the Englishman's face to darken. He turned suddenly and came striding swiftly across the yard towards her.

'Louis, my plans have been changed for me.' His voice was low enough for other people in the yard not to hear. 'It seems there have been several attacks on travellers using the road to Caen. There is to be an armed guard but I consider it wiser if you do not come with me.'

'Remain here!' she blurted out. 'But I do not wish to! For I have set my mind on going with you.'

He scrutinised her face carefully, before saying dispassionately, 'I am, of course, delighted that you are desirous to be in my company—but you still do not come with me.'

Louise was surprised at the extent of her dismay and for several seconds she just started at him, while his words penetrated deeper. 'Is it that you think I will be afraid? I am not. I can take care of myself,' she said emphatically.

'I've seen how you take care of yourself,' he said shortly. 'And I don't want to be worrying about you if it comes to a fight.'

A spark of anger gleamed in her eyes and she jutted her chin. 'You don't have to worry about me, M'sieur Milburn.'

'I do if you're riding pillion behind me. You might get in the way of my sword arm.'

'Then get me another horse and return my knife to me,' she said impatiently. 'I'm not afraid of chancing the road. After all, I travelled all the way to Calais alone.'

'Not without incident,' returned John grimly. 'But no doubt *you* do not fear the brigands about Caen, who have robbed, raped and slaughtered. Likely they might be counted among your acquaintances.'

Louise felt as if she had been slapped in the face. Her hand fell to her side and she stepped back from him with an angry movement. 'You insult me, *m'sieur*! If Frenchmen are driven to make such raids on travellers it is because they are desperate. So much of our farmland has been laid waste and the workers have fled in fear because of the same crimes you accuse them of.'

'That may well be so,' he said roughly, as he moved closer to the horse. 'But it is not hunger that causes them to ravish and slit the throat of a merchant's elderly wife, but a desire for revenge! I'm not saying I don't understand such an emotion, but it only creates a vicious circle which means more atrocities on both sides.'

'Of course it does,' she retorted, the colour coming and going in her cheeks. 'And to perform such a deed is cruel. But some of those living in the wild *are* ruffians and petty thieves. They, too, fled when the English advanced and at such times as these they take advantage of the situation and surface like scum on water. But most people living in the wild, while they might resort to stealing, do not kill unless they have to.'

'I take your word for it,' he said impatiently, swinging up into the saddle. 'But that doesn't change matters. You still aren't coming with me.'

'I see!' Her face was flushed with annoyance. 'Our ways part here, then?'

'That isn't necessarily so,' he muttered, glancing at her stiff, outraged figure. 'If you still want my help to find your sister, then I suggest that when the wind rises and veers to the west you go aboard the *Grace*. It will sail along the coast and up the river Orne to Caen. I will leave for England from there.'

His words took her by surprise. 'Why can't you sail with her?' she retorted swiftly.

'Why?' he murmured, having gained control of his anger. 'Because I daren't delay. The person I wish to see might leave the city.'

'I suppose it's business! If you are in such haste then you should have sailed straight to Caen in the first place,' she said annoyedly. 'It seems foolish doing it the way you are. Surely you must have noticed such ships as yours tied up at Caen when last you were there?'

'No,' he said shortly, his mouth setting in a hard line. 'If I had known it was possible I *would* have sailed straight to Caen. But the master of the *Grace* knows little of France's rivers, being more familiar with northern seas. He knew of the river Orne but not that it was navigable so far inland. He discovered it was so from some mariners he was drinking with last night.' He gathered the reins into one hand. 'I have spoken to

Thomas and while he is not . . . responsible . . . for you he
will help you in every way possible if you wish to take
up my offer.'

'I suppose I have no choice,' she said ungraciously,
her frowning gaze meeting his.

'If you wish to find your sister that is so,' he murmured in that silky voice that always spoke the truth and
made her feel discomfited. 'Be content, Louis. You are
to be relieved of my company and for that I thought
you would be grateful.'

'I am transported with delight, *m'sieur*,' she said drily.

A deep chuckle sounded in his throat, causing a slight
smile to crease her face. 'And if I'm killed on the road
I suppose you'll cheer?' he murmured.

'Unlikely.' Her long eyelashes swept down, hiding her
expression from him. 'For how then will I find the man
who knows my sister's whereabouts?'

He laughed shortly. 'Trust me when I say that I have
provided for that and every other eventuality.'

Louise was startled into looking at him. 'What of the
unexpected?'

He kept her waiting for an answer and the air seemed
suddenly vibrant between them. His eyes glinted. 'It's
the unexpected that's the sauce on the dish of life. If
this is adieu, Louis, then I'm glad we met. God grant
you a safe journey, and may your passage be smooth.'
A wave of the hand and he set the horse in motion.

His words surprised Louise and caused her unexpected pleasure. Her pulses raced jerkily as she watched
him go. Then she tore her gaze from his blue-clad figure
to turn it, with some displeasure, on the advancing
Thomas. Remembering their first encounter, she felt
certain that he would thoroughly disapprove of her.

He was a man of middle years, of medium height,
possessing a nondescript face, which at that moment
showed all the signs of his suffering from a fever. His
eyes were red and watery and he was in the process of

wiping his nose on the back of the brown sleeve of his padded jupon as he stopped in front of her.

'Well, lad—lass,' he said hoarsely in English, giving a sniff. 'This is a fine chase you've sent the master on.'

'*Pardon?*' Louise smiled patiently. '*Parlez Français,* Thomas.'

'*Je parle un*...only a bit—er—*m'sieur,*' responded Thomas, his creased face drooping in comical dismay. '*Mon monsieur* forget to *parlez vous* that.'

She stared at him in bewilderment. '*Pardon? Pouvez-vous parler plus lentement, s'il vous plaît?*'

'Pardon it is.' He sneezed and rubbed his nose with the back of his hand, blinking at her mournfully. 'How are we going to do here with you speaking no *Anglais et moi* no *Français,* that's worth mentioning?'

Louise could see some humour in the situation but she was also impatient of it. '*M'sieur Milburn est un imbecile!*'

Thomas's brows bristled. 'Master John's got a lot on his mind,' he said sharply. 'He's no fool—just harassed, trying to do the right thing. So look here! You'll have to learn some *Anglais*!'

'*Anglais?*' she questioned, staring at him down her nose, and folding her arms across her chest. 'No English.'

'*Vous* gonna *parlez Anglais*!' he said determinedly. '*Si vous allez à Angleterre.*'

At that moment Louise had doubts as to whether she would ever get to England, but she nodded and said, '*Ma soeur Marguerite est en Angleterre!*'

Thomas sneezed again, scrubbed at his nose and looked at her with a serious air. '*Ma soeur*—my sister, lass. I *comprends* that. *Votre soeur*—your sister!' he said emphatically, adding, 'Master John told me about her.'

'*Pardon? Ma soeur*—my sister?' Her spirits lifted a little and her hazel eyes twinkled. '*Votre soeur*—your sister.'

Thomas grinned and patted her shoulder. 'Good!
Bon!' He cleared his throat. '*Nous allons à*...the inn.
I could do with a hot drink of ale with some nutmeg
and honey in it. Master John said that if you're staying
then I'm to keep the room on for you at the Peacock.'

Her smile faded and she shrugged. '*Je ne comprends
pas.*'

'Ay, I can see that, lass.' He groaned. 'And we've either
got to find someone who can understand both of us or
give this up.'

'*Pardon?*' demanded Louise impatiently, tapping her
foot on the cobbles. If this went on she would go mad.

Thomas sneezed, and she came to a quick decision,
having no desire to catch his fever after just recovering
from a chill. '*Je vais!*' she declared, walking away.

Thomas quickly seized her arm and spun her round.
'You can't just *allez*,' he muttered with a worried frown.
'But what to do about you, that's the problem,' he added
with an air of uncertainty.

Louise sighed heavily before removing his hand from
her arm. '*Thomas! Je vais!*'

He shook his head at her and then his doubtful
expression lifted and he grinned. 'Right! *Vous allez!*'

'*Oui!*' She flashed him a quick smile. '*Au revoir!*'
Again she moved away but he pulled her back.

'*Attendre!*' Before she could free herself he reached
inside the neck of his jupon and took out a pouch.
'Master John wouldn't like it if I just let you go like
that,' he muttered, taking his hand from her arm so that
he could empty out a heap of coins from the pouch.
'But if I give you the money that I would have spent on
the room at the inn and feeding you then I'm hoping
that should satisfy him.' For a second he appeared
doubtful. Then he shrugged and held out a number of
sous and deniers, as well as pennies and farthings.

Louise stared at him, understanding a little of his actions, but not really wanting to take the money. *'Non.'* She shook her head for good measure.

'Oui!' He took her hand, pressed the coins into her palm and curled her fingers over them. *'Pour pain.'* He stepped back and shrugged and repeated, *'Pour pain.'*

Conflict surged inside her—to accept money from an enemy did not seem right, and really she did not want to accept it, because it made her beholden to him. Yet she would need to buy food. *'Merci!'* Her voice was husky.

He smiled and she smiled, before turning and walking away. She tried to estimate how much money he had given her for bread without being seen to be doing so. English and French money, and it was enough for several weeks by the feel of it. At least she would not starve and the clothes she wore still had a lot of wear in them.

But what to do? She was extremely reluctant to abandon her search for Marguerite, but her exchange with Thomas had shown her better than any argument how difficult it would be to go to England without Master Milburn's help. She supposed that she could stay in Harfleur and take the ship to Caen still, even though Thomas believed her to be leaving. What *was* she to do?

Torn by indecision, Louise trod the narrow streets of Harfleur, hardly feeling the cold because her thoughts were so taken up with her dilemma.

Eventually she found her way to the south-west corner of the town. Two English soldiers huddled by a brazier near the damaged barbican, exchanging desultory conversation in their own tongue. A black-robed monk, riding a donkey, crossed the drawbridge in company with a group of peasants carrying burdens of firewood on their backs. She gazed out on the bleak landscape beyond the moat, and found herself estimating the distance to Caen. Anything would be better than roaming the streets, waiting around the town and wondering whether she would be allowed on the *Grace*.

She hurried past the parish church that had almost been destroyed in the English attack and to a bakery that she had noticed. She had to use English money to buy some bread and a couple of veal pasties with crosses on top, from an English-speaking baker. Here in Harfleur, she realised more than ever before how advanced were King Henry's plans to anglicise Normandy. She placed the food inside her doublet and made her way to the south-west gate. The soldiers took little interest in her and she was soon over the drawbridge.

Louise reckoned that, walking, she could reach Caen some time on the morrow, all going well. As soon as she came to some trees she found herself a suitably heavy stick, balancing it in her hand before setting out again. A few hours walking and she reckoned to be in country that had become as familiar in the last eighteen months as the city of Caen had once been. Only then would she leave the road and cut across country.

She found herself not only thinking of Master Milburn, as she walked, but of the past two years, reviewing the youth's part she had played. It seemed a madness now and she wondered how many other people had known her for a maid, besides Pierre, when she had chopped wood, dug turves, and gone hunting. Yet when they had hunted in groups after boar or deer she had always managed to hold her own and keep up with them. She had been scared at times because there had always been danger in colder weather from prowling wolves, drawn by the smell of the kill. And there had been the chance of meeting up with a hunting party of English— that was what happened when Marguerite had been taken.

Marguerite! She thought of her small sister, who, despite all the hardships they had been through, had never lost her high spirits. It was Marguerite who had

cooked the small game, caught by Louise with home-
made snares and bow and arrows. She baked the black-
birds and thrushes, feathers and all, in clay. Old Marie
had taught her how, just as she had taught Louise the
easiest way to skin a rabbit. Old Marie, almost blind,
had known Louise's secret. It was her voice that had
given her away, said the old woman. She was wise in the
way of herbs and had taught both town girls how to
recognise plants and roots for flavouring and healing.
She had also comforted them when their father had died.
Still life had been harder after his death and would continue to be so if they returned to live in the forest, even
with Pierre's protection. But Louise did not want to think
of what she might have to surrender for such protection,
and instead gave her mind to her journey.

The hours wore away and eventually Louise sat down
in the lee of a hillock. Her feet, in the unaccustomed
boots, were hurting and a blister had burst on her left
heel. She ate one of the pasties and drank sparingly of
icy water from a stream as she viewed the empty road
that passed within twenty feet of the forest spread out
not such a great distance before her. No doubt Master
Milburn would be in Caen by now, having his supper.

Louise made her way to the deserted stretch of road
and limped along it. She was completly unprepared for
the carnage that met her when she rounded the bend.
Her eyes widened in shock as they took in the hacked
bodies in the bloodied grass and beaten earth. Nausea
seized her and for a moment she stood retching, her eyes
tightly shut. Then she forced them open, and, crossing
herself, prayed as she steeled herself to go and look at
the faces of the dead.

Some had been stripped of their clothing and their
private parts had been mutilated. Fingers had been
chopped off and she guessed that rings had been taken.
Not all were mutilated nor were they all English. It had
been a fierce battle and the attackers had not got all

their own way. She widened her search, going into the skirts of the forest, and found there more bodies with arrows piercing throats and chests. One of the men she recognised as belonging to the camp, but of Master Milburn there was no sign.

Louise went further into the trees; it was much darker beneath their cover and she had difficulty at first following the signs left by the attackers in the undergrowth. It would be reasonable to believe that Master Milburn had escaped, because the attackers had taken few horses—if the hoof marks were anything to go by. Compelled by a strong urge she went on, hesitantly at first but swifter as her eyes grew accustomed to the twilight under the trees. Something or someone had been dragged along the ground. It could be a dead horse taken for food, but she could not help thinking that if Pierre had been involved in the raid he might have recognised Master Milburn as the man who had slashed his hand through to the bone, just as she had recognised him immediately in Calais. If that was so and he had managed to capture the Englishman then he might have something other than a quick death in mind for him.

After a while it grew so dark that Louise could not see the trail but it did not matter because she knew where she was going. Soon the moon would be up and on such a clear night would provide some light. Her leg muscles were aching unbearably now and her heel was so sore that she gritted her teeth with every step taken. She began to wonder if her physical strength would give out before she reached her destination.

Still she kept on until at last the trees thinned and she came to a group of crude dwellings of turf and timber. Several fires could be seen and voices heard. Men and a few children huddled near the fires while the women busied themselves with the cooking.

Louise watched a moment, her eyes searching, before making her way round the backs of the hovels until she came to one set a little apart from the others. She listened a moment and then slid round the side and down through the opening into the single chamber scooped out of the ground.

A hunched figure looked up quickly. 'Who's there?' she said hoarsely.

'It is I, Louise Saulnier,' whispered the younger woman. 'I come for information, Madame Marie.'

'Louise, it is really you?' Her hand reached out through the dark and Louise crawled achingly towards her and submitted her face to the woman's searching fingers. Marie made a satisfied noise in her throat. 'Why have you come back?' Her hands dropped and her fingers found her spoon again. 'You have found your sister?'

'No. But I suspect that an Englishman who can help me in my search could be here.'

'An Englishman?' The spoon paused halfway to Marie's mouth. 'Now what do you know about the Englishman?'

'Then there is one here?' There was a hint of dubious excitement in Louise's voice.

'Ay. Matilde tells me that he has hair as black as the devil's soul and eyes as blue as the reflection of a summer sky in the river.'

A long breath escaped Louise and she sat back on her heels. 'It *is* Master Milburn, and I must know where they have put him and what Pierre plans to do to him.'

There was a brief hush and then Marie said, 'The Englishman is no longer here in the settlement.'

Louise's heart seemed to miss a beat. 'He is not already dead? I did not think that Pierre would kill him so swiftly!'

Marie muttered to herself and rocked backwards and forwards. 'Not dead—not yet.'

'Do you know where Pierre has taken him—what he plans to do to him?'

'He has not asked me for any poisonous brew this time, only an amulet and an incantation to ward off evil spirits.'

A chill flashed down Louise's spine but she concealed her sudden fear. 'Then you must know what he plans?' she insisted.

'Wolves.'

'Wolves?' Louise experienced the icy trickle of fear again. 'What of wolves?'

'The Englishman has been taken and staked out for the wolves' feasting. Already there is blood on him. They will smell it and come.'

'Where?' Her hand tightened on her stick.

Marie turned her almost sightless eyes on her. 'You should not go. It is haunted.'

The chilling fear spread. 'For Marguerite's sake tell me quickly!' said Louise in a frantic whisper.

'In the circle.' The old woman's voice was weary.

'May the mother of God bless you!' Louise kissed her hastily and dragged herself up and out into the frosty air.

She waited until she was out of sight of the dwellings and beyond the light of the fires before pulling off the boots and running. The moon was up, enabling her to see any obstacles in her path, although it cast shadows in places and twice she tripped over her cloak and fell.

Her hope was that Pierre would have already left the stone circle after the staking out. He was as fearful of the souls of the dead as any of them in the settlement.

By the time most of the trees were cleared and the hill was in sight she was gulping for breath and there was a stitch in her side. Then she saw Pierre and two other men coming out from between the stones and instantly she dropped to the ground and rolled into a patch of shadow. As she lay with her face buried in her arms, a wolf bayed. Sweet Jesu! The words were thought rather

than whispered, a whisper carrying on such a night. She
stayed perfectly still.

It seemed a long time between the next howl and the
barely audible tread of the three men. She had guessed
that they would not stay in the vicinity long in case the
wolves caught their scent. In the morning they would
return to see the results of their night's work.

Waiting for the men to get further away was difficult,
knowing that she would have to act soon and swiftly.
At last she could hear nothing and, getting to her feet,
she ran desperately up the hill. She came to a halt outside
the circle where pagan rites of sacrifice had once been
performed. Her fear was like an iron hand about her
heart. Slowly stepping round one of the standing stones,
she crossed herself and sent up a quick prayer. Then she
saw Master Milburn, completely naked, stretched out
on the ground.

She drew a quick breath and stopped abruptly. Slowly
his head lifted, and for several seconds they looked at
each other. Then he groaned and his head dropped back.

A series of howls sounding on the air galvanised her
into action, and as she crossed the grass her fingers were
loosening the brooch that fastened the cloak, so that
when he lay at her feet she was able to swirl it down
over his nakedness.

As she knelt on the grass to inspect the leather strips
that tied his wrists and ankles to stakes in the ground,
his eyelids fluttered open. '*Mam'selle*, how do you come
to be here?' he muttered.

She stilled, taken by surprise. Then, 'Quiet,' she said
in a low voice, darting a glance at his bloodied face. His
head moved slightly as if in acknowledgement and his
eyelids drooped.

As her fingers worked to loosen the knots they brushed
his cold skin, and she wondered if he might die despite
all her efforts, and anxiety replaced her embarrassment,
and fear of wolves and spirits.

It took Louise some time to free him and she broke several nails. His wrists and ankles were chafed and as bloodied as his face when at last she sat back on her heels, but he still lay motionless on the ground. She lifted one of his hands and rubbed it. 'Master Milburn, you must get up. We have to get out of this place.' He made no answer. 'Master Milburn,' she repeated urgently, dropping his hand and seizing his shoulders. 'Master Milburn!' She shook him hard. 'You must wake.' A low groan issued from his lips and his eyelashes flickered but did not open. 'Master Milburn! John! The wolves are coming and we must go!'

Slowly, as if it needed a tremendous effort, his eyelids opened. 'Help me—get up.' The words were barely audible, but they were enough to spur Louise on. She got an arm beneath his naked back, noting as she did so the cuts and abrasions on his shoulders and upper arms. Managing to lift him into a sitting position, she dragged the cloak under his armpits and pulled it right round him. Then, rising a little on to one knee, she lifted his arm about her neck and heaved.

He came up gradually, his feet scrabbling for a hold on the frost-covered grass—until at last, heavily leaning upon her, he stood. 'Good,' she gasped. 'Now with more effort we might get out of here.'

He nodded painfully. 'But—to where?'

'Up a tree?'

A noise that sounded like an attempt at a laugh barely stirred the chill air and she looked sidelong at the cut and swollen face so near hers. 'You don't have to walk far to reach the trees,' said Louise. 'It's our only chance! Besides, moving will warm you up.'

'True.' He lifted his cut cheek from her head. 'Later, I will ask questions as to how you got here,' he said jerkily, with a glimmer of a smile.

'Walk,' she said severely, 'and don't trip over the cloak.'

'Or drop it,' he murmured. 'I would not embarrass you further, *mam'selle*.' Louise made no response to that remark but a swift glance showed that he had a fold of the cloak wrapped about one hand against his chest.

It did not take so very long to reach the trees. Then she saw the glimmer of amber eyes in the gloom a short distance away and her heart seemed to leap into her throat with fright.

John had seen them too, so there was no need for her to mutter 'haste'. Besides, his blood had begun to circulate the swifter, warming his body and easing the stiffness in his limbs. He removed her arm from about his shoulder and pushed her towards the nearest large-branching tree. She needed no urging and despite sore feet she climbed swiftly and with agility as high as was necessary. He followed more slowly and painfully, and his feet caught in the cloak a couple of times. At last he eased himself up on a thick branch near the main trunk opposite and a little below the one she stood on.

They were not a moment too soon, as several wolves loped on to ground which they had trodden not many minutes ago. They snuffled in the grass, and a couple jostled to lick at a dark stain. One, with its nose to the ground, followed the trail out through the trees, up the hill and into the stone circle. The others wandered about, yelping, until one found its way to their tree.

Louise, peering down through the bare branches, saw the wolf place its front paws on the tree trunk and snuffle and lick before beginning to bark. She jumped and clutched at a branch. John, who had been resting his head against the trunk on the other side, opened his eyes. He was able to make out her face. 'Come closer,' he breathed.

'I can't,' she whispered, afraid to let go of the branch or move in case she fell. John carefully reached up and round the trunk. The wolf continued to bark and was joined by another. She began to tremble and her cold hands to lose their grip. Then John's arms went about her waist and his fingers hooked on to her belt.

'I have hold of you,' he said through gritted teeth. 'You can let go.'

With difficulty he managed to ease them both on to his branch and she sagged against him. Her head sank on to his bare shoulder and for several minutes neither of them moved or spoke. Then she shifted her head and her cheek felt the chill on his skin. 'How cold you are,' she stammered.

'And you,' he said unsteadily.

'Not as much as you.' She flushed even as she spoke, remembering the sight of him in the circle. 'If the wolves do not get us, then the cold will surely finish us off.'

'We can try and keep each other warm,' muttered John, slackening the grip he had on the cloak. He eased it free of constriction and Louise was forced to sit upright. Her heart steadily increased its beat, for although she did not look at him directly she was aware of him lifting the garment high above his shoulders so that it hooded his head, and enfolded her as well.

Neither of them spoke as they shuffled closer. His arm round her shoulders held her tightly. Closing her eyes seemed to make inching her arm around his waist easier. She was conscious of broken skin on his back. He winced as her fingers gently explored the extent of his wounds but he made no complaint. Where he was not hurt but only cold she rubbed him, and his body felt warmer to her touch. Her other hand roamed over his chest, fingered and pulled at nipples there, wondering why men had them when they did not feed babies. He trembled and she wondered if he liked being touched there just as she had last night. Was it only last night? Her fingers stilled in an awful awareness of what she doing. Then he took her hand and placed it on the chilled skin of his hip. She rubbed vigorously down to the curve of his damp buttocks. How long and hard were the muscles there.

Her mind opened on the picture of him naked and her hand stilled again. Her cheek rested against his bare chest and she could hear the increased heavy thud of his heart.

She jumped when his fingers touched her throat just as they had last night and she lifted her head. His cool lips found hers unerringly in the warm damp darkness beneath the cloak. His mouth moved almost hungrily over hers, rousing within her overwhelming uncomprehensible desires. He loosened her buttons and tore her shirt open. Her pulses raced crazily as his chest brushed her breasts, rubbed against them slowly before they were squashed as he brought her hard against him.

His tongue forced her lips apart and entered her mouth, teasing her tongue, sending thrills through her. She had never experienced anything quite like it—had warded Pierre off with a knife when he had ventured to touch her thigh. This man seemed to be demanding the very essence of her being and in that moment she could not have denied him. All thought of his being an enemy was forgotten as was the sinfulness of what they were doing. They could die this night and she needed and wanted him.

His fingertips rubbed her breast, caressing her nipple, pulling at it, and then he lowered his mouth and suckled it. A moan of pleasure escaped her, and her hand, which had stilled, restarted its stroking, warming his chill loins and tentatively, curiously, running her fingers up the source of his masculinity. It grew beneath her touch and he groaned and, taking her hand, he placed her fingers firmly round it and whispered encouragement as she caressed it. Then he reached inside her hose and stroked her belly, reaching lower and lower, and exploring inside her secret place, rousing her to a fever pitch of enjoyment and a need for his deeper exploration.

His lips found hers again and their kisses were as feverish as their actions. They swayed perilously on the branch, heedless of their danger—from falling or the wolves—as they pleasured each other. Caught up in each other's arms they overbalanced and crashed through the branches to the ground.

CHAPTER FOUR

LOUISE, more than a little dazed at being brought down to earth so abruptly, struggled to rise even as John did, and they both came up together, entangled in the cloak as they were. Fortunately they had not fallen far and had landed in a heap of dead leaves, and, but for a few bruises and having the breath knocked out of them, were unharmed. The wolves had gone, although they could still hear howling and barking.

They looked at each other and shamed embarrassment caused her cheeks to pinken. She had had no idea that men and women could give pleasure to each other just by kissing and being close, and caressing their secret places. What must he think of her? She loosened her hold of the cloak and stepped away from him.

'May I have your belt?' His voice was quiet.

Louise unfastened it and handed it to him. He girdled it about the cloak, but did it so that the opening was to his right side and he had an arm free. 'What now?' he said, easing his shoulders in a way that revealed that they caused him pain. 'I presume you know your way about this forest, *mam'selle*?'

She nodded and relief flooded through her because he did not refer to what had happened. 'I can take you to Caen.'

'Good. The sooner we move the better. We might be warm now but we'll cool down if we stay still.'

Her colour rose again at the thought of how they had warmed each other. She cleared her throat. 'What of the wolves?'

The muscles in his face tightened. 'I don't doubt that they have found easier eating on the road.'

Immediately she realised what he meant and a shiver passed through her.

'Try not to think about it,' he said roughly. 'And button yourself up or you'll be chilled.' A faint, tired smile tugged at his mouth.

Instantly that smile infuriated her as she realised that the front of her shirt and doublet were wide open. What had she been thinking of to allow him to take such liberties and to return them? She turned her back on him and fastened and tucked in her shirt, still feeling slightly light-headed. Adjusting her doublet, her fingers suddenly found, halfway round her back, the pasty and loaf that she had placed inside her doublet. The pasty was crumbling and the loaf had been flattened, but as she pulled them out she realised just how hungry she was.

Facing John, she said stiffly, 'I have some food.'

'You think of everything to comfort a man,' he said quietly, watching the colour flood her cheeks as he tore off part of the loaf she proffered. What was she—an innocent or a wanton? He was uncertain. 'Where did you get this food and how did you get here?'

'Later I will tell you,' responded Louise, squaring her shoulders and tilting her chin. 'Best we keep quiet. It's unlikely that Pierre is still around, but——'

'Pierre is their leader?'

She nodded. 'You have met before and he nearly lost a hand.'

His brows drew together. 'That would explain why he was so determined to make me suffer a little before putting an end to my life,' he said lightly, biting a chunk out of his bread and beginning to walk. 'He considered it amusing to tie me naked to a horse and have me dragged along the ground.'

'Oh!' She involuntarily glanced down at him. 'That— that must have been—painful.'

'I managed to turn myself around a few times so that certain places did not get damaged too much.'

She blushed, guessing at what he referred to. They both fell silent and did not speak for a while, their own thoughts keeping them company. Wearily they forced their stiff limbs to keep on moving. Eventually they came out on to the road, a couple of miles or so further on from where the attack had taken place. There was a huddle of boulders several yards from the road, giving some kind of shelter from the elements, and without saying anything they both came to a halt. Louise dragged herself up from the frozen ground and on to one of the boulders. She hunched her knees and dropped her head on her folded arms.

John joined her on the rock, which was in the lee of a higher one, and tucked the hem of the cloak under his cold feet. 'I'm glad that you didn't stay at Harfleur,' he murmured, 'but why didn't you?'

She told him in a voice slurring with tiredness, adding, 'I almost wish I had stayed there now. Because—maybe Pierre will find us after all, *and* he will kill me as well as you, and what will happen to my sister then? At the least if he learns of this night's work he would not allow Marguerite and me under his roof when we get back from England.'

'There is something between you and this man?' he rasped.

She lifted her head and looked at him, then wished she had not because the blue eyes were regarding her with a great deal of annoyance. 'He would have me be his woman,' she said with some dignity.

'You have not lain with him already?' he demanded.

'No,' she said coldly. 'Not that it is any of your business, *m'sieur*.'

'Isn't it?' he said softly. 'It seems foolish for me to help you, if all you are going to come back to is life in the greenwood with a cut-throat brigand.'

Louise's eyes flashed. 'He is a patriot! And will fight to the last drop of his blood.'

'Whose blood?' John countered grimly, wincing as his back brushed against the rock. 'I vow that he has killed more innocents than I have. Besides, what can he offer you that's worth having? I can offer you more.'

'You!' For a moment she could not think what else to say. Then, 'I would not take anything from you, for surely you will want something in return.' She folded her arms across her breasts and her eyes smouldered.

'I presume you think that I'll want you.' He frowned at her. 'You flatter yourself, *mam'selle*. But anything I could give you would be ten times better than life in that miserable settlement with a man who fears spirits more than God.'

His words touched a nerve. 'You know nothing about him,' she snapped. 'And a hovel, living with him, would be preferable to living in a castle with you.'

There was a brief silence before John said in a weary voice, 'I don't live in a castle, but I could see you safely settled in a house with your sister. I could find you work. You will not even be bothered much with my company. I am not so often in England.'

She stared at him, not sure exactly what he was suggesting. She was not blind to her position. No man of means would wish to take her for wife. But if it was what he hinted at, then really she knew that she should be more affronted than she was, because of what *he* was, but she was not and that shocked her. 'You really believe that I would wish to live in England?' Her voice shook. 'I *hate* the English.'

'It would be a damn sight more comfortable—and safer—than living under a tree,' he mocked. 'And maybe sometimes, if you got over your seasickness, I could take you journeying with me—perhaps to Danzig in the north. Or to Bruges—surely, if your father was a clothier, you've visited Bruges?'

Louise did not answer because his words had made her furiously upset, bringing back memories that still had the power to hurt. For a moment she allowed herself to dwell on old times, remembering the great fair at Bruges and a particular length of lemon silk, brought overland by the Venetians, that her father had purchased. She had made an undergown and embroidered it with tiny white flowers. How she wished now that she had one such gown and that her hair was down her back. Then she would show this Englishman that she was worthy of being some man's wife and not his whore!

'You do not fancy Bruges? Or Danzig?' John's insidious voice broke into her thoughts. 'You really would rather share a hovel with that murdering brigand?'

'He is a fellow countryman,' she said tersely.

His smile did not quite reach his eyes. 'And I am the enemy. I'm glad that I didn't fool myself into believing that you came to my rescue for any other reason than because you needed me to find your sister. Even so I can't believe that you find me utterly distasteful.'

Louise could have hit him. 'You have no sense of delicacy,' she muttered. 'You were cold and it was your suggestion that we—we kept each other warm.'

His blue eyes gleamed. 'I'm cold now. So are you.'

'Don't touch me,' she said hurriedly, wishing he would not look at her in such a way that it did strange things to her heart.

He raised his eyebrows. 'You are safe. I have taken a vow of chastity not to bed a wench until I have fulfilled a quest.'

'You—have taken a vow?' A mocking laugh escaped her. 'You surprise me, *m'sieur.*'

He smiled. 'Almost I forgot it—if we had not been up a tree then I...' He left the sentence unfinished and his eyes closed as he leaned back against the rock.

'You seem to forget it very easily,' she said unsteadily. 'How long have you known I was a maid?'

'Almost from the moment we met,' he said dispassionately. 'But I did not let it bother me, and I considered that you would be happier thinking I still thought you a lad.'

'How did I betray myself?'

'You felt different in the water.'

Anger showed in her face and she crossed her arms defensively across her breasts. 'You touched me—before I even knew you. How dared you?'

His lips twitched. 'I could hardly rescue you without touching you.'

'No. But…' She scowled at him and dropped her voice, saying awkwardly, 'You make it sound different from ordinary touching.'

'It was hardly that different,' he said, almost apologetically. 'You didn't even notice.' Not looking at her, he added in a murmur, 'Not like before.'

She reddened. 'I—I thought we were going to die.'

'In that case you would have surely been wiser to have confessed your sins and prayed for absolution?' he mocked.

Louise had not thought of that and was mortified, and furious, because she could not think of anything to say in answer, and was relieved when he straightened up with some difficulty and said, 'Perhaps we should continue, however slow the pace?'

'Ay.' A long weary breath escaped her and she eased herself to the edge of the rock and slid to the ground. 'Pierre——'

'Might find us yet,' he finished. 'And neither of us wants that at this moment if we are to find your sister.'

Louise made no answer, only forcing already stiffening muscles to work. Finding Marguerite was uppermost in her mind once again and now she worried about having antagonised John and whether he might change his mind about helping her. She would have been wiser holding her tongue.

They trudged on. Dawn came and the wind seemed
less cold. Louise did not remember falling asleep on her
feet and John almost despaired of them both surviving
the night then. He managed to keep her going by half
dragging her. Then he saw a ruined hamlet and roused
her. They stumbled up the slope towards the tumbledown
buildings. Most of the houses had been razed to the
ground, but an ancient stone barn had defied all at-
tempts to destroy it. Inside it was less cold and there was
a heap of straw in a distant corner from the door. They
collapsed into it, not caring whether there was vermin.
Louise went instantly to sleep but John paused to cover
them with a warm layer of straw. Then he, too, slept.

It was the sound of voices, indistinct but near, that
woke Louise. She looked down at John, and was taken
aback by the bruising and swelling on his face. A moment
she stared at him, distressed, then she shook him awake,
keeping a hand over his mouth as she did so. He was
instantly alert, and, removing her hand but keeping hold
of it, helped her to her feet.

She almost cried with pain as they limped their way
over to the door. They stood behind it, listening. Then
John let out a long breath. 'They're English.' Opening
the door, he went out into a damp grey day. Louise, her
face set, followed slowly and stood, leaning, against the
wall of the barn.

Several men, wearing padded jupons, chainmail hoods
and flat steel helmets, broke away from the group and
came towards John. One had a pike at the ready.

'God grant you a good morn,' called John, raising a
hand in greeting as they approached.

'It's gone noon, mate, and you've been in the wars
by the look of you,' said the one with a pike, staring at
him curiously. 'And what's that you be wearing?' He
grinned unexpectedly.

'You catch me at a disadvantage.' John smiled
lopsidedly in response to the man's obvious amusement.

'We were attacked on the road and barely escaped with our lives.'

The man's face darkened. 'Several men reached the city last night with the news. And Sir John Popham has sent us out in search of the thieving, murdering swine.'

'I'm glad to hear it. You'll find signs of their slaughter a few miles back,' said John, regretting that he could not help them further than that. He had no positive information to the brigands' whereabouts. 'Do you think there's any chance of a horse to get us back to Caen?'

The man pursed his lips and shook his head. 'Most of us are foot soldiers; only Sir Edmund and several of the archers are mounted. But you should be safe walking from here and it's not that far.'

John thanked him and beckoned to Louise. She walked awkwardly over to him, avoiding the soldiers and doing her best to disguise her feelings. 'Well, *m'sieur*?' she muttered. 'What help?'

'None,' he said briefly. 'But we haven't got far to go.'

'That I knew already,' she said stiffly. 'Let us get away from this place.'

They went, hungry, thirsty and footsore, and it was not too long before they saw Caen ahead with the towers of its white-walled donjon showing on its hill. What appeared at first sight to be hundreds of church spires pierced the grey sky. Outside the walls stood the great Abbaye-aux-Dames, where William the Conqueror's wife Matilde lay, and where Henry V had set up some of his cannons.

Despite their aches and pains and weariness, their pace quickened as they drew nearer. Now could be seen the gleam of the river Orne, which encircled the lower, newer town, the Ile St Jean. The two parts of Caen were joined by a bridge spanning one of the arms of the Orne, which was guarded by the fort of St Pierre.

The riverside was busy, the *quais* thronged with people. Cargoes were being loaded and unloaded. There were vats of wine, and bales of cloth in oilskin wrapping, as well as chunks of the same white stone used in the building of the castle. They kept the wooden cranes occupied, swinging back and forth from ship to shore.

John was aware of the curious, sometimes pitying or smiling glances as they were jostled. He turned to Louise, who was gazing about her with differing expressions flitting across her face. 'The *Grace* might not be here for some days, and I must have some clothes.'

She turned her hazel eyes on him. 'Then it makes sense not to dawdle but to go to your house immediately.'

He agreed with the barest of hesitations, and allowed her to go a little ahead of him. She turned on to the bridge past clusters of beggars, and they forced their way along in company with tradesmen, priests, liveried officials and housewives, careful to avoid the rumbling, heavily loaded, metal-rimmed-wheeled wains.

They went along streets where shop owners cried the merits of their wares. There were tailors working in the front rooms of their homes, and shoemakers hammering pieces of leather into shape on lasts. And, to Louise's annoyance, on every side could be heard the English tongue.

A pieman rang a bell, while he balanced a tray on his head. John signalled him and she purchased a couple of bacon pies.

They ate hungrily, walking slowly up a street of tall houses with casement windows and steep, tiled roofs. Here and there gaps showed in the rows, proof of the battering that the lower town had received during the siege two years ago.

Stopping before one such space filled with rank grass and weeds and littered with broken wood, bits of plaster and stone, Louise said in a voice tight with strain, 'This was my home two years ago.'

He glanced at her slender, suddenly pale features. 'Would you live in Caen again?'

She gave him a startled look. 'You jest, *m'sieur*! It would mean accepting your king's rule. Impossible!' She turned from him, limping round a corner and up another street.

John grimaced, and followed her. From several directions came the clack of looms and he gazed about him with interest. Women stood in some of the doorways, distaffs in hands, spinning. Halfway down the street he halted before a black front door. He did not hesitate but raised a fist and hammered on the door. The sound echoed through the house but nobody came to answer it. He knocked again.

Louise returned to his side and stepped back to take a better look at the house. Lifting her eyes she saw the figure of a woman at an upper window. For a few seconds they stared at each other before the woman drew back into the shadows.

Frowning, Louise said, 'Try again. There is someone upstairs.'

John obeyed but it seemed a long time before footsteps sounded inside, and the door was opened.

A woman stood before them, clad in a crimson houppelande over a rose-coloured undergown. Her dark hair was smooth and looped up about her ears, and on her head she wore a crisp white head-dress. She winced as she looked at John. 'Pardon? Can I do anything for you?'

Before John could speak, Louise said 'Clotilde?' She could hardly believe her eyes.

The woman flashed her a swift glance, inspecting her briefly. 'You know me, *m'sieur*?'

'It is I, Louise Saulnier!'

The woman's mouth fell open and for several seconds no sound came out, then she squeaked, 'After all this time—I don't believe it!'

'Pardon!' John's sharp voice drew her attention swiftly. 'May we come in?'

She looked at him again. *'Mon chér?'* she asked in a faltering voice. 'But what has happened to you?'

'We were attacked,' he answered, and immediately she was all solicitude, placing her plump white hands on his bare arm. 'Come in! Come in! But what a terrible thing to happen. Where did it take place? My dearest, your face, it is unrecognisable! And you are filthy! And where are your clothes?' While she was speaking, John was being hauled inside a room where a wood fire burned cheerfully in a large fireplace. She urged him into a carved oak chair and put a cushion to the back of his head. 'Your poor feet—where are your shoes? *Mon dieu!* You should not have gone down to the *quai* alone. Did you fall in with thieves? Tell me immediately!' Before he could answer she had rushed away and was bringing back a pitcher and a goblet.

Louise stood indecisively just inside the door, watching a smile come over John's face as he stretched his legs towards the fire. Clotilde was pouring out wine and bewailing the damage to his face. Warring emotions fought inside Louise's breast. Seeing her old friend had given her a severe shock, for it was obvious to her that Clotilde was on very friendly terms with Master Milburn. How could she behave in such a way? And Master Milburn! He was lapping up her attention like a cat when it got at the cream. Almost she had forgotten that he had admired Clotilde and raped her at the storming of Caen. Now it seemed the pair of them had set up home together. Was he married to Clotilde—or was she his mistress? She could not ask, and neither of them were taking any notice of her! Tears pricked the back of her eyes. Probably Master Milburn had a string of mistresses in different ports! She pressed her hands against her eyes. She would not cry! Not over a whoring Englishman!

Turning swiftly on her heel, Louise walked out of the house. She wandered about the streets trying to empty her mind of all thought, but it was not easy. She was cold and tired and her feet were very sore and she wished heartily that she had never met John Milburn.

She wandered down to the *quais* to watch the ships being loaded, and, although she doubted that the *Grace* could have arrived, limped along the waterfront, looking at the names of the vessels. She stopped to admire the figurehead and the fine carvings on the *Christopher* of Hull.

It was just as she was turning away that she heard Master Milburn's voice. Instantly she whirled round and saw him, standing on the deck. Hardly able to believe that he could have changed so quickly and come down to the *quai*, she could not take her eyes from his now clean face and tidy figure in a damson doublet and red hose.

He suddenly seemed to become aware of her stare and looked straight at her, unspeaking. Then he presented her with his back and carried on with his conversation.

'M'sieur Milburn!' The name burst from her.

Slowly he turned and faced her, and the cool blue eyes ran over her dishevelled appearance. 'I think you make a mistake, lad,' he said in English.

'Parlez Français,' she demanded. 'How did you get here so quickly, and your—face...' She paused and realised the truth.

'My face?' he asked in French. 'What is wrong with my face?'

'It is nothing.' Her voice was harsh. Why couldn't Master Milburn have told her that he had a double? She turned and walked away.

'Hey!' he called. 'Wait a moment!'

But Louise did not want to wait—did not want to talk to the man who was party to her sister's abduction. She began to run, but he caught up with her and swung her round. 'What is this, boy?'

She wrenched her arm out of his hold and backed away from him. 'I made a mistake!' And she would have walked away again.

'Not so fast!' His hand shot out to seize her wrist and his blue eyes gazed intently into hers. 'You spoke a name that I know and seem to believe that we are acquainted.'

'A mistake, *m'sieur*, as I told you. I thought you were someone else.' She attempted to free herself but he held on.

'A mistake? Ay,' he murmured softly, sounding extremely like Master Milburn. 'But perhaps it can easily be rectified. This man so like me—you have seen him recently?' He spoke the last few words with a sudden sense of urgency.

Her eyes ran over his features, reluctantly marvelling at the similarity to John. 'Yes,' she muttered. 'He is here in Caen and I think that he has been looking for you.'

He freed a long breath. 'You know where he is?'

She nodded coolly. 'You are kin to Master Milburn?'

A smile lifted the corners of his mouth. 'You could say that. Take me to him.'

'No.' She came to a quick decision. 'But I tell you that you will find him in Clotilde's house.'

'Thank you.' He frowned down at her as he released her. 'Haven't we met before?'

'We have not been introduced,' she said stiffly, moving away from him.

He followed, gazing intently at the profile presented to him. 'But we have met and you weren't so well clad—although even now your clothes look a little the worse for wear.' A flush darkened her cheeks but she had no intention of satisfying his curiosity. 'I hazard that it was not a friendly encounter,' he pressed.

Still she remained silent and tried to walk a little faster, but her muscles refused this time to exert themselves.

'If you know Clotilde—then you must be a citizen of
Caen?' he questioned. 'Where have I met you? And how
is it that you know my brother?'

Louise could not resist a swift glance and a smile lit
his face. 'Now here's a mystery. You know my brother.
Where did you meet and how?'

'Calais!' she said roughly, realising that there was little
to be gained by not talking. 'My sister was taken during
a skirmish in the forest a few weeks ago. And I thought
your brother was you.'

'Not so fast.' His forehead was knit in concentration.
'You've missed a lot out—but let's leave it for now. Just
tell me—my brother realised pretty swiftly your mistake
and so he came looking for me?'

She slowed her pace, and her eyes darkened. 'He said
something about my being mistaken, but never told me
that he had a brother.' Her voice was strained when she
added, 'That is the reason, I suppose, why he said he
would help me.'

'Help you? What's this, boy? Why should you need
my brother's aid?'

'Because you were party to my sister's abduction a
few weeks ago.' She scowled. 'He said he would help me
find her but he insisted on coming to Caen first,' she
said fiercely. 'Now I know why, and also the reason for
his not knowing the name of the man who has
Marguerite.'

'Marguerite?' Realisation flickered in his face. 'A
young girl?' He returned Louise's regard without any
sign of discomfiture. 'And John said he would help you?'
A smile twisted his mouth. 'That's my brother. He'd
help a lame dog jump through a hoop.'

Louise's expression hardened. 'I am not a lame dog!
Nor do I need your brother's pity. If you could just tell
me the name of the man who took her,' she rasped.

His brows drew together in a familiar fashion. 'What
good would it do you, lad? Best forget your sister. She's

better off in England than living the way she was.' He quickened his pace.

She hurried to catch up with him. 'I don't believe that is true,' she said angrily. 'You must tell me!'

'Must?' He shook his head. 'You might have persuaded John to help you, but I never do anything unless I want to.'

Louise's temper flared. 'Have you no conscience, *m'sieur*? No heart? Think of the child that my sister is, alone in a foreign land. You are all that I called him! A thieving, ravishing abductor!'

His stride faltered and a smile flickered over his face. 'And what did my brother say to that?'

'What does it matter what he said?' she said impatiently.

A laugh escaped him. 'Sweet Jesu! I would have enjoyed seeing his face when you said all that! Respectable! That's John! And he never believes in using violence unless there's no other way. It was the devil's own work trying to get him to hit back when we were lads. You must have made him really mad.' He gazed at her with interest.

'I do not find this situation amusing, *m'sieur*,' she said through gritted teeth. 'Your brother has some virtues, it seems. But it appears that you possess none of them.'

'Ay! John is a much better man than I,' he said lightly. They came to the house and his eyes narrowed. 'How did you know where to find me? Was it Clotilde who sent you to the *quai*?'

'No!' she exclaimed. 'She had her hands full looking after your brother—so I . . . just left.'

His eyebrows rose sharply, but he said no more, only opening the door and going inside. She hesitated, before, with a great deal of reluctance, following him.

There was nobody in the room but, as the door closed behind them, footsteps sounded overhead and several moments later Clotilde came through a door to the rear of the parlour. Warm colour was in her cheeks and her eyes sparkled. She stopped abruptly. 'Harry! Your brother is here, so there will be no need for you to try and get to England.'

He interrupted her ruthlessly. 'The lad told me. Where have you put Jack?'

'The lad?' Clotilde's face was suddenly abrim with amusement. 'You do not know that this...so trim...young man is a girl? Or that she has no liking for you, *mon chér*? Not only are you English but you knocked her senseless at the Fall.'

Harry turned swiftly to Louise. 'Does my brother know you are a girl?' His voice showed a lively interest.

'Of course,' she said icily.

His eyes sparkled. 'His sense of propriety must have found that a challenge. Are you a virgin?'

Louise felt the hot colour run up under her skin and she said fiercely, 'I suggest, *m'sieur*, that you keep your nose out of my affairs and go and see your brother!'

He grinned. 'Now does that mean ay or nay?' He turned to Clotilde and a nerve twitched near his mouth. 'Where have you put him?'

She lowered her eyes. 'I thought you would want him to have the best, *mon chér*, so I put him in our bed.' She toyed with the pomander at her waist. 'His voice so like yours, Harry, and the blue of his eyes. But such bravery—the quick jest even when I knew that I was hurting him. He has many cuts and bruises. Although he was a little hesitant about letting me see the full extent of them.'

Harry swore softly but did not delay any longer. Within seconds they heard his feet on the stairs.

Clotilde turned her attention to Louise, and her smile faded. 'He said that you saved his life! I would never have believed it of you, my dear friend. You! Who hated the English! But I'm sure you had your reasons...' She paused expectantly.

Louise was not only angry but exhausted. 'May I sit down?'

'But certainly.' Clotilde shrugged and sat in the chair vacated by John. Louise took a stool and held out her hands to the fire.

'He is a finely made man, of course,' said Clotilde, pushing a great handful of starched veil from her shoulders. 'I do not blame you for accepting his protection.'

'I did not seek his protection,' muttered Louise. 'I did not know that he knew I was a woman till yesterday. He said that he would help me find Marguerite. Today I have discovered that he never knew where she was but used the information I gave him to come to Caen in search of his brother.'

'He has explained to me,' said Clotilde, 'how he was certain that it was Harry from your reaction to him, and that he had lost touch with him several years ago.'

Louise's anger flared again. 'He could have told me about his brother—but he kept me in the dark!'

Compassion flickered across Clotilde's face. 'Perhaps he thought that you would not believe him. Even I, who know Harry intimately, marvel at how alike their voices and eyes are. Whether their faces are so alike——'

'They are,' Louise murmured, gazing into the flames, as it struck her anew that he was innocent of the crimes that she had accused him of. 'He should have told me,' she muttered.

Clotilde laughed merrily. 'Does it matter? I cannot get over it—you saving his life. You, who once said that the only good Englishman is a dead one!'

'I had to save his life,' she countered defensively. 'I have explained. But no doubt now he'll change his mind about taking me to England. His brother is not in favour of it!' She lifted her eyes to her old friend and was suddenly hesitant. 'I did not expect to see you here. At the storming——'

'I know,' interrupted Clotilde, frowning. 'So Harry raped me that day, but at least he allowed no other to touch me, and he did not discard me. Almost two years I have kept house for him, and I think I have made him happy.' She gnawed at her lower lip and played with her pomander. 'Although there have been times when I have feared,' she added slowly, 'that eventually I will lose him. He longs for England and yesterday he swore that his brother was in danger and that he must find a way to get home.'

'How strange,' said Louise in a stilted voice. 'Master Milburn was in danger.'

'I know.' Her mouth trembled. 'But he is out of danger now, and I am hoping that seeing his brother safe might make Harry settle again. He has tried to leave before, saying he will return, but I don't know if I believe him. Fortunately it is not easy for him to go. Their king has made it difficult—all must have passports, and none can leave without his licence, which is hard to obtain.'

'But you believe that he will try?' said Louise softly.

She was silent, tapping a dainty red-leather-clad foot on the rush strewn floor. Her lips firmed. 'Yes,' she said quietly. 'But I would find a way to stop him.'

They stared at each other. Then Clotilde laughed unexpectedly, tilted her head on one side and scrutinised Louise's appearance. 'You must tell me what has been happening to you. And I must find you some clothes.' She hummed a light air, and, getting up, she went over to a great oak chest near the far whitewashed wall.

Louise did not follow her. Almost asleep, she gazed into the fire, picturing Clotilde's face as she talked of Master Milburn's brother, and in that moment she vowed never to care for a man so much that she could not face life without him. Annoyingly John came into her thoughts, only for her to angrily dismiss him. The sooner he was out of her life the better!

CHAPTER FIVE

JOHN was sitting on a four-poster bed, fastening up one
of Harry's doublets, when the door opened. He looked
up quickly, and relief lightened his damaged features as
his brother entered. For a moment neither of them spoke.
Then Harry swore softly under his breath before moving
swiftly over to the bed. 'I knew something had happened
to you. That youth, or maid, who found me at the
quai . . .' he gave his brother a searching look ' . . . hinted
at you being in something of a mess.' He clapped him
on the shoulders.

John winced. 'Go easy, brother.' His voice was rough.

'Sorry.' Harry grimaced. 'What happened?'

John told him his story from the moment he had met
Louise in Calais, omitting certain happenings. 'It's been
a long search.' He surveyed Harry keenly. 'I was
borrowing some of your clothes—your arms are still
shorter than mine, brother—to end it. That wench of
yours said something about your trying to get a ship to
England.'

A rueful smile twisted Harry's face. 'Not so easy as
you would think. You wouldn't believe the stranglehold
that the King has over Normandy. He doesn't want
anybody deserting the great cause.'

'That bad?' John frowned. 'How did you go over to
his side in the first place? I know our family have always
had links with the Lancasters but when this Henry's
father killed King Richard it changed things somewhat.'

'It's a long story,' said Henry in clipped tones. 'How
have things been with you? How's dear Dorothy and my
godson?'

'Dear Dorothy is well as far as I know. I am seldom in England.' John's voice lacked emotion. 'As for Peter, he is apprenticed to a wool merchant in Burford. I did not consider it fair to remove him from his mother's care completely.'

A muscle throbbed in Harry's neck. 'Have you heard any news of Dykemore in the last year?'

'I have seen him but once in the last eighteen months or so, and that was in Burford when I was there on business, and he was in Dorothy's company.' His face darkened. 'He would still interfere in my affairs, and is still active in his search for Lollards. But never mind what's been happening to me! What about you? Five years, it's been. Mother's fretted. Even though I have been able to reassure her as to your safety.' Puffed and bruised blue eyes questioned blue.

'You still get those feelings too?' said Harry sharply, wriggling his shoulders. 'They're damned uncomfortable.'

'And inconvenient,' murmured John. 'I was in the Baltics when I last knew you in deep trouble two or three years ago and lost a customer or two in my haste to get home.'

Harry perched on the bed, and stared down at his hands. 'I went to Glyn Dwr. You know well how little love the Welsh have for Henry of Lancaster. But Oldcastle was there and it was the same thing all over again. Get rid of the Usurper—put the rightful heir on the throne. And what was the outcome this time but betrayal by the heir himself? March just doesn't have the stomach for a fight to gain what's rightfully his.' He laughed bitterly. 'Grey and Scrope lost their heads. I tell you, John, that it was then that I wondered why I was involved in it all!'

'So you went over to Henry of Lancaster's side?'

Harry shook his head. 'Not immediately. I suppose it was when the news of his victory at Agincourt reached us that I began to have doubts about risking my life for a cause I was no longer certain would win the day. It really seemed that God was on Henry's side. It was like a miracle when he beat the French—David against Goliath! Of course since then I've learnt a few things about that battle, and it appears that half the French just drowned in mud. Too heavily armed and too many of them to manoeuvre properly in terrible weather conditions. But going back—I stuck it out in Wales for a while—then Oldcastle was captured and several of us with him.'

John's mouth tightened. 'So that was what happened to you. It was bad.'

'They roasted Oldcastle alive.' Harry's voice was expressionless but his eyes were stormy. 'And I had a visit from Dykemore.' John's head jerked back but he said nothing, waiting for his brother to continue. 'He brought along the good friar Nester, because, as you know...he can cause such exquisite pain with hot pincers.'

A muscle twitched in John's neck. 'What happened?'

'Fortunately the King was short of men for his wars. We prisoners were offered a free pardon if we joined Henry's host. I was a fair archer—so I told the sergeant. And somehow I managed to prove it to him, despite these!' He held up his hand and John saw now the couple of scarred fingers with the nails removed. 'I had to recant, of course,' continued Harry in a light tone, not looking at John, 'and no doubt the good friar was disappointed, as was our friend Dykemore. They doubted my sincerity, as well they might. But the sergeant had no interest in doctrine and religious squabbles and so he won the day.'

He laughed. 'Sweet Jesu, if only I'd known what I was in for. The King is so determined to have his own way, and is utterly ruthless. Yet the men love him. He's a damn good soldier, although they made no mistake when they called Henry the Prince of Priests. He sets up altars wherever he conquers and it's believed that he's taken a vow of chastity—that he won't sleep with a woman until he weds the princess Catherine.'

John smiled grimly. 'I made a similar vow, which is ended now I've found you.'

Harry cast him a quick look. 'So that girl downstairs——'

'I have not taken her. She could be a virgin.' He smiled slightly. 'She remembers you from Caen.'

'I know that now.' Harry rested his head against the bedpost and closed his eyes. 'I still smell and hear the horror of that day sometimes. The gutters ran with blood, but at the time I didn't take it in. It was as if it were happening to someone else. The French burnt one of our men to death, almost in front of me, smothering him with burning straw. You know how I feel about the flames. That made me really mad so that I had no mind for mercy when we entered the city. I led the way with a man called Ingles and took his name afterwards. My bravery was noted and I was awarded a house in the city.' He smiled wryly. 'I had gathered a few treasures here and there, so I applied myself to being a clothier. It's strange, isn't it? I didn't want to be involved in the trade at all when it was what father wanted, but now I find I like living in a town rather than on the manor. Still...' He was silent a moment before adding, 'How are Mother and Father?'

'Wishing you would come home. Five years is a long time to not know where your son is.'

Harry nodded, and his chin quivered slightly. 'I wanted to go home, John. Often!' he said unevenly. 'But after Father and I quarrelled——'

John interrupted ruthlessly. 'That is the past! Mother and Father would be overjoyed to see you. I await the *Grace*'s coming. You can sail with us.'

Harry was silent a moment, then said slowly, 'It won't be easy. All ships are checked and my face is known.' He stared at his brother. 'It's fortunate that at the moment you don't look like me. Otherwise you might have trouble. I tried today to get passage on a ship going to York, but without permission from the King's officials it's going to be difficult.'

'Perhaps not as difficult as you think,' said John softly. 'I find it useful to travel under more than one name at times. I have several sets of papers.'

Harry's expression relaxed slightly. 'It might work.' He paused. 'What of the lass below? Do you really intend taking her to England?' There was a note in his voice that caused John to frown.

'If it weren't for Mam'selle Saulnier I might never have found you,' he rasped. 'She saved my life and I gave her my promise.'

Harry's eyes narrowed and he tapped a nail against his teeth. 'To find this sister of your wench, you would have to go to Kent.'

'Where?'

'I've sent her to Wat Fuller and his missus. They lost their daughter and were bemoaning their lack when last I was there. You know how they need every pair of hands they can get.'

John started. 'If you'd been caught, Dykemore would have found some excuse to have you strung up and to light a fire to toast your toes. Accept that Cobtree was the price Father had to pay for our freedom. We have lost that manor for good.'

Harry's eyes sparked. 'I don't know how you can talk like that. You always held Cobtree dear. It was your favourite place. And even I was content there.'

'You didn't act contented.' A slight laugh escaped John. 'You turned him down and got caught up in some wild venture.'

'Which you tried to save me from—and we both ended up in trouble.' Harry grimaced.

John shrugged. 'It's behind us now. And if we are honest, brother, we might have escaped if I had not been Father's obedient son.'

Harry frowned. 'Dorothy?' He rubbed his chin. 'You were the elder. One of us had to act in a responsible manner. But that still doesn't make it any safer for you to go to Cobtree.'

'I'm going.' John twisted a button absently. 'We'll sail to Dover and you can go on ahead with Thomas to Yorkshire. Best if one of us gets there as swiftly as possible. Consider, Harry; soon it will be the Christmas feast. Imagine Mother's delight.'

Harry stared at him pensively. 'Never mind painting joyful scenes for me, Jack. I don't like what you're doing. This Mam'selle Saulnier—what kind of wench is she, to be going about dressed as a youth?'

'Don't try to dissuade me, Harry,' said John, his mouth tightening. 'And don't interfere! I've given my word. I will not go back on it.'

'Fool,' said Harry in a hard voice. 'Do you trust this *mademoiselle* not to stick a knife in your back? Has Dorothy not taught you that women can't be trusted? Clotilde said that she hates the English.'

'The *mam'selle* needs my help. I'll make sure that there are no daggers handy when we're alone.' He stretched himself out on the bed and closed his eyes.

Harry got up. 'How long since you've had a woman? You say you took a vow.'

'Mind your own business,' said John shortly. 'I presume the fair Clotilde is your mistress?'

'You presume right.' He smiled wryly. 'Dammit, John! She counts herself lucky that I've set her up comfortably.'

'If you say so.' John twisted his head and stared at him thoughtfully. 'Where is Mam'selle Saulnier?'

'Downstairs with Clotilde. She looked none too happy. I do believe that, despite my telling her that you were respectable, her opinion of both of us isn't high.'

A smile lurked about John's mouth as he pulled a blanket over him. 'She pretends to loathe me.'

Harry's brows shot up. 'Pretends?'

John got beneath the covers and closed his eyes. 'She could do with some rest. Is there another room? Another bed?'

'Then there is nothing between you?'

John yawned again. 'She needs rest, I said.'

'You're mad! Have her and get her out of your system, then leave her here with Clotilde.'

There came an indistinct murmur from the bed and for a moment Harry continued to stare at his twin's battered face. Really! Sometimes his brother needed protecting from himself! He turned and went thoughtfully down the stairs.

As he entered the parlour Louise and Clotilde lifted their heads from the depths of an enormous chest. Heaps of clothing were piled on the chair and cushioned settle. There were linen chemises, and long-sleeved, full-skirted corsets with tight-fitting laced bodices, woollen, samite and Venetian cotton houppelandes and surcotes—some heavily embroidered, others dagged round the edges of sleeves and hems. There were reds, blues, greens and saffrons. Louise had not enquired where such finery had come from, but the words 'spoils of war' had occurred to her.

'What are all these out for?' demanded Harry, fingering a heavy silky samite houppelande in pale green.

'Louise has need of something different to wear, so I am searching for one of my old gowns that might fit her,' informed Clotilde quietly. 'That one will not fit her.'

'Nonsense,' retorted Harry, smiling at Louise. 'You've gone fatter. This would be fine. This green will suit her colouring perfectly.'

'But—that gown is one of my favourites!' said Clotilde in a trembling voice. 'It is hardly suitable for her needs, Harry.'

He nodded. 'Perhaps you're right. Something warm and sensible, that's the best. But she'll need a good linen chemise and a corset—and some warm stockings.'

'And shoes and pattens,' declared Clotilde, smiling now that he had not given away one of her most expensive gowns.

Louise, concealing well her disappointment concerning the samite houppelande, seized hold of a plain saffron woollen. 'This will do.'

'You will have that and this,' said Harry, bundling a dark green surcote into her arms. 'Now find yourself some good underclothing. Clotilde has more than she needs—thanks to me. Then go and get changed in the kitchen. My brother is sleeping upstairs and I don't want him disturbed.' His smile did not quite reach his cool blue eyes.

Louise wanted to ask whether John was still taking her to England, but this brother's eyes were so cold, and, turning, she left the room.

It was warmer in the kitchen and an old woman, whom Louise recognised as Clotilde's mother, was turning a carcass on a spit over a fire. Fat and juices caused the flames to crackle and spit and the smell was so appetising that her mouth watered.

Louise murmured a greeting to the woman, who smiled and raised the long-handled basting spoon. Louise walked stiffly to a corner of the room where there was a scrubbed table with pots and platters on it.

She put the clothes down and with aching arms rid herself of the soiled garments she wore. She took the remainder of the money Thomas had given her and

placed it on the table. She wished that she could have
washed before dressing. Then she noticed the pail of
water on the stone floor under the table and, taking a
corner of her discarded shirt, she dipped it in the water
and scrubbed at her face and hands. A bath was what
she would have liked but knew that was out of the
question. She dried herself on part of the shirt before
pulling the linen chemise over her cropped head. In that
moment she realised that she would need a veil or a
headdress to conceal the shortness of her hair, otherwise
people might believe she had committed some great sin.

On with fine woollen knitted stockings and satin
garters. Clotilde did herself well, thought Louise, picking
up the white corset. It fitted snugly about her hips and
waist but as she laced up the bodice she made sure that
it was not so tight that it flattened her bosom. Then she
pulled on the saffron surcote, which was sleeveless and
had a scooped neckline, and eased it down over her hips
before fastening the belt about her slender waist.

She picked up the coins from the table and slipped
them into her pocket. Then it was feet into soft leather
shoes. Louise was now ready except for a hair covering,
but she had not been given one. She felt excited but a
little strange wearing long skirts after such a long time.
Her father had wanted her to go back into skirts after
they had left Caen but she had possessed none. Besides,
she had considered herself safer wearing youth's garb.
Wishing that she could have looked at herself in a
polished metal mirror, and squashing the desire to have
John in the parlour instead of his brother, she ignored
the astonished stare of Clotilde's mother and quit the
kitchen.

Harry let out an oath on sight of her, and exchanged
a swift glance with Clotilde, who bit hard on her full
lower lip, before saying, 'Your hair, *ma chére amie*, but
it is terrible!'

Louise's face fell. 'I know it is,' she responded rue-fully. 'But it will grow, and in the meantime if you could lend me one of your headdresses? But for the rest—do I look acceptable?'

Before Clotilde could say anything, Harry stepped forward, a faint smile in his eyes that reminded Louise instantly of John. 'But it is wonderful! A perfect trans-formation.' She flushed with delight, allowing him to lift her hand to his lips, only to draw back when he added, 'But you must not let my brother see you like this.'

'Pardon!' The light in her face faded. 'What do you mean? Why can't I...?' Her voice trailed off at the seriousness of his expression, and her heart sank.

Despite her unwillingness Harry took her arm and drew her a little to one side. 'If he sees you like this then he might weaken and decide to take you to England after all.'

'He has changed his mind?' Louise suddenly felt faint. 'But why? He gave me his word,' she stammered. He was silent. 'It is you who has changed it for him!' The accusation was flung at him as she gathered her wits together. 'I don't believe that he would do such a thing!'

Harry was more than a little taken aback by her vehemence. 'No. He changed it himself,' he said strongly. 'Think, woman, do you really want your sister to go back to the life she was living?' He paused for effect, before adding softly, 'Unless it is that you would turn her into a courtesan such as Clotilde? It is a part you could play well yourself and it would be much more comfortable than living in the forest.'

'I think you are insulting both of us,' said Louise, keeping her voice steady with great effort.

Harry shrugged. 'No. Not all women can play the part well. Common whores can be had six a penny. But you aren't that kind. I could find you a protector here.'

She had paled. 'Ah, now you are not even suggesting
my sister is part of this! You and your brother want me
to forget her utterly!' Her eyes held his. 'Perhaps it is
that you are lying to me? I would like to hear him tell
me that he will not take me to England.'

'My brother is weary and you know what he has been
through.' His voice was frosty. 'In his weakened state
he could so easily be persuaded by your tears if you
begged him to take you.'

Louise's mouth firmed. 'I have no intention of weeping
or begging Master Milburn to do anything for me,' she
said strongly. 'But he gave me his word!'

He scowled at her. 'I will not have you bothering him.
You will leave this house now. I have friends in Caen
with whom you can stay. I will give you money, and
once John and I have left Caen then if you wish you
can come back here and live with Clotilde.'

Her eyebrows seemed to disappear into the curling
copper-coloured tendrils of her fringe. 'You really do
believe that I would be content to be some man's
mistress?' she hissed, her eyes blazing.

'It's not a bad life, and what else is there for a wench
such as you?' he hissed back, a line of scarlet running
under his skin. 'You would have a home in thanks for
saving my brother's life!'

Her hands curled into fists. 'I don't want your thanks!
I would rather take my chances in the forest!' She turned
from him, her skirts brushing the floor, and, almost
tripping over them, she marched across the room and
pulled the door open. Clotilde called something but
Harry remained silent. She slammed the door so hard
behind her that the whole house seemed to vibrate.

Upstairs John stirred.

Heedless of the curious stares of vendors, passers-by,
and a woman standing in a doorway, Louise picked up
her cumbersome skirts and ran up the street, not caring
where she was going. Tears blurred her vision and she

savagely wiped them away with the back of her hand. She hated him! Hated both the brothers! How dared they think they could use her and discard her when they wanted? It was back to the forest for her. At least there she could tell at a glance which was the ravening beast and which was not!

Louise came to the bridge and crossed it. She noticed suddenly that it was later in the day than she had realised. Despite her sore feet she began to run once more, quite desperate to reach the city gates before they closed at dusk. With the breath burning in her throat Louise came too late. Her knees gave way and she sank to the ground. Her skirts swirled round her and she buried her face in her hands.

There was a tap on her shoulder, and slowly she lifted her head and looked wordlessly at the guard. He only had one eye and a scar ran down the side of his face. She rubbed at the tear-stains on her cheeks as she shrank back from him. 'Now what have we here?' he said.

'*Pardon, m'sieur,*' she replied unthinkingly.

The guard slanted a sly glance at his mate, 'A Frenchie,' he muttered, and caused her to jump as he fingered the fabric covering her bosom. 'Well dressed! Should be in her shift with that hair! Must have sinned mortally. Perhaps they've just cropped her and she got away before they could strip her?'

'We could do it for them,' suggested the other man with a grin, crouching down the other side of Louise and lifting her skirts slightly. She reacted violently, slamming her fist into his face. He swayed and clutched at his jaw. 'Streuth!' he groaned. 'You little bitch! I'll have you for that!'

Louise did not need to understand English to get the meaning of his words and she sought to get to her feet hurriedly to escape him. If it had not been for the other guard she might have managed it, but he seized hold of her sleeve and pulled hard so that she toppled over and on to her back. They were on her quickly and she screamed.

Still struggling and screaming she was hoisted to her feet and dragged into the shadows beneath the wall. Several other guards had come out of the guardhouse to see what the noise was about, and they stood watching, laughing as she kicked and bit, and cursed the two men attempting to get her down on the ground again, away from the prying eyes of folk hurrying home in the bleak November day.

'Perhaps she's a damned heretic!' called one of the men who had got close enough to see her cropped head. 'They're possessed by demons, Ralphy! That's what makes them so strong! Better watch she doesn't give you a poisonous bite or cast a spell on you!'

'You'd better hurry up,' shouted another. 'Or the frairs, wanting their bit of her flesh, will be here before you get going.'

The one-eyed man swore as Louise's teeth found a fleshy part of his arm again, and he seized her hair, yanked her head up and slapped her face so hard that she bit her tongue. Her ears rang dizzily and she felt herself sliding down through the man's hands. But as she sank to the ground and the man pushed up her skirts and straddled her, there came a seething voice she barely recognised, cutting through the air like a knife. 'What the hell do you men think you're doing?'

Louise was relieved of the crushing weight almost immediately as the man was dragged forcibly off her, and sent sprawling against the wall. 'Is this what Englishmen have come to?' his voice roared at them. 'Attacking defenceless women?' There was a sudden hush. 'What would your king say?' he demanded. 'He has forsworn women! Could you not at least treat them with compassion for their weaknesses?'

'This one ain't weak,' called a voice in the group. 'She's strong—possessed by demons for certain.' His words were greeted with an approving murmur.

'She's a witch,' muttered the guard, hauling himself up from the wall.

'Don't be daft, man,' said John, frowning at him. 'If you were scared to death you'd fight tooth and nail. Haven't you ever gone into battle and had to summon up the last ounce of strength in you?'

'Ay, but—that's different!' The guard rubbed his chest where John had pushed him.

'How's it different?'

'King Henry told us God be fighting on our side and we be fighting against the Devil. And she's a Frenchie.'

John laughed incredulously and slapped the man on the shoulder. 'My good yeoman, that would surely make her scared of you.' He smiled. 'The King is desirous of marrying a French princess, no less. I doubt he would be pleased if you called her a witch.'

Several of the men, who huddled near the wall, murmured agreement and they began to shuffle towards the gatehouse door. Someone commented on how cold it was outside and that he was for the fire and his ale inside. There was a general drift away from the figure lying on the ground and the two guards.

John stared at the two men. 'I would mind the gate if I were you,' he said softly, and, taking no more heed of them, he bent over Louise, and sliding his hands beneath her lifted her in his arms.

'Who is she to you, anyway?' the younger of the guards asked suspiciously, stepping in front of John. His jaw still ached from Louise's punch.

'My cousin,' said John, adding without hesitation, 'The reason that her hair is cropped is because she has a skin disease. I pray that you don't catch it.' On these words he brushed past the man, who drew back hastily, and he headed for the bridge, praying that the guard he had bribed to let him cross would still be waiting to let him back over.

Louise stirred in his arms halfway across the bridge and forced her unwilling eyelids open to gaze up at him. 'How?' she muttered.

He glanced at her then looked ahead again. 'The door slamming roused me,' he rasped. 'I got up and looked out of the window and saw a woman running as if there were demons at her heels. I recognised it was you by your hair. It was easy to find someone of your description—you didn't pass exactly unnoticed.'

'But why did you follow me?' Her eyes were bemused as they stared up at his shadowy face. 'Your brother said——'

'Damn my brother. I guess he upset you. I didn't pause to ask questions.' Louise was silent, reluctant to tell him the truth.

'Well?' he demanded. 'I know he thinks I shouldn't take you to England. Was that it?'

Louise looped an arm about his neck as she slipped a little in his grasp. The act brought their faces closer together and she smelled salve. 'Yes,' she replied in a low voice.

'So you ran away and instantly got yourself into trouble.' His voice was as quiet as hers. 'It seems that you need protecting from yourself, *mam'selle*.'

'It was these damn skirts,' she muttered. 'I would have escaped if it weren't for them. But—I am very grateful that you came to my rescue.'

He halted. 'So you should be.' There was the slightest hint of laughter in his voice. 'You never fail to surprise me, *mam'selle*.'

Her other arm went up about his neck, and their breath mingled. His mouth touched hers briefly, butterfly-light. She stared at him. 'You could put me down. I can walk,' she said unevenly.

'But you might trip again.'

'Perhaps,' she whispered, and her head drooped against his shoulder. His arms were strong and she felt safe.

They did not speak again as he carried her through the darkening streets. They came to his brother's house.

The door was opened immediately in answer to their knock. Louise expected him to put her down on the settle but he did not, and she was as astonished and speechless as Harry and Clotilde when John brushed past them and carried her through the parlour, and on, up the stairs.

CHAPTER SIX

THE bedchamber was in darkness but Louise could see clearly the outline of the four-poster bed with its curtains. Her heart was beating so fast now that she thought that she would suffocate. Had John only saved her from the soldiery for himself? She found that hard to believe, considering the days she had been in his company when he had made no advances to her at all.

He toppled her on to the bed rather than placing her there, and collapsed beside her. For several minutes neither of them moved and she could hear his rapid breathing. She managed to lean up on one elbow in an attempt to see his face in the curtained seclusion of the four-poster but could barely make out his profile. 'M'sieur Milburn,' she whispered, 'why have you brought me up here?'

'You need to rest,' John retorted in a barely audible voice. 'I will get up in a moment and leave you.'

She doubted him capable of movement for some while. 'I will find somewhere else to rest,' she said softly, and would have removed herself, but he stretched out a hand and hooked it about her neck and pulled her down beside him. She attempted to free herself but his other arm slid about her waist and his hold on her neck slackened as his head shifted on to her shoulder and he brought her closer to him. His overwhelming masculine presence had already caused her to be the target for conflicting emotions on the journey from the gateway, and so again she attempted to free herself.

He muttered indistinctly and his arm tightened about her, as he said in a slurred voice, 'Stay—please.'

Louise realised that he was almost asleep with exhaustion. Rescuing her had drained the remainder of his strength. She allowed herself to relax and a long breath escaped her. It seemed that she was fated to spend the night in his company once again, and if aught else happened she supposed that was the price that she had suspected all along she might have to pay to find Marguerite. A yawn escaped her and, reaching down, she pulled the bedcovers over them. Maybe she could trust in his vow this night? Weary with the events of the last two days, she slept.

For hours she slept peacefully but then dreams assaulted her and she was running, filled with a dreadful fear, reliving the moments by the city gates. She awoke with a start and lay rigid in the bed, staring up at the dark canopy overhead.

Within moments she was fully awake. How stiff she was—and hungry and thirsty. She slanted a glance at John's motionless figure—he lay on his side, facing away from her. Pushing back the covers, she slid out of bed. Going over to the window she saw that there was a line of orange, silver and white beneath the grey above the roofs to the east. Without delaying any longer she made her way over to the door.

All was silent, and almost noiselessly Louise felt her way downstairs to the kitchen. The fire was nearly out on the hearth, but her nose led her to the remains of the pork beneath a covered dish on the table. Finding a knife, she managed to cut herself several slices of the meat.

Remembering the layout of the kitchen from earlier she went over to a shelf and took down a corked earthenware container and poured some cider into a tankard. Then she set about enjoying her feast.

She was just finishing off her meal when the noise of quiet footsteps on the stairs almost caused her to drop the tankard. Several seconds passed before the outline of a figure appeared at their foot, and, without noticing her, moved like a shadow towards the entrance to the front room.

Louise could not understand why she did not make her presence known to Clotilde, but when she heard the bolts pulled on the front door she allowed her time before going over and peering into the parlour. There was nobody there and she decided that it was really none of her affair why Clotilde should be leaving the house so early in the morning. She stood a moment thinking before quietly going back upstairs. Wrapping a fold of her skirt about the latch, she silently opened the bedroom door.

Sitting on a chair by the window, Louise puzzled over why Clotilde should be out alone at this time of morning.

'What are you doing over there? Why did you go downstairs?' John's whisper startled her. He had pulled the curtain aside and was sitting up against the pillows. She winced at the sight of his face. 'To the kitchen for something to eat and drink,' she said slowly. 'I'm sorry if I woke you.'

'That's all right.' He smiled lopsidedly. 'I wish you'd brought me something.'

'I never thought.' She added hesitantly, 'But if you want me to I can fetch you some food and drink now.'

'I'd like that,' he drawled.

Louise was there and back within minutes. She laid a tray before him and sat sideways on the bed, watching him take a deep draught of cider. 'Did Pierre have the men beat you before dragging you on the ground?' Her voice was concerned as she gazed at him.

He glanced at her and for a moment was silent. 'If I'd been in his position I'd have probably done the same to an enemy. It's of no matter. I'll live.'

'Your brother said that you are not a violent man.'

'Did he?' He gazed at her and then down at his food. 'You don't want to believe everything Harry says.' His tone discouraged further discussion.

She sat watching him eat, wondering about him. At last he finished the food and leaned back against the bed. A painful gasp escaped him and he quickly bent forward.

Louise frowned. 'You are in pain.'

He drained his tankard before saying, 'I will have Clotilde look at it.'

'Clotilde?' She was suddenly vexed. 'Why should you wait for her to minister to you? She has gone out. I will see to it. Take off your houppelande,' she ordered briskly, 'while I go and fetch some water.'

She hid a smile at the expression on his face as she left the room quietly. It was not long before she returned with some cloths and salve and a small cauldron that steamed.

John had managed to remove his houppelande and doublet, and unfasten the buttons on his shirt, but he was having difficulty removing it. He grimaced and she hurried over to him. 'Allow me,' she murmured, gazing on his linen-covered shoulders and back where blood and ointment had stained the fabric. She began to dampen it with warm water, before slowly and gently easing the material off. In some places it stuck stubbornly to his skin and she was aware from the clenching of his fists and his indrawn breath just how painful it was for him.

To take his mind from his discomfort Louise began to chatter about the last time she had been to the great fair in Bruges, and of the sugar loaf, the kid gloves and fabrics she had purchased. He began to talk of the countries he had seen. Of the cold northern lands, and of Iceland, which he had only visited once. He spoke of how different it was from other places he had visited. It was a land of legend, wreathed in warm mists, not completely ice as one would think from its name. He spoke of the people in their animal furs, whose main livelihood was fishing their icy waters, and of the strange creatures that dwelt in the sea.

Louise listened with as much attention as she could, although she did not catch everything he said, as she smeared the ointment on his back and shoulders. She could not help noticing that there were several scars on his back. Her fingers started to trace the shape of one but he reached round and caught her hand. 'Don't,' he said roughly.

'What is it?' she murmured.

'Nothing for you to concern yourself with.'

'But it is a perfect "J".'

'So I've been told.' His voice was taut. 'Hurry up with your task, *mam'selle*, I'm getting cold.'

'I'm sorry,' she said stiffly, and skilfully finished binding up his wounds.

He seized her hand as she passed him his doublet. 'I'm sorry if I sounded impatient just now. I am grateful for your tending me.' He kissed her wrist.

'Don't!' she said huskily, trying to snatch her hand back.

He kept hold of it. 'Just a kiss, Louise. It is nothing,' he murmured, pushing up her sleeve. His lips caressed the underside of her arm.

'Please—you mustn't touch me,' she whispered.

'You don't like me touching you?' His eyes scanned her face over her arm.

'No!' Then, with a little less certainty in her voice, 'I—I—it is wrong.'

'You find it pleasant, though?'

She looked away from him. 'You should not ask me such questions.'

'How am I to know what pleases you—if I don't ask and you don't answer?' he said quietly.

'Why should you be concerned about what pleases me?' she stammered. 'To seek the pleasures of the flesh is sinful. We should be thinking more about our immortal souls.'

'When I look at you I can't help but consider the pleasure we could give to each other. You made a pretty boy, *mam'selle*, but you make a lovelier maid.' He leaned forward and his lips brushed her cheek before finding her mouth. It was a gentle kiss; even so, it sent a precarious thrill of excitement shooting through her.

She drew back swiftly. 'Is it that you would seduce me, sir?' Her voice held a hint of breathlessness. 'I'm not blind to the position I have placed myself in because I need your help to find Marguerite.'

'Bedding you was never part of my promise to help you, *mam'selle*,' he said with a sincerity that she wanted to believe in as his fingers touched her cheek and traced a line down her throat. He took hold of her shoulders and she allowed him to draw her closer. His lips brushed hers briefly, tantalisingly. She knew that she should pull away as his hands explored the contours of her body, but she did not. His gaze was on her face as if he watched for her every reaction. She moistened her mouth, thinking she should say, Stop! when his fingers toyed with her fastenings. Her heart leapt into her throat as he eased the surcote from her shoulders but still she was silent. It was almost as if he had bewitched her.

When he started on her corset it was a different matter; she stirred and clutched at the lacing of the bodice. 'Please, I don't think I want you to go further,' she said in a stifled voice.

'No?' he whispered, against her mouth, stopping any further protest with another kiss, and removing her fingers one by one. He loosened her ties, saying softly, as his hands felt the shape of her beneath the clinging chemise, 'This would have been easier if you were still dressed as a youth.'

She felt a hysterical laugh rising inside her, and said unsteadily, 'Why do you want to remove my clothing?

It's not needful if you wish to just lie with me. Take me quick and have done with it, Master Milburn!'

'I did not say that I would lay with you,' he murmured. 'But I would like to feel your flesh against mine just as it was the other night in the tree.'

'You should not remind me of that again!' Her voice shook with a mixture of excitement and mortification, and she gripped his arm with both hands in an attempt to prevent him going any further.

He made a noise in his throat. 'Why? Because it was enjoyable for both of us?'

'I never said that was so,' she whispered, trembling a little.

'It wasn't necessary.' He laughed and, leaning forward, he caught her lower lip between his teeth before hungrily covering her mouth again. His fingers caressed the nape of her neck and tickled her ears, before baring her shoulders and kissing the hollows beneath her collarbones. Almost of its own volition her body arched back over his arm and his lips discovered her breasts so that she had cause to swallow in an attempt to control the rising thrill of pleasure as his tongue and mouth teased her nipples. He brought her up straight and dragged the chemise over her head and flung it on the floor. For a moment they looked at each other as they knelt on the bed and she trembled because he had roused such desire within her, and she did not know how to control it. Then he enfolded her in his arms, breast against chest, and she embraced him, shivering with a mixture of cold, excitement and apprehension.

She could not think coherently as he laid her down and stretched out beside her. He pulled the covers over them before his mouth claimed hers. His hand stroked her hip and her stomach, soothing even as he roused and rolled her on to her back. His fingers gently explored inside her, spreading pleasant tingles through her loins. Her body moved of its own volition beneath his touch and there was an overwhelming need inside her to reach out and draw him closer. Her hand sought the bare skin between his bandages and stroked it as his fingers caused pleasure to pulsate through her. She had a desire to caress his loins as she had last time, except now they were covered. 'I would please you,' she whispered urgently.

'Surely,' he said tenderly, ridding himself of his hose, and bending over her. It was not quite what she expected when he brought her hips up to kiss against his and parted her thighs. Then she realised what was going to happen and her mind struggled against the stronger urge inside her. His root of masculinity penetrated her secret place and a moan escaped her. Her hands flew to his chest in an effort to ward him off. 'Please don't.' Her voice was a shivering whisper.

He moved gently inside her. 'Trust me to take care of you, Louise.' His mouth lipped her throat and she gasped as he thrust deeper inside her, mixing pain with pleasure. Even as her mind told her she should be struggling, her arms were enfolding him and her body was arching to join in the rhythm that throbbed inside her, and she urged him on. Then her body was flooded with a pulsating ecstasy that caused her to cry out, and ended in a shudder that raced through him into her.

John lay on his stomach next to Louise, one of his arms stretched across her. She was trying to think through what had happened. It had been like nothing else she had ever experienced and because it had been so delightful she had surrendered her virginity to him with barely any resistance. Why him? He was English, so deserving of her hatred. Why could she not have welcomed Pierre into her body in the same manner? She could not understand the overwhelming attraction John had for her and felt shame because she had given in to her lust. 'I have become your whore,' she said in a dull voice, 'and I am damned forever.'

'No more than I.' His voice was muffled. 'I cannot blame you for tempting me, although you did.'

'I would be blamed less for my sin if one of the men at the gate had taken me,' she murmured. 'You saved me from them for yourself and seduced me with soft words and gentle hands. I was chaste and you have ruined me.'

There was a silence and he lifted his head. 'You would rather I had left you with them?' There was a disbelieving note in his voice.

'No!' She turned her head and looked at him. 'But I would you had needed to force me!' Her voice quivered.

Because he did not speak in a whisper, when his words exploded in the air they seemed very loud. 'Force? Dammit, woman, I was deliberately gentle with you. I could have taken you roughly and with passion and you would have fought me this first time. Instead I wooed you and you allowed it because of that! Was it not pleasurable for both of us?'

'Ay! But what we did was wrong! My enjoyment makes it a worse sin.' She sat up abruptly, clutching the blanket to her breasts. 'Your gentleness undermined my resistance,' she said strongly. 'And I trusted in your vow that you would not go so far.'

His eyebrows shot up. 'My vow was at an end when I found my brother.'

She stared down at him, taken aback. 'You should have told me.'

'And how should I have done that?' His voice was soft. 'Perhaps I should have said, Mam'selle Saulnier— or Louise—I lust after you, so I'd better warn you that my vow of chastity is at an end.'

'You mock me,' she said hotly, her hazel eyes sparkling.

'A little.' He smiled crookedly. 'Because you are being quite ridiculous, my sweeting. And besides, would it really have made that much difference?' He added silkily,

'Be honest and admit you wanted me to take you in the inn in Harfleur.'

Hot colour darkened her cheeks. 'I! Want an Englishman?' she said, almost choking on the words because they were perhaps shamefully true. 'I hate you! And if it were not for Marguerite I would wish to never set eyes on you again.'

'I hardly expected you to say that you love me,' he retorted, getting out of bed. 'But hate?' He stood, naked, gazing down at her, his hands on his hips. 'It is a strong feeling, Louise, as vigorous as love. I doubt there can ever be passive emotion between you and I. The trouble is that love and hate make demands on a person. But hate always destroys eventually, whereas love conquers and builds up. You have to make up your mind which it is you feel towards me, and I suppose till then I will have to bear with your moods of blowing hot and cold.'

'You bear with me?' Louise sat up with a violent movement, and her voice was frigidly controlled because looking at him made her want him all over again. She felt sick to the stomach at the thought. 'I was a virgin! It was the only thing I had to give to a husband and you have taken that from me. And you dare to talk of love!'

He was silent and then he inclined his head. 'So be it. I will not talk of love. But as for your being a virgin, I was not sure—not until it was too late—and even then I was not sure. I took it that in your guise of youth you mixed much with men. But why you dressed in such a way—you have never explained.' He started to button up his shirt, his gaze on the far wall. 'Anyway, lass, be glad that I was the first. I vow that it would not have been as enjoyable with anyone else.'

She ground her teeth. 'You have a fine conceit of yourself, sir! And it was my father's idea that I dressed as a boy before the storming of Caen. He thought that it would protect me from the likes of you. Afterwards I had no other clothes to wear, and I considered it not such a bad idea to continue in such garb for my own protection. I did not want to become your wh——' The word stuck in her throat, and she came out with, 'Woman!'

'You knew the risks you took,' he said in a clipped voice, going over to the stand where there was a pitcher of water and a bowl. 'But be assured, *mam'selle*, that I don't regard you as my woman. If what we did is so utterly distasteful to you, then there is no need for you to be subjected to it again. Our liaison is over.'

Louise felt as if she had been doused with cold water. 'Then I might as well leave now,' she said in a voice that quivered despite all that she did to control it, 'if you are not going to help me find Marguerite.'

He paused in his washing. 'I did not say I would not help you find Marguerite. I gave you my word and I intend keeping it.' He shook water off his arms, and began to dry himself.

'Then—you just mean——' she began, getting out of bed, clutching a blanket to her breast.

'I mean, *mam'selle*, that you will come to England with me if I have to drag you there by the hair.' His slitted eyes glinted. 'I owe you something for saving my life.'

'You saved mine,' she said quietly, 'when you threw me in the sea, thinking me a thieving rogue.'

'My life might have been less painful and complicated if I had left you there.' His mouth eased into a smile.

'And perhaps I should have left you to the wolves.' She could not help returning his smile.

'But you didn't,' he murmured, picking up her chemise from the floor, and holding it out to her.

There was a silence as she took it. 'How do I know I can trust you to keep your distance?'

'You don't,' he said quietly, looking suddenly very weary. 'You'll just have to believe me when I say that I want you as little as you want me.'

Louise stared into his face, before lowering her gaze to his bare muscular thighs. She took a deep steadying breath. 'Then I suggest, sir, that you get dressed and leave me to perform my toilet alone.'

'A good idea. I wish to see if the *Grace* has tied up yet.' His hand brushed past her as he reached for his hose and she turned her back on him hurriedly. A few minutes later she heard the door open and close.

CHAPTER SEVEN

LOUISE was just lacing up her bodice when Clotilde entered. She was wearing a scarlet bagpiped-sleeved surcote that swept the floor, and her dark hair was loose about her shoulders. 'So you are awake at last,' she said brightly. 'I brought you a clean surcote.' She tossed one of dark green on a heavy carved oak chest, before seating herself on its lid. 'The men have gone out so we are free to talk of whatever we wish. Harry asked me to try and persuade you to stay here with me. He is under the impression that he is leaving for England and that I will be lonely. But I don't want you to stay, so I thought I would tell you that immediately.'

Louise stared at her, a little surprised. 'I have no intention of staying. We both have changed and I doubt we would suit. But surely it is true what Harry says— and you will be lonely without him?'

Avoiding her eyes, Clotilde said, 'Without him—ay! But perhaps he will not go after all, and in that case you will not be needed here.' She slid off the chest, and picked up the soiled saffron surcote that Louise had discarded. She tuttered and held it away from her skirts, her dainty nose wrinkling in disgust. 'I don't know how you managed to get this so dirty so quickly. Or why you had to run off the way you did yesterday. What was it Harry said to you?'

'Nothing for you to concern yourself about,' murmured Louise, picking up the green surcote.

The other woman stared at her, her lower lip pouting. 'He asked you to stay, didn't he? What else did he suggest?'

'It is of no importance. I am not staying,' said Louise.

Clotilde frowned, and, going over to the window, she drummed her fingernails against the pane. Then she turned and gazed at Louise. 'He cannot desire you,' she said abruptly. 'It must be that he pities you because you were an oddity in those boy's clothes. That *must* be the only reason for him taking an interest. Harry never suggests anything without it being directly to do with his welfare. Have a look in my mirror and you will see that your looks can't compare to mine.'

'I don't have to.' Louise's voice was quiet. Her careful fingers smoothed the fine, almost cobweb-like woollen skirts of lyraigne.

Clotilde gave a glittering smile and walked over to the mirror to stare at her reflection. 'Do you really think that I've lost none of my looks? Lately I've wondered...' Her voice tailed off and her brows knitted.

'You'll lose them if you keep frowning like that,' said Louise, coming to stand next to her, and comparing her rosy face to the pale complexion of her old friend. She wished that her hair would grow quickly.

A heavy sigh escaped Clotilde. 'It's because I worry. My looks are my life now, Louise. If I lose them—who will want me? If I allowed Harry to go——' She stopped abruptly and Louise stared at her.

'Can you stop him?'

Clotilde smiled. 'I have an—acquaintance of influence.' She shrugged, and toyed with her nails. 'Harry says that he will return, but if he gets home to England who knows? I have heard the emotion in his voice when he talks about that country.'

Louise said quickly, 'It is natural that he cares for his own country. And would you not think that it would make him understand better why I want to find Marguerite and bring her home?'

Clotilde suddenly smiled. 'Ah, Marguerite, always so cheerful even when everything was going wrong. She was not the least like you, *ma chére amie*. I wager that even living in England will not lower her spirits for long.'

Louise's mouth lifted. 'That is why I miss her so much. I could never get too depressed when in her company. I *must* find her!'

'And when you do?' said Clotilde, moving away from the mirror. 'What then? Will Harry's brother still provide for you? No, Louise, I do not think he will.' She sat on the bed, hugging herself. 'Last night Harry told me that his brother had taken a vow of celibacy and that it came to an end yesterday. No wonder he wanted a woman! Any woman would have done,' she said carelessly. 'You were fortunate to be at hand. Make the most of it, for it will not last. He will tire of you eventually. And what then?'

Louise took the insult, concealing her emotions well. 'He said that he will find a home for me and Marguerite,' she said calmly.

Clotilde's eyes widened. 'And you would be happy in such a position? He is an Englishman, remember, and you hate them all.'

Louise looked at her squarely. 'I turned his offer down. When I find Marguerite I will return to France.'

Clotilde's smile came and went. 'Then I presume you gave yourself to him for his promise to help you find Marguerite. How noble of you.' Louise shrugged but said nothing, having no intention of telling her friend the truth of the matter.

Clotilde continued. 'But do make sure that you have something from him to provide for some kind of future for you and Marguerite. He is the older twin and not a poor man, but the whole family are heretics and already they are the poorer because they have had to pay fines to their king.'

'Pardon!' Louise stared at her, taken aback. 'Harry has told you he is a heretic?'

'Men like to unburden themselves in bed.' Her eyes hardened. 'And what do I care for what the Church says? They condemn me for being alive. They would rather I starved in the gutter while half of them live immorally and wear miniver and scarlet. The Church needs reforming but its priests are slow to put their own house in order. And they would destroy any that seek change! Harry would have been burnt alive if he had not recanted and joined the Usurper's army.'

'And John—has he recanted?' Louise asked through stiff lips.

Clotilde shrugged and avoided her eyes. 'I know little of his affairs. But at least Harry knows now that he is safe. He was telling me that they feel it when the other is in some kind of trouble. He will soon settle down again. But you—you must go with his brother, Louise.'

But Louise was not listening properly because she was trying to take in that John was a heretic. In her mood of distraction she murmured, 'My father would never listen to the debates of the heretics, but covered his ears, fearful that he would become possessed by the demons possessing them.'

Clotilde got up from the bed. 'Do you believe the brothers possessed?' A tinkling laugh issued from her painted lips. 'I do not! And I doubt John would try to persuade you into believing what he does. He's only interested in your body, not your soul.'

'My body, not my soul. Ay,' murmured Louise, an unexpected ache inside her. 'But Harry isn't only interested in your body if he has talked to you about such matters.'

'He talks to me because he has nobody else he trusts. And men must talk!' Clotilde raised her eyes to the raftered ceiling.

Louise could not help wondering whether Harry was right to trust her friend. She seemed very certain that he would not be leaving for England. Who was this acquaintance she had mentioned, and where had she gone earlier?

Clotilde put her hand through Louise's arm. 'Sometimes men's talk can be very tedious. Let us instead speak of food.' Her expression lightened. 'There is roasted pig and truffles and plenty of cider.'

'Surely it is not time for dinner? Besides, the men have not returned yet.'

'That is true.' Clotilde shrugged. 'But food has to be prepared. And if you are sailing to England then you must get ready.' Without another word she swept Louise out of the bedchamber.

A couple of hours later John and Harry returned with the news that the *Grace* had not yet docked.

'Perhaps it will not come,' said Clotilde brightly.

Louise darted a glance at John.

'Of course it will come,' he murmured, taking the platter of meat and bread from her. 'After dinner, if you so desire, you can walk with me to the *quais*. My brother has some business to attend to.'

Warmth flooded her because he seemed concerned to reassure her. 'I would like that,' she said, considering that if the opportunity arose she might mention her suspicions about Clotilde. She wanted nothing more to delay her getting to England.

They talked little as they walked through the streets, but he asked her about the two abbeys outside the town walls. One he knew contained the remains of Matilde, the wife of William the Conqueror. 'Ah, the other holds the remains of her husband,' said Louise, smiling. 'The pope at the time forbade their union. William was a bastard and he behaved in a manner that displeased the Church. Even so they married and in the end Holy Church countenanced it—at a price. They both had to pay to have an abbey built. So that is why there are two. It always seems sad to me that they fought to live together and yet they lie apart in death.'

'Yet they will rise together at the end of time. It is a romantic tale,' said John pensively. 'But do you not consider it interesting that this same William of Normandy conquered England and now a king of England is doing the reverse? William was as little welcome in England, then, as Henry is here and now.'

She glanced at him, her expression startled. 'What is it that you are saying? That it is just that your king conquers?'

'No. I'm saying that French and English blood has mingled much in the past despite the power games that kings play. That there is kinship and friendship and trade between both countries as well as enmity.'

Her eyes darkened. 'It is not that easy to think of friendship when you lose your home and your father, and your sister is abducted by the enemy.'

'No. But it is easier to let hate go when you allow the enemy to become a friend.'

'A friend?' She looked at him, and flushed slightly. 'I doubt you could call it friendship that binds us.'

'I do not like the thought of you hating me, Louise,' he said with a spurt of impatience. 'And if we are not going to be lovers then let us be friends.'

She felt suddenly shy of him. 'Can a man and woman be friends? I have never heard of such a thing.'

'Then let us be different.' His smile grew, and he caught her hand and swung it. 'Friends help each other and I would help you all I can, Louise, because you have helped me in the manner of a friend, despite all your talk of hating me.'

She averted her profile because looking at him affected her breathing in a peculiar way. 'Perhaps I don't hate you as much as I thought I did,' she murmured. 'But we have come to the *quais* and perhaps we should be giving our attention to finding your ship.'

He agreed and they walked along the riverside, scanning the ships tied there and avoiding men unloading goods.

'There it is!' Louise indicated with her left hand. John still held her right. They hurried over to where the *Grace* was tied up, its sail furled.

A man came off the ship even as they came up to it and would have walked past them if John had not seized hold of his arm. 'Do I look that unrecognisable, man?' he demanded.

Thomas stared at him. 'Master John?' His voice was shocked as he grasped John's hand and shook it fervently. 'By all that's holy, what's happened to you?'

'It's a long story to be told another time.' John smiled ruefully. 'But my brother is here so all is well.'

Thomas looked relieved. 'That's good news for me, Master John. Because I have to tell you that the maid went off.'

'Is that so?' He looked vexed for a moment and then laughed. 'Thomas, may I introduce you to Mam'selle Louise Saulnier?'

Louise gravely inclined her head in its starched linen head-dress, but her eyes twinkled. *'Bonjour,* Thomas.'

'Well, I'll be damned,' the servant muttered, frowning and scratching his ear. 'I really believed I'd seen the last of you, missy.'

'Pardon? Parlez-vous Français?' she responded.

'Now don't you be starting that again, *mam'selle*!' He appeared discomfited. 'I hope the master's thought of teaching you some *Anglais*?' He slanted John a look.

John nodded. 'Yes, I have. But I need to talk to you of more serious matters. My brother will be sailing with us—the sooner the better, because there could be difficulties.'

Thomas scowled. 'We've already had some clerks aboard, nosing about and asking what our business is here. The master told 'em we just came to fill up with water, and get fresh food if there be any available, and to pick up a couple of passengers. He seemed to think we'd come out of our way just for that and wanted to know who the passengers were.'

John frowned. 'Did you tell him the name we agreed on? And did he ask to see the master's papers?'

'Ay,' he said tersely. 'And mine. Seems that everything's getting tightened up at these Anglified Frenchie ports.'

'You still have the false papers safe?' said John. 'My real ones were taken from me.'

Thomas nodded and grinned. 'A fair collection I've got tucked away where only I know about them.'

John nodded thoughtfully. 'We'll have need of them. Get me ready the ones referring to the Bertrands. Apparently the King doesn't like it when his subjects change their minds and want to return home.'

Louise tugged at his arm; not understanding a word of what was being said had become a little wearisome. 'M'sieur Milburn,' she said quietly. 'If you would be so kind as to——'

'Hush, woman,' he muttered. 'Don't call me by that name here. I am now Master Bertrand and don't you forget it. And that reminds me.' He smiled slightly. 'You will not object to playing the part of my wife for now?'

'Your wife?' she stammered.

'Ay. I have papers for a wife. But I won't expect you to put body and soul into the character,' he said drily. He turned to Thomas before she could say any more, and spoke rapidly. 'You will tell the master I wish to depart this evening.' Thomas nodded and John took Louise's elbow and led her away.

'Do we return to your brother's house now?' she demanded.

'Ay. There are matters to be sorted out before we can leave Caen.'

'You have papers for Harry?'

John nodded. 'But you must keep quiet about them, Louise. Do not speak of them even to Clotilde.'

Louise said hesitantly, 'She does not want your brother to leave.'

'That is understandable.' His brows drew together. 'Yet he will leave her well provided for. She really has nothing to complain about.'

'They have lived like man and wife,' she could not help saying. 'Parting is bound to be a wrench.'

He stared down at her, and his expression had hardened. 'It is not always so between husband and wife. Many are glad to live apart.' He paused, before adding, 'You believe, though, in Harry's—and Clotilde's—case that she will perhaps miss him for more than what material benefits he has brought her?'

'I think Clotilde might try to stop him leaving,' she said quietly, as he hurried her past a creaking wain and over the bridge.

'He will not be persuaded to stay by her tears. Harry has made up his mind to leave and will do so. My brother has a will of iron when it suits him.'

'I was not thinking of tears,' murmured Louise, gnawing at her bottom lip, considering carefully before she added, 'She left the house early this morning and she has spoken to me about having an acquaintance of some influence. She seems very sure that Harry will not be leaving.'

John's grip on her arm tightened. 'You think that she has informed someone of my brother's intentions?'

Louise barely hesitated. 'Ay. And the quicker he is informed the better. He could have told her already about your false papers—the name of the ship. She knows your real name—perhaps she could cause trouble for you both that way. If you are heretics——'

'She has told you that?'

Louise nodded. 'It is true?' she asked tentatively.

His eyes narrowed. 'The less you know about such things, *mam'selle*, the better. My brother's a damn fool for all his talk about *me* where women are concerned. Come, let us not tarry.'

She wondered what he meant by women but had little time to think on it because as they neared the house she noticed a couple of men standing on the other side of the street who did not seem to be doing anything in particular. 'Do you think——?'

'Ay! Avert your face.' He presented the man with only the slightest glimpse of his profile before they went inside Harry's house.

They were instantly confounded to find Harry entertaining a visitor. John sensed immediately that Harry wished them out of the room. He did not speak, only nodding curtly and telling them that Clotilde was in the kitchen and for them to help themselves to a drink.

Clotilde was sitting by the fire with some sewing. There was no sign of her mother. She looked up at them. 'So you are back already? Is your ship in?'

John trod warningly on Louise's foot. 'No, *mam'selle*,' he said, grimacing. 'Alas, it looks as if it might not come until the morning.' He pulled up a stool and indicated that Louise sat. She did and he stood just behind her and faced Clotilde. 'Who is that man with Harry?'

Her eyelashes swept down, concealing the expression in her brown eyes. 'I—do not know. But he is probably a customer. Harry does not tell me everything—or introduce me to everybody.'

Louise did not believe that she did not know the man, but she sensed enough from John's manner to keep quiet about it. A few minutes later Harry entered the room, an almighty scowl disfiguring his face. 'That was a damned cleric from Popham. Would I call on him in the morning! Information about my movements has come to light and he would like to discuss it with me.

It's a polite way of telling me that he knows what I'm about and is going to prevent it.'

'Oh, Harry!' exclaimed Clotilde in distressed tones. 'How disappointing for you.'

'Isn't it?' said Harry, his mouth tightening. 'But I'll be damned if I'll let him stop me going to England. There must be a way.' He looked at his brother. 'John, those papers——'

'No,' interrupted John quickly. 'You'll just have to accept, Harry, that this time you can't come with us. Maybe next time I have business this way.'

Harry stared at him, and Louise saw the warning look that John flashed to him. 'I suppose you're right,' said Harry, setting free a heavy breath. 'Clotilde, get us a drink and bring it through into the parlour.'

'I'll do it,' said Louise quickly, rising from the stool. She was not fooled by the men's talk but hopefully Clotilde was. If her smile was anything to go by then they had tricked her into believing that her plan had worked. Yet they still had to find a way of getting Harry to the ship without rousing the suspicions of the men outside.

As Louise entered the parlour, her eyes fell on the trunk from which Clotilde had brought out all her finery yesterday, and an idea came to her. She went over to John, who was gazing out of the window, and said in a low voice, 'Do you have papers for two women?'

John glanced at her, and then at Clotilde, who was talking gaily to Harry about the coming Advent festivities. 'Only the one. Why?' he murmured.

'I was thinking of your brother disguising himself in women's clothes.'

He was silent and then a slow grin eased his expression. 'It's a good idea. But we only have one set of papers for a female. Which means, little as you like it,' he said with deliberation, 'you will have to pretend to be a youth again, Louise.'

'But——' she began, placing the tray on a stool, and wishing she had kept quiet.

'Just do it,' he said gently. 'You can take the clothes you have with you. In truth I think it wise if you pack for my brother several gowns and head-dresses and some underwear.'

Louise looked at him and experienced a moment's joy. Did he mean them for her eventually? Then she switched her attention to his brother and giggled. 'You think he will agree?'

'He's got no choice,' murmured John. 'But he'll have to get Clotilde out of the way first.' Without further ado he left Louise and went over to his brother.

He drew him aside and a few minutes later an expressionless Harry went over to Clotilde and pulled her to her feet. 'My love, there is something I have bought you upstairs. Come and see it.'

'Now, Harry? It'll soon be suppertime.'

'Now,' he said in a soft, insistent voice. 'Or I shall give it away to——?' For a second his glance rested on Louise, and Clotilde's eyes followed his.

'I shall come,' she said quickly, a slight pucker between her dark brows.

'Good.' He pulled her hand through his arm and kissed her cheek and they left the parlour.

'We must leave here soon,' said John, turning to Louise. 'You go now and find the clothes you discarded.'

'I have seen them in the kitchen, hanging near the fire.' She left him, her pulses beating faster.

With regret she took off the green surcote and the head-dress, her corset and chemise, and once more donned the shirt, doublet and hose. As she rolled up the discarded clothes, her thoughts were of John saying, 'You made a pretty boy...but you make a lovelier maid.' Perhaps it was just as well she no longer wore skirts.

When she went back into the parlour John had the chest open and was rummaging through the clothes there.

He looked up at her, his dark brows drew together and a sigh escaped him. 'I pray that you won't have to wear them too long. But I've been thinking that maybe it would be wiser if you are dressed in such garb if we are to be travelling much in each other's company alone. Still!' He smiled. 'We'll take some of these for when you discard your hose.' He threw several garments her way.

She suffered a pang of guilt. 'Do you really think we should be taking so many? I feel sorry for Clotilde. I think she is very fond of your brother.'

'I think he likes her well enough in his way too,' replied John, 'but it's time he was thinking of finding a wife.'

Louise's hands stilled on a lemon silk chemise, and her voice contained a note of anger when she spoke. 'And you do not consider Clotilde suitable, I suppose? She is good enough to keep house for him here and to warm his bed, but not to bear his children or his name!'

'It has nothing to do with me,' said John, as cool as she was heated. 'And no doubt she doesn't expect marriage from him. It is you who might desire it in her position.'

'No, *m'sieur*,' she retorted, her eyes glinting. 'I'm not such a fool as to expect you to make an honest woman of me.'

'That is wise of you,' he said, a muscle tightening in his cheek, 'because I couldn't. Come here and help me to choose what Harry can wear tonight, and then find us something to eat that we can take with us.'

Louise was tempted to say more, but she knew from the set of his mouth that he would not be drawn on the subject any further.

She chose a blue houppelande and then went into the kitchen. She was wrapping bread and meat in a napkin when Harry came downstairs. There was a grimness about his expression that reminded her vividly of John when he had thrown her into the sea. He nodded in her direction. 'So the masquerade is to be played.'

'Yes,' she murmured, and added impulsively, 'Do you have any regrets leaving Clotilde?'

'Regrets?' A slight smile passed like a shadow across his face. 'I have a mother at home whom I have not seen for five years, who has waited faithfully for my return. I have a father to face whom I quarrelled with. They are both getting old. Clotilde thought by scheming to stop me leaving. But I have tied her to the bedpost with a few scarves. She didn't try to understand that I must leave, now that John has brought me to a realisation of how little time I might have to spend with my family.'

'She fears that you will not return.'

'We all have our fears for others, *mam'selle*.' His eyes met hers. 'I fear that you can lead my brother into danger in this quest for your sister.'

'What danger?' she asked, a puzzled expression on her face. 'He has mentioned no danger to me.'

'John wouldn't.' His voice was low and angry. 'Has he told you he has a wife in England?'

'A wife!' The room seemed to spin around her.

'He hasn't told you.' He smiled. 'Draw back, *mam'selle*, before it is too late. There is still time for you to change your mind about staying here just as a friend to Clotilde. I will see that you are well provided for.'

Louise eased the tightness in her throat, and said coldly, 'From the moment we met you have been determined that I should not go to England with your brother. Can't you understand that I must go and find my sister? Did your brother not come looking for you?'

'Ay. But that's different.' Harry frowned. 'Your sister is better off in England.'

'In this place where there is danger?' She laughed harshly. 'I think you exaggerate any danger. Anyway, even if I changed my mind—which I won't—your brother has said that he would force me to go to England with him. So you see he has made the decision for both of us.'

'It's worse than I thought,' muttered Harry, and fixed her rigidly with his gaze. 'I almost wish that he had never met you.' He turned and went into the parlour.

Louise, angry and hurt, picked up the parcel of food and followed him.

'Now, brother,' John was saying, 'this should not be too difficult. Remember when the mummers came to perform on New Year's Eve and we used to dress up? We were able to trick Mother and she knew us better than anyone.'

Harry agreed in a resigned tone, but added, 'She recognised us eventually.'

'Naturally. Because we pranced around waiting for her to do so. No one here is expecting you to be dressed as a woman,' said John softly. 'So we should get away with it. We will leave at dusk, which will make it even more difficult for anyone to see your face at a distance. Which means we have little time for you to change and practise walking.'

'He will make a very tall woman,' said Louise in a strained voice. 'Do these papers say that Mistress Bertrand is *your wife*?'

John shot her an enquiring look and stilled. Their gazes held, and he said quietly, 'We originally had them forged for my mother in the event of our family having to flee England at a crisis in our life.'

Louise raised her eyebrows. 'Your mother? Then I suggest that Harry becomes your mother—that way it will look quite acceptable if he stoops—and maybe he could have a stick to lean on and he can keep his head down.'

'Perhaps I should blacken a few teeth and place a false wart on my nose,' said Harry.

'This isn't a game,' said John harshly. 'Don't let your sense of the ridiculous land us in hot water as it has before.'

'I did not know then that dear Dorothy was a spy in the camp.' Harry picked up the blue houppelande. 'Is this what I'm wearing?'

'It will match your eyes,' rasped John.

Harry groaned, bundling the clothes under his arm before going into the kitchen. Immediately John turned to Louise. 'You know about Dorothy, don't you?'

'Dorothy?' she said calmly, her eyes stormy. 'Is that the name of your wife?'

'Ay, dammit!' he said roughly. 'And don't be looking at me like that, Louise. If I could change matters I would. But I can't, so there's an end to it.'

'You realise that we've committed adultery.' Her voice was stiff.

'The sin is mine. Not yours.' His hands curled on the clothes he was stuffing into a bag. 'The match was arranged between her mother and my father, and I was fifteen to her twenty years when we married. I have lived to regret making such a match, but don't let that affect your decision to come with me. Finding your sister is, after all, why you are making this journey.'

'Ay,' she muttered, picking up her cloak. 'And the sooner it is over with, the quicker we shall say farewell and I shall be on a ship back to France. Now where is that brother of yours?'

Harry made an entrance by almost falling flat on his face. 'I'll be damned if I'll ever get the hang of taking dainty steps.' He clutched at the arm of a chair and pushed up the green steeple-shaped hennin he wore fastened to his head with a white veil. 'Well? Are we ready to go?'

John nodded silently, and picked up the baggage.

'What about Clotilde?' said Louise.

'Her mother will be in soon enough and will find her,' said Harry. 'Besides, I didn't tie her up that tightly. So let's get out of here.'

They did so forthwith.

The two men still stood opposite the house, blowing on their cold hands and walking up and down. As the three of them left, the men exchanged looks and crossed the street. 'A cold evening, master,' they said, looking John over.

'Ay. Not fit to be out in.'

They both nodded. 'You've come from Master Ingles's house.'

'Ay. My name's Bertrand,' said John, 'and this is my mother and brother.'

'Good even to you, young master, mistress.' Their keen eyes ran swiftly over Louise and then the bent figure of Harry, before they stepped back and waved them by.

Louise nodded her head briefly and Harry waved his mittened hand vaguely in the air before walking slowly on, tap-tapping with the stick.

Once round the corner, he said, 'You were right about them. Now let's go swiftly. I don't think I'll relax till I get aboard ship.'

Louise knew how he felt because her nerves were strung up, and they hurried to the *quai* in the gathering gloom. To her dismay as they approached they could see a couple of soldiers standing not far from the gangplank. When they drew closer Louise recognised one of them from the other morning, and it appeared that he recognised her and John.

'I've seen you before, lad,' he muttered, inspecting him with interest. 'And you, master,' he addressed John. 'A nice pair of eyes you've got there. Didn't catch sight of those murdering swine yesterday. But we'll get them in the end. Don't you fear.'

'I'm certain you will.' John smiled and would have brushed past him to go up the gangplank but he took his arm.

'Are you a citizen of Caen? Because I'll have to see your papers.'

John sighed heavily. 'I am not a citizen of Caen, nor is my brother or my mother. As for our papers, they are aboard this ship. Will you allow my mother on board while I get them for you?'

'Don't see any harm in that. We ain't looking for no old woman. You can go aboard, mistress.' He smiled kindly at Harry. 'Here, let me help you.' He seized his arm and perhaps it was the feel of it that roused his suspicions and caused him to peer closer into his face— to touch it and rasp his fingers on his chin. 'Hey, you're not——' he began, only to be grabbed by John from behind and spun round. A left upper-cut to the jaw dropped him. Harry caught him and laid him flat on the ground, just as the other soldier moved in. Louise put her foot out and he went flying over it. Harry hit him on the back of the head with the walking stick, and he collapsed on the ground.

'Too much drink, young man,' he cackled as a couple of men passed by.

'Stop acting,' hissed John, pushing him up the gangplank with one hand and seizing hold of Louise's fingers with the other. 'Tell the master to cast off, man!' he shouted to Thomas, who was standing on the poop deck, grinning at them.

'He's doing it now,' called Thomas. 'It's good to have you aboard, Master Harry. I just hope that you and Master John between you don't get us into any more trouble before we see England.'

'What trouble could I get up to?' retorted Harry, whooping as he dragged off the head-dress. 'It's my brother and the *mam'selle* you'll have to watch, man.'

'Ay. She's got plenty of spirit,' said Thomas gruffly. 'But it's downright unseemly the way she's clad. And you, Master Harry.'

He laughed as Louise and John reached his side, and the three of them gazed at the *quais* and the town with the donjon on its hill as it receded into the distance behind them.

'We're on our way at last,' breathed Louise, holding her face up to the wind that filled the sail.

John said against her ear, 'Let's pray that your hopes will not be disappointed.'

'I'm sure they won't,' she said, determinedly pulling her hand free from his grasp. 'We'll find Marguerite. I'm certain of that.' He made no answer, only standing at her shoulder as she turned her head and faced the direction they were going.

Next port of call was Dover—England!

CHAPTER EIGHT

LOUISE shivered in the wind that blew in from the Channel, and pulled the fur cap as far down as she could over her ears. She glanced about her. 'So this is Dover.' It looked much like any other port she had seen, with its ships and its castle on a hill, its huddle of houses and inns, and seabirds being blown about the grey skies like scraps of parchment against the chalky white cliff.

It was more than a week since they had left Caen and the crossing had been rough. She had spent most of it in the cabin, convinced she was going to die. The woman's curse had been upon her, and she had been thankful that she had thought of putting into the baggage linen strips for John's wounds. Fortunately both men had had their hands full helping with the ship in the stormy seas and that had afforded her some privacy, although they had all shared the cabin, there being little room on the ship. She had not taken her clothes off and would have dearly loved to immerse herself in a tub of warm water, but that had been, and still was, out of the question. 'It is very cold.'

'It'll be colder in the North.' Harry rubbed his hands together and huddled into his squirrel-trimmed scarlet houppelande. 'But you won't have to suffer that, *mam'selle*.' He looked towards his brother. 'You have sent Thomas on ahead to your agent to have some horses ready for us?' He spoke in English.

'Ay. We'll do what I planned in Caen,' said John, glancing at Louise in her travel-stained youth's garb. 'I will take Mam'selle Saulnier to Cobtree Manor, while you travel north with Thomas and the packhorse. The sooner one of us reaches Yorkshire and reassures Mother concerning our safety the better.' He picked up some of the baggage placed on the quay. Harry and Louise did likewise, then they began to walk.

Harry frowned. 'I can't change your mind about taking the *mam'selle*?'

'No.' John's look was one of cynicism. 'Why suddenly all this concern for me? Five years it's been, Harry, and I've managed to stay out of trouble on my own. Most likely I shall experience no difficulties in finding the girl.'

'Hmmph! I wish I were going with you. Anyway, be on your guard. Most likely Dykemore will be at Oxford, having left his steward in charge of Cobtree, but you never know.'

'I have thought of that,' said John patiently. 'Now let's have an end to debate and be on our way. We can travel together as far as Canterbury.'

'And then it's Thomas and I? And you and the *mam'selle* alone again,' murmured Harry. 'Do you really think that's wise?'

'Dammit, Harry,' said John, his temper rising, 'you'd think I was the one always getting myself up to my neck in hot water. She's not going to stick a knife in my back!'

'I wasn't thinking of that.' Harry's gaze shifted from his brother to Louise's slender face, flushed with the wind. Some wisps of copper-coloured hair had escaped the cap's confinements and curled on her forehead and cheeks. 'She makes a lovely lad.' He smiled and she responded with a look of enquiry. Walking between them, she had tried to understand some of what they were saying by watching their facial expressions and picking up some words here and there. 'When you put her on the ship back to France, try to persuade her and her sister to live with Clotilde,' murmured Harry. 'It would be such a waste her going back to the forest.'

John's mouth tightened and his eyes glinted. 'I'll do no such thing. Isn't it time you settled down, brother?'

'Let Father find me a nice little wife, as he did you?' murmured Harry.

'I was unlucky,' said John in a clipped voice. 'You're old enough to choose your own wife. Our kinswoman Blanche has been widowed and has been left a tidy fortune and a business.'

Harry looked thoughtful. 'I haven't seen her for years. But from what I remember, Jack, she was always dogging your heels.'

John shook his head. 'She couldn't tell the difference between us. She'd have you if you offered for her.'

'Perhaps,' he said with a rueful grimace, and quickened his pace so that he drew ahead of the other two.

Louise contained her impatience no longer. Now she turned to John, noticing how the grazes were healing on his face and that the swelling had gone down. There was still a hint of purple on his eyelids and a line of yellow beneath one eye. She realised how difficult it would be telling the brothers apart once all physical sign of injury had disappeared. 'How far to the place where Marguerite has been taken?' she asked, stumbling over the English words.

'We shall be there today,' said John. 'And hopefully Wat Fuller will have your sister under his roof.'

'Good.'

He stared at her and his eyes twinkled slightly. 'Are you so impatient to make the sea voyage to Caen again?'

She shuddered expressively and closed her eyes briefly. 'I have to suffer it if I am to return home.'

'You could wait till the spring,' he said quietly.

She glanced at him and away again quickly.

'Spring, Master Milburn?' she questioned forcefully. 'And what would my sister and I do with ourselves till then? Where would we stay?' Suddenly there was a sparkle in her hazel eyes. 'I cannot see your wife enjoying

our company.' She tossed the words at him with an air
of disdain, in a mixture of English and French.

His forehead knitted. 'I thought of taking you both
north so that you could spend a couple of months in my
mother's house,' he said impatiently. 'She would have
much sympathy with your situation. She has suffered
through the violence of men herself, having lost her
father when the peasants rose on his manor when she
was your age. They murdered him and she buried him
with her own hands!'

She was lost for something to say because his
suggestion had astonished her, as did the information
concerning his mother.

'Well?' he demanded.

'I cannot see why you should want to do such a thing,'
she said in a bewildered voice.

'Don't you?' His expression softened. 'Is it that you
don't consider living in the forest in winter pure misery?'

Her throat moved and she moistened lips chapped by
the wind. 'I don't want your pity.'

His face darkened. 'I'm not offering you pity. My
mother would enjoy your company. She never had a
daughter, and my stepsister lives in Ireland and we
seldom see her. Accept my offer, Louise,' he urged. 'I'm
sure it will be beneficial to you both.'

She was silent a moment, before saying, 'But what
would you tell her about us? It is not right that you take
me to your mother after what we have done. What will
she think of me?'

A sharp laugh escaped him. 'How is she to know?'

Her cheeks pinked. 'I feel it is written in my face,' she
said unsteadily. 'It is a grave sin and I cannot get it out
of my mind.'

'Can't you, Louise?' He stopped and took her chin
between his fingers before she could draw back. His blue
eyes scrutinised her countenance. 'I can't forget it either.
But you look no different from when I met you.' A smile

of singular charm eased his face. 'Except that you are not so thin, dirty or ragged.'

'You *do* pity me,' she muttered, considering it unfair that his smile and touch should have such an effect on her senses. 'I cannot do it. Besides, whatever you say, she is going to question your motives in taking two French females to her.'

'She would never suspect what is between us, having the highest opinion of my moral standing in the world. Fortunately mothers aren't always the best judges of character when it comes to their children.' He grimaced and dropped his hand. 'Shall we catch up with my brother?' He lengthened his stride so that she had to run to keep up with him and she knew that her refusal had upset him, but could see no way of accepting his offer.

They came to the agent's house, and there they were offered refreshment while their horses were made ready.

Within the hour they were on their way, travelling at a canter along the old Roman road used by pilgrims visiting the tomb of Thomas à Becket. The conversation was desultory and concerned mainly with the landscape, sheep and fruit trees, as well as cloth-making on Cobtree Manor for Louise's information. They also talked about Canterbury, which they came to after some two hours' journeying.

They entered by the Riding Gate, finding their way through the back streets to the high street, and Harry dismounted outside the Chequers Inn. He looked up at John, who was still on horseback. 'You are not stopping? I thought that Thomas and I could break our journey for dinner here and rest the horses.'

'We will not delay,' said John. 'Tonight we will probably have to return here with Marguerite.'

Harry, a slight smile playing round his mouth, looked up at Louise, who was sitting astride a grey palfrey. 'I pray you find your sister. But I won't say *au revoir*, *mam'selle*. It's possible that we will meet again in France, if you are the woman of sense I take you to be.'

'And what is that supposed to mean, *m'sieur*?'

'The offer I made you still stands,' he said softly.

Impatiently she gazed down at him. 'You, *m'sieur*, do not know how to take no for an answer.'

He shrugged. 'I share that trait with my brother, so be on your guard.' He lifted the hand resting on the pommel and kissed it.

Louise snatched it back, aware of John watching them. 'People will consider your kissing a youth's hand very odd, *m'sieur*.'

Harry laughed and John scowled. 'We must be on our way,' he said bitingly. 'God grant you a safe journey, brother, and tell Mother and Father that I will be with them as soon as I can.' He set his horse in motion towards the Westgate.

Louise followed him and now she was looking forward to the moment when she would see Marguerite again. Soon they would be together and she would concentrate on that thought, not on the parting to come with John, knowing that it had to come some time and it was better sooner than later.

They travelled along the road for a short distance before turning off. He set his horse to a gallop across a field and she imitated him, aware of a growing excitement as the ground flashed beneath the beast's thundering hoofs. After a while he slowed his pace and she managed to draw alongside him.

'You will be relieved to know that it's not far now.' His gaze met hers. 'And I'd best warn you now that if when we reach Cobtree you see a man in red robes— short, fat, with a face like a cherub, and silver hair beneath his hat—avoid him. Hide if you must. He is dangerous and not a man easily fooled.'

She shivered slightly. 'Who is he?'

'He is the lord of the manor. Named Dykemore, he is a cleric who hates all Lollards, but particularly ones named Milburn, and especially me. I married his niece, you see, and a tidy fortune slipped through his fingers because my wife's mother did not wish him to see a groat of it. She was his sister and had suffered from his cruelty as a girl. A timid widow woman, who knew my father through the wool trade, she found the courage to thwart her brother's plans by allying our families. And Dykemore never forgave us or her. She is dead now and he would like nothing better than to see us in the same state.'

'So Dykemore is the danger your brother spoke about?' said Louise slowly. Her expression was pensive. 'I thought Harry only said it to frighten me. Why did you not tell me?'

'Because most times Dykemore is not here but in Oxford. He is a fellow of the university, where he teaches theology; that is when he is not pursuing heretics throughout the south of England.'

'But why is it that your brother sent my sister to this Cobtree?'

'Because it once belonged to us.' The muscles in John's face tightened. 'My father had to sell it to pay for a pardon from the King for Harry and I. We had no idea that it was Dykemore who bought it. He used an agent, knowing that we would never have sold it to him.'

'How long had it been in your family's possession?'

'It belonged to my mother's father, and his father before him. But it is smaller than it was in those days. A parcel of it was given to my uncle Hugo and aunt Rose. They died a short while ago, but one of my cousins, Adam, is steward there for his brother Hugh, who lives in Yorkshire.'

'It sounds complicated.'

He smiled. 'There is a story behind it—too long to tell now. Let's ride. The days are short and we will most likely have to return to Canterbury this night.'

They rode swiftly until John slowed the pace and Louise looked with increased interest about her.

Orchards, their trees stark, gnarled and black against the grey sky, appeared more often and sheep grazed on tired-looking turf beneath their branches. A little further on there was a bridge, and beyond that a village. A dog barked as they crossed the stone bridge. There were few people about. A woman toiled at freeing a cabbage from the frozen earth. She looked up, smiled and called a greeting. John returned it but did not go to speak to her.

As they travelled past the houses Louise became aware of the sound of metal on metal. They came to a stone building and John called a halt and dismounted. Louise followed suit and entered after him what she guessed was the smithy. The man inside was tall with broad shoulders and strong arms, and he was in the process of shoeing a horse. A girl was using the blowers to kindle the flames in a brazier.

'Well met, Matthew,' said John, smiling warmly.

The smith looked up and his pleasure was obvious to Louise, who had moved over to the other side of the brazier and was holding her hands out towards its heat. 'Why if it isn't Master...' He paused and screwed up his eyes.

'It's John. And it's been a long time,' he said quietly.

'Ay! Master John.' He grinned. 'It's been too long, sir.'

'Much too long.' There was a silence and John cleared his throat. 'Is all well with you?'

'Well enough.' Matthew pulled a face. 'The new steward's all right in his way. It's his lordship the villagers have mixed feelings about. Sweet as honey one visit, going to be like a father to us all. The next time he's rooting around as if he's got a swarm of bees on his tail and then it's everybody look out,' he said grimly. 'Only last week he was here with that friar. They took away Wat Fuller.'

Louise looked up at the name. She met John's eyes and moved closer to him as he swore softly, and asked, 'For what reason?'

'The only reason that his lordship ever yanks people away from their homes for. Heresy!' Matthew's lips tightened. 'I'm not one of you, Master John. But I say, why can't people be left to believe what they like if they ain't doing anybody no harm, but are behaving like Christians? Likely it was because he was preaching a sermon outside here the other Wednesday. As good as any you'd hear in church.'

'Do you think the steward reported him?'

'Might have mentioned it without thinking. *He's* not a damn witch-hunter. He likes his ale and the wenches too much.'

John was silent. Louise tugged at his sleeve. 'Master Milburn, what of Marguerite?'

He covered her hand with his, and nodded. 'Matt! Did any man bring a French maid to the village—looking for Wat?'

The smith's brow furrowed. 'Not that I know of. But if they'd come on the day Wat was taken off they could have been missed. I do know that there's no French maid here now or I'd have heard about it. You're best having word with Wat's missus.'

'She's still here?'

'Not in the village. Gone to your cousin's manor, and is staying with her sister there, as far as I know.'

Louise tugged on John's sleeve again. 'What is he saying?'

He gazed down at her. 'Marguerite is not here in the village. But it's possible that she's with Wat's wife across the river on my cousin's land.'

Her spirits sank. 'But why should she be there? What has happened?'

'I'll explain on the way. Go outside and mount. I'll be a few moments.'

Louise did as she was told. When John reappeared she waited only until he had mounted before demanding information from him. He told her all that Matthew had said, adding, 'Don't start worrying until we speak with Maud.'

They crossed the river and rode beside it for a short while. On the other side Louise could see some wooden tubs which she guessed were used for fulling cloth. They came to a group of thatched cottages, built mostly of clay daub. A few hens pecked in the straggling grass in front of them. John dismounted and knocked on the door of a cottage. It was opened by a woman with a distaff tucked into her belt and a baby under her arm. With her free hand she plied her spindle.

John smiled. 'Is your sister here, mistress?'

'Ay, sir.' Shyly she returned his smile.

'Could you get her for me?'

'If you'll wait, sir. Crying all week she's been, and perhaps you can find words to comfort her.'

John's smile faded and the lines in his face deepened. Louise, who could only make a guess at what was being said from what he had told her earlier, sensed his concern. Impulsively she slipped her hand into his and squeezed it. He looked down at her and his eyes warmed, and his fingers returned the pressure on hers before releasing her hand.

The next moment a woman, perhaps some ten years older than Louise, appeared in the doorway. She was dark-haired and her face was drawn and pale. Her eyes lacked lustre. 'It is you, sir. For a moment I didn't believe our Meg,' she said dully. 'You've heard what he's done to my Wat?' Her voice broke suddenly. 'He didn't deserve that, sir,' she wailed, throwing her apron over her head and sobbing into it.

Louise moved and put her arm round her, feeling it was the least she could do to comfort her. John pulled her away. 'You are forgetting your situation,' he said in an undertone. 'Wat must be dead.'

Maud suddenly ceased her crying and lifted her head. She scrubbed at her eyes. 'Dead he is, sir. Had him hung he did on the Lollers gallows and lit a fire under him.' She paused and swallowed. 'He consigned him to hell's fire, but I don't believe he's there, sir. He's sleeping now and he'll be raised at the Last Day with the Saviour. That I do believe!' Her voice had strengthened. 'That's right, isn't it, sir?'

'Ay, mistress.' He squeezed her shoulder. 'And that same Saviour will give you strength to go on. But you and your sons must not return to Cobtree. It won't be safe for you. Stay here with your sister for now, and I will have a word with my cousin about building a cottage for you.'

'Thank you, sir.' She scrubbed at her eyes again.

He waited a moment to allow her to compose herself before saying, 'Good mistress, I must ask you if a stranger called at your home last week. This young master is looking for his sister. A French maid of the name Marguerite—about twelve years old. My brother was sending her to you and Wat to help you out.'

Maud's eyes swivelled from John to Louise and there was a silence, then, 'There was a strange maid with a lad,' she said slowly, 'standing on the edge of the crowd, but I had no mind to heed them properly that day. But I know I never saw them again afterwards.'

Louise tugged on John's arm. 'What is she saying?'

'That there was a maid but she hasn't seen her since.' He frowned.

'Ask her was she flaxen-haired and whether she wore a russet gown.'

John did so.

'Ay, she could have been fair. I think she was. As for the colour of her gown, now that I don't remember,' said Maud, her eyes going from one to the other.

'My thanks to you anyway.' John dug in his pocket and pulled out some coins. He pressed them into her palm. 'I will not forget to speak to my cousin.'

A watery smile brightened her face and she lifted his hand and pressed it against her cheek. 'God bless you, sir,' she muttered huskily.

John stepped back and Louise looked at him. 'Well?' she demanded. 'Tell me everything you said.'

'Up on your horse first and we'll talk on the way to my cousin's house.'

'Your cousin's?' she said quickly. 'Is that where Marguerite is?'

He shrugged. 'I have no notion of your sister's whereabouts, but it could be that Adam knows.' He dug in his heels and pulled on the reins, lifted a hand in farewell, and left Maud staring after them.

John told Louise of the exchange between himself and Maud. 'It could have been Marguerite,' she said eagerly. 'At least she has been here.'

'A week ago—probably,' said John cautiously. 'But to say where she could be now would be purely guesswork.'

'But your cousin——'

'That is a long shot, Louise. It's unlikely he'll know anything definite. After all, what happened wasn't on his manor. But news does get round, and although Adam has little to do with Dykemore I gather from Matt that there is some interchange between him and the steward at Cobtree.'

'Then perhaps it would be best to see the steward,' she pressed.

'Only as a last resort,' he murmured, his eyes narrowing. 'I would not like it to get back to Dykemore

that I've been asking questions of his steward. Actions
and words can be misconstrued, twisted and used against
one. It's happened in the past to me and I've no intention
of giving Dykemore the satisfaction of toasting my toes
on the gallows.'

She gazed at him and her eyes were sombre. 'I'm sorry,
John. I have done what your brother feared.'

He smiled slightly and shook his head. 'I've lived with
that danger stalking me for years. Dorothy was
Dykemore's tool. She betrayed me when I went to warn
Harry five years ago when he got himself involved in a
plot to capture the King and his brothers, and to demand
drastic changes in the Church. I know my enemies and
that is my greatest weapon against them. It was when I
believed him a friend, and Dorothy a faithful wife, that
I nearly lost my life.'

'Tell me,' Louise asked quietly. 'I would try and
understand.' There was a silence and she sensed his
reluctance. 'You do not trust me?' she murmured.

'It is not that. It's just that we are here at my cousin's
house and I can see him. Later! I will tell you later.' He
urged his horse into a canter.

With that she knew that she had to be satisfied, as she
followed him up the winding path past a small green
swathe of lawn with flower-beds. She reined beside him
outside a stone house. It had glazed windows and stood
foursquare against the weather, its upper storey jutting
out over the lower. The door was open and a man of
perhaps some thirty years came slowly down a couple
of steps towards them.

'Jack?' His deep voice contained a note of enquiry.
'Or could it possibly be Harry?'

'You had it right the first time, coz.' John grinned and
held out his hand to the fair giant standing at his horse's
head. 'Is all well with you and your good wife and
brood?'

'I could wish them less noisy but it's to be expected with the festive season approaching. Where have you come from?'

John dismounted. 'France. Come from Dover today. Let me introduce you to Master Saulnier. We seek his sister—a French maid of some twelve years, named Marguerite. Harry sent her to Wat Fuller, but I presume you know what happened to him.'

Adam frowned. 'It's a pity he couldn't keep his opinions to himself and he could have saved his hide. He was a good worker. But that's the trouble with some Lollards—they like to shoot off their mouths.' He nodded in Louise's direction. 'Frenchie, is he?'

'Naturally,' said John politely, 'if his sister is French. I just wondered if you'd heard anything about the wench?'

Adam rasped a hand across his large square chin. 'You say Harry sent her?' John nodded. His cousin sighed. 'That was made plain, I hazard. You'd best come in, both of you. You'll be ready for a drink and a bite to eat. You're just in time for supper and I don't doubt you'll be needing a bed. It'll be dark within the hour. I'll get one of the men to take your horses round to the stables.' And without another word he turned on his heels and went inside the house.

'He knows something about Marguerite,' said John to Louise, holding a hand up and helping her dismount so that she came down close to him. 'Just what we'll find out when he's ready.' His voice was low as his fingers brushed her cheek. 'You can't rush my cousin Adam.'

She looked up into his intense blue eyes and felt a moment's breathlessness. 'But at least you're certain he can tell us of Marguerite's whereabouts?' she murmured, experiencing a desire to press against him and have his arms around her which caused her to instantly back away.

He shrugged and began to unfasten the baggage from behind her saddle. 'As certain as I can be.' He took her arm and led her up the steps and into the hall.

It was filled with activity. The trestles had been put up and platters and bowls were being placed on the table by several serving-maids. A couple of boys were kicking a ball at the far end of the hall, and a girl was playing with a doll sitting near the fire on a stool, close to an elderly woman. A larger boy was grooming a hound, and Adam was talking to a plump woman wearing a surcote of pale blue. She glanced towards them and, after patting Adam's arm, she hurried over to Louise and John.

'You are welcome, Jack.' Her smile warmed her large brown eyes as she stretched up and kissed him. Then she turned her attention to Louise.

'Mistress Ann, this is Master Louis Saulnier.' John made the introductions again.

'Ay! So Adam said,' murmured the mistress of the house, scrutinising Louise's face. 'He's a pretty lad. And there's that man of mine speaking of him as if he were one of the devil's minions. But now that's because there's been warring over one thing and other between our countries for heaven only knows how long.' She smiled. 'Come, lad, and warm yourself by the fire for a few moments before supper. We won't expect you to change your raiment.'

John took Louise's arm, translating swiftly what Ann had said. She smiled and thanked her in English, and went gladly with him to warm herself by the flames that burnt vigorously on the hearth. She eased off her gloves and folded them into her belt before pushing back her cloak over her shoulders to allow the heat to penetrate the better her chilled, stiff body. They were both silent as they stared into the fire. It had occurred to Louise that if the family considered her a youth then it was likely that they would expect her to share a room with either their boys or John. But before she could give much thought to the situation they were called to the table.

A bowl of water was brought to them by one of the sons of the house. They rinsed their hands and dried them on the towel presented to them by another son. Grace was said by the priest sitting a few places up from Louise and next to the old woman, whom John informed her was Ann's mother. They were served a soup, rich with peas, barley and chunks of rabbit meat, in treen bowls. It was followed by slices of heron in a vinegar and ginger sauce on thick trenchers of wheatmeal bread. There was also sliced brawn in a wine and honey syrup. Little talk spread along the table as they all ate their fill. Only when warm spiced wine and sweetmeats were set before them did the children begin to chatter and the grown-ups to talk.

Louise had to be content to listen to the hubbub of noise, only understanding few words here and there. She hoped that later John, who was in deep conversation with his cousin, would give her the information that she wanted.

It was to be much later it seemed as the two men sat on, talking, while the women rose and took the children to their beds. Louise got up too, went to the privy and came back. The women, returning also, sat with their sewing, close to the fire. The priest left the table, and only Louise remained, dozing over her wine, weary with the day's travelling. Then a frowning John hoisted her up.

'The servants want to clear away the trestles,' she heard him say, as his arm went round her shoulders and he led her to a door in the right-hand corner of the room. 'And if we want to have an early start then it's bed for us.'

'Where are we going?' she muttered, as a cold wind whipping along a narrow passage set her cloak swirling. They began to mount a wooden staircase.

'We are guests—we have a bedchamber to ourselves. The girl and her grandmother are sharing a room with Adam and Ann.'

Louise paused and blinked at him. 'I knew this would happen. Are you sure you know what we're doing?' The words were slurred. 'What about Marguerite?'

'I'll tell you everything once we're alone,' he said soothingly.

'Alone. It's not right for us to be alone. Is it good news or bad?'

'Both.'

'I don't understand.'

'You will.' His voice sounded grim. They had come to a door to the left at the top of the stairs. 'Now quiet. We don't want to disturb the boys when we pass through their room to ours.'

'Won't say a word,' she muttered, gathering her cloak around her.

John smiled slightly, put his hand over her mouth, and, placing his arm around her waist, he lifted her off her feet and carried her past the slumbering boys to a door at the far end of the room. He put her down and dragged her through the doorway, closing the door quietly behind them.

A small lamp, burning rancid mutton fat, cast a tiny circle of yellow light on the bed that took up most of the space. Louise's nose wrinkled with distaste. 'Where are we?' The fingers of one hand curled about his wrist.

'I've told you, and it doesn't matter,' whispered John. 'Get into bed.'

'Pardon?' She sought to pull herself together.

'It's all right,' he muttered. 'You can trust me. I'll sleep on the floor.' He trod softly over to the bed and took off the top blanket.

She nodded, flung back the covers, scrambled on to the bed and into it fully clothed.

'Your boots, woman,' he hissed.

Louise scowled at him and stretched out her legs in his direction. The corner of his mouth lifted and he tossed the blanket over his shoulder and pulled off her boots, before covering her. He wrapped his blanket round him and sat sideways on the bed. 'Your sister was here,' he said quietly.

She gazed at him from bleary eyes. 'Was?'

'At Cobtree. Dykemore ordered the lad to take her to Burford.'

Louise attempted to sit up. 'Why? And where is this Burford?'

'Oxfordshire. And the "why" is because Dorothy has a fever, and so apparently have several of the serving-maids. Your sister's been sent to help in the house, according to Adam's information, which he had from Dykemore's steward.'

There was a silence and Louise forced her eyelids wider. 'The bad news is that you don't want your wife to see me, I suppose?'

'No,' he said shortly, frowning. 'Haven't you been listening? They all believe you to be a pretty lad. It wouldn't occur to them that I would deceive them in such a manner. The bad news is that the fever is partic-ularly nasty and virulent.' He hesitated.

'What are you saying?' She leaned forward and seized his arm. 'Are people dying of it?'

'I have not heard so,' he lied. 'But I thought you'd best be prepared. Your sister could go down with it and it will take us at least four days to get to Burford. You might have to stay in England longer than you thought—till she has recovered.'

Louise freed a sigh of relief. 'Is that the bad news? I thought you were going to say that you would not take me.'

He smiled. 'I've given you my word, haven't I?'

'Ay.' She returned his smile, and loosened her hold on his arm. He caught her hand and, lifting it to his mouth, pressed a kiss on her palm. His eyes met hers over their joined hands and sweetness trickled like warm honey through her veins. 'Perhaps,' she whispered, 'you could sleep on the bed. It would be more comfortable.'

'Do you consider that wise?' A smile deepened the creases about his nose and mouth.

'No. But it'll be a lot warmer,' she muttered sleepily, lying down, her hand still holding on to his. He stretched out beside her, his chin resting on her hair. Despite the layers of covering between them, she could not help thinking of how it had been in the four-poster in Caen. In the morning, she would have to be mindful of his having a wife.

CHAPTER NINE

DAYLIGHT was already streaming into the room when Louise woke, and the place beside her was empty. She heard the door latch being lifted, and, groaning, turned over.

'I thought you'd be full of aches today,' John said, smiling cheerfully as he placed a bowl on the floor. Over his arm he had a towel and some clothing. He closed the door behind him. 'Also that you might want to wash and change your raiment.'

She eased herself into a sitting position, her legs over the side of the bed. 'But I have only women's wear! What have you there?' She leaned forward curiously and he placed the clothes on her lap.

'I have exchanged what you have on for these clothes of Adam's eldest boy and a pair of riding boots. You said the ones you've been wearing are too big.'

Gratitude flooded her as she fingered the garments. The woollen shirt, padded jupon, and the russet houppelande felt soft and warm, and—she lifted them to her nose—fresh. Her eyes met his, and they were moist. 'I have felt dirty and smelly for so long that you can't begin to imagine how grateful I am for your consideration in fetching these for me,' she said in almost passionate tones.

'Don't you think I've felt the same?' he said ruefully.

She gazed at him appraisingly. His hair was damp and curled on his forehead and he had shaved. The houppelande he wore was green, fur-trimmed, and split up the sides for easier movement while riding. Beneath it showed a doublet of saffron. It was a pleasure looking

140

at him and perhaps her feelings showed in her face, because his eyes twinkled as he said, 'I've also brought
some salve for your chapped lips and cheeks—and for
any other places on your anatomy that you would like
to anoint.' He took a small jar from his pocket. 'Ann
said it's goose grease and yarrow.'

She grimaced. 'I think I would need a larger jar to
cover them all, but I am very grateful.'

John smiled. 'I'll wait outside. The older boys are at
their lessons with the priest. But the younger children
just might come in for curiosity's sake to look at the
"Frenchy lad".' He lifted the latch and left her.

Louise had not expected such thoughtfulness and
courtesy. During the night he had made no advances
towards her, and, to her dismay, as she stripped off her
soiled clothes her thoughts strayed to how pleasant it
would have been if he had. She chided herself—she must
not think in such a way! Kneeling on the floor, she
washed her hair with the tablet of Castile soap provided,
before washing her body. Yet as she dried her breasts
her remembrance was of how he had touched and kissed
her. Shaking her head, she tried to rid it of the pictures
there. He had surely bewitched her if such sinfulness
was still in her mind. Consider his wife, she ordered
herself, towelling the rest of her dry. His sick wife! A
wife who had betrayed him! said another little voice in
her head. 'Still a wife,' she said it aloud. 'Remember
that, Louise!'

The door opened and she covered herself with the
towel hurriedly. 'Did you ask for something?' John's
gaze slid over her throat and bare shoulders—her legs.
And came back to her face.

'I was talking—to myself.' Her voice was husky, as
she struggled to free her eyes from his gaze. 'I will not
delay you much longer.'

'We don't have to wait to break our fast.' He moved slowly towards her. 'Ann has prepared us some food to take with us so that we can eat on our way.'

'I'd best make haste, then,' she whispered, her hand searching for the woollen shirt on the bed. He picked it up and placed it about her shoulders, before lifting her free arm and easing it into the sleeve. Not daring to look at him, she changed hands on the towel and slipped her other arm into the other sleeve, before submitting to his buttoning the shirt with fingers that quivered.

He picked up the woollen hose and linen slops and held them out to her. The towel slipped from her fingers as she took them, and he bent and picked it up, with his eyes still on her face, only to drop it on the bed.

Somehow she was in his arms, his hands clasped behind her back, her fingers laced behind his. She lifted her face, and his mouth brushed her sore lips, nuzzled her throat, before hugging her to him, and nestling her head against his shoulder. For several minutes they stayed in that position and she waited, her pulses racing, for him to make the next move. His hands strayed beneath the shirt to her buttocks, and he pressed her against him. She knew that he wanted her just as she wanted him, could feel him trembling.

He released her abruptly so that she fell on the bed. There was an expression in his face that caused her heart to leap into her throat. 'I'll go downstairs and bring the horses round,' he muttered. 'Don't be long.'

Louise picked up the clothes from the floor with shaking hands, and sank on to the bed. Now she truly knew what temptation was! The only answer was for them not to be alone and to keep their distance. And that was going to be impossible! Sooner or later he would take her again, and to her shame she knew that she would not be unwilling. She was damned unless she confessed and paid penance and resisted.

With fingers that still shook she took the tiny jar of salve and rubbed it on her lips and cheeks, on the chafed places on her inner thighs and inside her knees. Then she finished dressing hurriedly, gave her hair a final rub, pulled on her fur hat, and, carrying the towel and the bowl, she quit the bedchamber.

Louise's thanks to Ann and Adam were perhaps a little effusive, due to her overwhelming sense of guilt for deceiving them, and for what might have happened under their roof. She was glad when she and John had left their manor, and Cobtree, behind, retracing their journey of yesterday. John was silent and withdrawn and, although she was extremely hungry by the time that they reached the London road, she kept quiet, and tried to stir up some interest in the landscape through which they were passing. It undulated gently and there were more fruit trees and sheep.

When at last John spoke it was to inform her, in a voice that showed he was making an effort to behave as if nothing had happened between them, that during the great rebellion thirty years ago his father and mother had fled from the peasant army along this selfsame road after her father had been killed. 'Were they married?' she asked.

He shook his head. 'She was betrothed from girlhood to his brother and he was taking her to him.'

'Then how did they marry?' Her gaze shifted from the road to his face and away again, having him so close she possessed a desire to reach out and touch him.

'They fell in love and my mother determined to marry him.' His voice was bland.

'I presume she got her way,' said Louise brightly.

'Father used to say that once Mother decided then he didn't stand a chance. It almost caused a scandal but they managed to avoid that and it all ended happily enough.' He had slowed his horse to a walk and now took out the napkin with the food from his saddlebag.

He balanced it on the pommel and handed Louise some bread and sheep's cheese. She ate hungrily.

'I cannot say that my parents, or even my grand-parents, ever caused any scandal in our family,' she said, almost wistfully, in between mouthfuls. 'Their lives always sounded extremely dull the way my father used to tell it. In truth he made marriage sound an unenviable state.'

'It can be,' said John grimly. 'I went into marriage, believing that our relationship could be like that of my parents. But Dorothy made it clear from the beginning that it was due to her being a dutiful daughter to her mother that she had made a match that was merely one of convenience.'

'And then she betrayed you?'

'Ay,' he said shortly. 'I'd hidden Harry, who had escaped from a disastrous plot, in our stables. She told her uncle of it and we were both imprisoned. He took the opportunity of torturing us in an attempt to find out the names of any Lollards we knew who were actively involved in spreading the gospel. Fortunately the King had a change of heart and for a price we gained our freedom. He needed the money, you see, to finance his wars in France.'

'And how did your wife behave after you were freed?'

A sharp laugh escaped him. 'She told me that she had had no choice but to inform her uncle! The skin was still raw on my back from the hot irons when she said that! Not that she would look upon my naked body. The flesh is unclean,' he said sarcastically, 'and she could never understand why God couldn't find a different way for mankind to beget children. And in like spirit she told me that she betrayed me so that my immortal soul could be saved from hell's fire. And that could only be done by my being persuaded of the error of my beliefs by my suffering.'

Louise's eyes sparkled. 'How could she bear for you to suffer so?'

He looked at her, and his face softened. 'Has it still not sunk in, my sweet? She cares nothing for me, for all her talk of being concerned. So what if I suffered pain? She inflicts pain and discomfort on herself with continuous fasting, and with scourgings by her uncle.'

Louise flashed him a look. 'Her uncle whips her? Why do you allow it?'

'How am I to stop it when I am away from home?' he said grimly 'She has said that she is proud to suffer just as Jesus did.'

A shiver raced through Louise. 'I do not like pain. There is too much of it in life.' She hesitated, before adding, almost reluctantly, 'There was a time when I was betrothed.'

John glanced at her. 'What happened?'

'He died in a squabble between the Armagnacs and Burgundians. He was a follower of Duke John, who was murdered recently in Paris and the Dauphin was implicated.'

'Harry told me about that. It caused a storm among the French.' He frowned. 'Apparently there was hope of the two sides joining forces and halting Henry's progress.'

She said vehemently, 'It's so stupid! The Armagnacs' quarrel is years old and should have been put aside for the good of France.'

'True,' said John lightly. 'Especially when it's all over a woman.'

'You know about it?' Louise was taken aback, and not a little dismayed.

'Your queen had an affair with Louis of Orleans, the King's brother, after already having had John of Burgundy, the King's uncle, for her lover. There was bound to be a fight sooner or later, especially when he who has the Queen's support controls the King when his madness is upon him.'

'You are well informed, Master Milburn.' Her chagrin showed on her face. 'What hope is there for France when its nobility behaves in such a way?' she said angrily. 'Now it's rumoured that the Queen has taken the Burgundian side and they are allying themselves with Henry—that a marriage will be arranged between the princess Catherine and Henry, and that he will be declared heir to the throne instead of the Dauphin.'

'It's common talk that the Dauphin might not be the King's son anyway, but a bastard by one of her lovers,' said John. 'If Catherine and Henry have a son, maybe——'

'And which throne will this son sit upon?' she asked tersely. 'England's, or France's? You said yourself some such words as it would be impossible for one king to rule both.'

'Perhaps it would be best if we talked of something else,' he said quietly.

'Ay,' she muttered, wishing that she had never mentioned her betrothed, whom she could barely remember now.

A silence fell and they did not speak for some time.

They came to Faversham, crossing the river Swale, and still neither of them had spoken. Louise felt depressed, wondering whether she was quite mad to have started on her quest to find her sister. The weather was cold and grey and she was completely dependent on an Englishman for all her needs. She felt a need to stir up her old hatred of the English, because of such dependence. It would be so easy to begin to rely on him totally for all her needs. Had he not offered her rest and comfort with his mother? It had been a kind thought but she must not ever consider acceptance.

It was just upon dusk when, weary to the bone, they stopped at an inn. It was noisy inside, and the smoke

from the fire caught Louise's throat, and hurt eyes
already watering from the cold wind. John fell into conversation with a couple of travellers as they sat at the
table over a supper of pottage, bread, herrings and ale.
She was cut off from their talk because she knew so little
of the language. She felt more than a little angry at
feeling an outsider, as they went upstairs to the commu-
nal bedchamber. Fully clothed, she fell asleep immediately on the straw pallet, next to John's, on the floor.

Stiff and sore, they set out next morning with several
other people, whose destination was London. Louise
resigned herself to passing the time with nothing to do
but look at the landscape. But they had not gone far
when John terminated his conversation with a pilgrim,
and turned his attention upon her. His dark brows were
knit in a frown. 'You have hardly spoken since yesterday
morning. Are we enemies again because of our conversation yesterday?'

'How can we be enemies when I have accepted your
help?' she muttered, her hazel eyes glinting a little. 'If
I have not spoken, Master Milburn, it is because I *cannot*
join in the conversation when you speak to your fellow
countrymen.'

He stared at her and nodded his head. 'Forgive me,
Louise! I was so caught up in seeking to find out how
matters have stood in England while I've been away that
I did not think. Perhaps we could use this time for you
to learn some English?'

'It could be useful,' she agreed, thinking that there
might come a time when she could find herself without
him near at hand.

'Good lass.' The intense blue eyes were warm as they
rested on her face, and she could not help but respond.

'Let the lessons commence,' she said gaily.

In such a mood the journey passed pleasantly enough.
Rochester came in sight and by then Louise was in

command of a little more English. John had proved a good instructor, patient but persistent.

The December days were short, so John called a halt at an inn in the city. After they had stabled their horses, Louise said hesitantly, 'I would like to go to confession and Mass before I sup. Perhaps you could come with me?'

His blue eyes were thoughtful as he took in the expression on her face. 'I'll take you to the cathedral.'

They walked along the narrow high street, made up of gabled buildings, to the cathedral. 'It is dedicated to St Andrew the Apostle,' he informed her. 'Mass is held in the nave for the common people. There is talk of a parish church being built because since the great rebellion there have been frequent disputes between the Benedictine monks and the townsfolk.'

'It's a magnificent building,' she murmured, glancing up at the turreted west front with its rich arcading and elaborately carved doorway. There was Christ in majesty, supported by his angels and the symbols of the Evangelists. 'Will you come inside with me?' she asked hesitantly.

His eyes narrowed, but he took her elbow and they entered the building. 'There is a shrine to St William of Perth in the eastern transepts,' he said softly, 'if you are interested in saints. They say many miracles took place after he was murdered, and buried here.'

She nodded vaguely. 'Will you make your confession?'

'To a priest? No,' he said softly. 'We have a great high priest, who has passed into the heavens and stands on the right hand of God. It is to the Father through the Lord Jesus that I will confess, man to his Lord.'

She stared at him in astonishment. 'But how can you do that? We are not worthy to pray directly to God. And besides, who will tell you what penance you must pay for your sins?'

'I know what God asks of me already.' His face was serious. 'A contrite heart, and—that I go and sin no more.' He pressed her arm. 'Louise, what I believe now I did not come to without a lot of thought. This my parents encouraged.'

She was silent, considering how her father would cover his ears, rather than listen to what he called blasphemy and the babblings of the Devil. 'Yet you still sinned,' she murmured.

'Ay.' His voice was low and passionate. 'Tempted by the flesh, I fell. And sorry I should be to confess that I do not regret a moment of it.'

'You should not say that in here,' she whispered, feeling her blood stirred by his words and the look in his eyes. She gazed up at the soaring roof and the beautiful raised choir and presbytery and was awe-struck. 'Let us get out of here,' she said in a scared voice. 'I do not feel that I have prepared myself for righteous confession.'

'Forgive me.' He was penitent. 'It is my fault for making you say such things. You have done no great wrong.' He lifted her hand and kissed it.

'You shouldn't be doing that here either,' she whispered, closing her eyes tightly and praying for ice in her blood instead of heat. Even so she pinched John's arm and nudged him in the direction of the door.

'What now?' he asked, once they were outside. 'Shall we go back to the inn and have supper?'

'What else is there to do on such a dull, dreary evening?' she replied, letting out a heavy breath, wishing the journey over, and knowing that she should want it so because then she and Marguerite could be on their way back to Normandy.

The food was good and hot, and there was a juggler and a minstrel, on their way to entertain the nobility in London, staying at the inn. They practised their arts on a willing audience, some ribald jokes were made, and

the artistes were rewarded for their talents. Louise's body
drooped with weariness and she was already half asleep
when they retired to the sleeping chamber upstairs.

She woke in John's arms. But there was nothing lover-
like about his embrace, so she told herself, despite the
look in his eyes as she dragged herself out of his arms.

The next day passed in much the same fashion. They
stayed a night in an inn in Southwark, and then they
were on the road again. Louise felt as if she had been
in the saddle half her life. One more night they spent in
an inn, and then they were on the final stage of their
journey to Burford. John became withdrawn and Louise,
instead of being excited at the thought of seeing her sister,
felt nervous and low-spirited.

They skirted Oxford and travelled several more miles
before they came to a valley, set among rolling hills, filled
with the shadows of late afternoon.

Burford's high street was broad, with some houses
built of yellow stone and others of timber and thatch,
sweeping down towards the church. They walked their
weary horses part way down before John turned off the
street and up an entry into a courtyard. There was no
sign of activity but a light shone through a leaded bay
window on the ground floor of the large stone-built house
before them. John glanced about him and up at the
house. A dark shadow passed an upper window. He
dismounted and helped Louise down from the saddle.
'It's unusually quiet for this time of day,' he said in an
undertone.

'Perhaps they're all ill?' She clung to his hands a
moment, before straightening her aching back.

He made no answer, only indicating silence, before
moving soft-footedly in the direction of the lighted
window. She followed just as quietly, sidling along the
wall of the house in like manner to him, watching as he
peered round the side of the window. He drew back
swiftly and bumped into her, then, seizing her hand,

hurried her away past the main entrance, and round the side of the house. 'What is wrong?' she whispered.

'It's Dykemore and Bradshaw, our man of business. They've always been as thick as bees in a hive. I wager they're plotting something.'

'What of your wife? Was she in the room?'

John shook his head. 'She never interferes in business matters when I'm home, but I always suspected when I was away those two got their heads together.' They came to a narrow doorway and he opened the door quietly.

Louise glanced about her as they entered what appeared, from the jars and flagons on floor and shelves, to be the buttery. They passed through it and came out on to a narrow stone passage. The low murmur of voices could be heard coming from a room along the passageway to the left and near the front door stood a couple of men who wore weapons, but who were not looking their way. John took her hand and led her in the opposite direction until they came to a flight of stairs.

They went up it in the dark and John paused a moment, listening, then headed along a passage till they stopped in front of a door. He lifted the latch but the door did not give under the pressure of his hand. Then he noticed the key in the lock and, turning it, pushed open the door.

A boy, dressed soberly in a black surcote and hose, who had been pacing the floor in the darkened room, looked up quickly, and the misery on his face was replaced by surprised delight. 'Father, you received my message, then?' he demanded. 'They said you wouldn't—were furious at me for sending one!' He flung himself at John, and his voice was muffled against his shoulder, as he added, 'But you have come faster than the wind, and swifter than I prayed for! And I'm glad because it will annoy Uncle Dykemore no end.'

'Hush, Peter,' John said quietly. 'Why are you not with Master Fulcombe? Where is your mother? And the servants—there seems to be nobody here but the two downstairs, some guards and yourself.'

The boy pulled a little away from him. 'So you didn't get my letter. I wrote to you care of your agent in Kent. Mother's dead! Over a week since and the funeral already been, and her buried in the churchyard.' His square chin quivered. 'The fever has raged here. Several people have died of it. Old Will! The new baby just down the high street! Jimmy, the shepherd's brother!'

John's hands stilled on the boy's shoulders and there was a stupefied expression on his face. 'Your mother is *dead*?'

Peter nodded, his eyes on his father's face. 'Have I not said so?' he burst out. John hushed him and he went on in a whisper. 'And I knew not about it until too late. Then Uncle Dykemore came and took me away from Master Fulcombe's house, and brought me here. He sent Mab and Giles away, the only two not sick, and we have had only those guards wait upon us. He said that he's taking me to Oxford and that I can be a scholar and learn under him. But I don't want to, Father! I want to be a merchant venturer like you! And now that Mother's dead perhaps I can be!'

'Perhaps,' muttered John, hugging the boy to him. His eyes met Louise's wondering gaze over his head. 'But what about your prenticeship, and your learning your grandfather's trade, so that you can take his place here?'

Peter's blue eyes were uncertain. 'I don't know. I just want to get away from here and be with you. I don't want to become a priest like Uncle Dykemore says and burn people.'

'Is that what he said to you?' asked John in a tight voice.

'I told him that it was cruel to burn people. Told him that I'd run away and find you.' He pulled a face. 'I should have kept quiet about that because he locked me in here, and said that I'd get nothing but bread and water for a week.' He paused to draw breath and John put a finger against his lips.

'Enough for now, son,' he said softly. 'I think I have the gist of things. Let's get out of here before your uncle realises that I'm here.'

'Aren't you——?' began the boy.

'Hush,' whispered John. 'Later.' He released his hold on him and looked at Louise. 'Keep as quiet as you can.' She nodded, aware of Peter's curious gaze as they moved towards the door, wondering why John hadn't told her he had a son. Perhaps he considered talking about anything connected with his marriage a sore point.

They were along the passage, down the stairs and just inside the buttery, when they heard the door of the room further along open. It seemed as if they all stopped breathing as footsteps went past the buttery door in the direction of the stairway. John waited only a moment before seizing hold of Louise's and Peter's arms and hustling them through the buttery and outside.

The horses were still where they had left them, their heads drooping a little. John put his hands together for Louise to put her foot in, and she sprang into the saddle. Peter was helped up behind her before John vaulted on to his horse. They were out of the courtyard in minutes and riding up Burford high street and on to the old packhorse way that ran along the crest of the hill.

Louise followed, having no idea where they were going, or what had happened to her sister. The news that John's wife was dead kept playing over and over in her head.

It was Peter, hanging on tightly to Louise's belt, who demanded to know where they were going.

'Yorkshire,' said John briefly.

Both Peter and Louise stared at him. 'Yorkshire!' they both exclaimed, almost in unison.

'I'm taking you to your grandparents for Christmas.' He smiled. 'They haven't seen you for an age.'

'I'm glad about that.' The boy grinned. 'But where shall we stay tonight, Father?'

'There's an inn a few miles on. We'll stop there.'

The boy seemed satisfied but Louise was not. 'Why did you not stay and confront Dykemore and this Bradshaw? It is likely from what you said that they are out to cheat you. And you could have asked him about Marguerite.'

John stared at her, and he hesitated before saying in French, 'You forget the guards. I couldn't fight four men single-handed. And besides I wanted Peter completely beyond his reach, and Yorkshire should be far enough at this time of year. It was a different matter leaving him in Burford when he was in Master Fulcombe's care being trained to follow in his grandfather's footsteps—because it was one of the few things that Dorothy and I agreed on, and she stood up to her uncle about. I don't know how much of what Peter said you were able to understand, but Dykemore would try and use my son as a weapon against me. I want him safe before I confront the pair of them.'

'What about Marguerite?' Her expression was anxious.

'Perhaps she never arrived there.' He addressed Peter. 'Did you hear of a French maid calling at your mother's house? She'd be in the company of a youth. They were sent to help in the house.'

Peter shook his head.

Louise fixed John with her gaze. 'Then how can we find her?' she demanded.

'Only by going to Yorkshire,' he said emphatically. 'Harry only told me what you already know—that I'd find her in Wat Fuller's house. He never told me the name of the man who brought her to England.'

'So I *have* to go to Yorkshire with you,' she said slowly.

'Ay!' His expression revealed little of his feelings. 'I'm sorry to disappoint you but you'll have to put up with my company a while longer. I only pray that my brother doesn't prove awkward about giving me the information once he sees you again.'

'What do you mean?' She was puzzled. 'Surely he will have no objection in telling us the name of the man?'

'One wouldn't think so,' he said lightly, forcing a smile. 'Don't worry. We'll find your sister sooner or later. Now let's ride.' He dug in his heels and urged the horse on.

Louise followed, wondering when her search would end.

CHAPTER TEN

THE journey had been long and tiring, but the intimacy that was still forced upon Louise and John each night was tempered by the presence of Peter. Even so she sensed a change in the man: he seemed preoccupied, which she supposed was natural in the circumstances. He has lost a wife and, despite what he had told her about Dorothy, she almost expected to see some evidence of his regretting her death, but if he was he kept his emotions well hidden. She was uncertain how to behave towards him now. There was a struggle going on inside her because after being in his company so much her feelings towards him had warmed and deepened instead of abating. Even his handling of his son drew her admiration. Her English lessons had continued and he had involved the boy in her teaching, which helped to take his mind off any sense of loss he was suffering.

The further north they had travelled the colder it had become. Now they were beyond the borders of Derbyshire and in Yorkshire itself. With a great deal of curiosity Louise stared about her at countryside that seemed to consist mainly of hills. So many hills, some dotted with sheep, others wooded. There were great swathes of moorland but few towns. They passed Knaresborough with its castle held in the King's honour, set high on its knoll overlooking the river Nidd.

'My cousin Hugh has a manor not far from here,' said John, easing his shoulders.

'Will we be staying there?' asked Peter eagerly, turning on his perch behind Louise. 'It's ages since I've seen Nat and Dan.'

John exchanged glances with Louise. 'We'd best break our journey. There'll be no moon tonight, and although Father's manor is not far from Hugh's I wouldn't recommend the ride over the fells in the dark.'

'Will there be many people in your cousin's house?'

'And how am I to know that?' He smiled. 'But it is Christmastide, so it's likely that my cousin will have family and friends gathering for the days of feasting.'

'What if your brother called there and told him about me?' Her hazel eyes were clouded.

His brows knit together. 'It depends on what he told them—if anything. But does it matter? Your father had you play the part of youth for your own safety. So cease your fretting, Louise.'

'It's not that easy not to be concerned.' Her hands twisted restlessly about the reins. 'They might question why I'm still dressed like a youth. They probably will not like me because I'm French. As well as that my English is not good and I have an accent.'

'A charming accent.' A slight smile eased his mouth. 'And we don't have to tell them that you're a woman if they don't know. It'll only be for the one night. If you can pass muster with Peter then why worry about my cousin and his family?'

'Do you really think Peter doesn't know I'm a woman?' she asked in French.

He shrugged. 'If he does, it doesn't bother him. But he's asked no questions about you, beyond why you are travelling in my company. My telling him about your sister seems to have satisfied him.'

Louise fell silent, annoyed with herself for caring whether John's kinsfolk liked her or not. Why should she care? Yet she knew the answer but did not like admitting it.

They came to a valley and John paused at the top of a hill to gaze down on a huddle of grey stone buildings. 'My cousin's house.'

'It looks so forbidding,' said Louise, shivering in the chill wind that blew over the bleak landscape.

'That is because it's fortified. The Scots have been known to raid as far south as this. Although there's been little trouble from that quarter for some years because their King James is a guest—to put it politely—of Henry of Lancaster.'

'And less politely?' she asked.

'He's a hostage. The King's father had some difficulty when he took the throne from Richard, and the Welsh and Scots took advantage of it. Trying to keep our neighbours out of England is how Henry learnt his siege craft.' He set his horse in motion down the hill.

They cantered up to a gatehouse, passing under its stone archway to enter a cobbled courtyard. A hound bounded forward, freeing a flurry of barks, only to be sent about its business by an elderly groom, who stopped and stared at them. A slow grin split his ruddy face. 'Your double be here, Master John. And your father and mother! Staying here for all the twelve days of Christmas and hoping you'd get here in time.'

Louise exchanged a quick look with John but before he could speak a door opened at the top of a flight of stone steps that ran at an angle up the side of the wall of the house. A man came out, followed by a woman. They froze when they saw the riders, and it did not need John's cry of 'Mother? Father!' and his swift descent from his horse to tell Louise who they were.

The likeness to John was there in the face of the upright figure coming down the steps, his hand gripping his wife's, steadying her as they reached the bottom. He had need to release her as John swept his mother off her feet and into the air and kissed her. She scolded him for being away so long, but hugged him as she did so. He set her on the ground and embraced his father. The two men began to talk.

John's mother turned towards Louise and Peter. She was small but neatly made, dressed in a creamy woollen gown and deep blue surcote. Her headdress and veil were crisp and white, and the curls that peeped out from beneath appeared to be spun from silver. 'Is that my grandson I see?' Her tone was one of disbelief. 'I did not look for such a surprise.' She hurried over to them, her arms held wide as Peter dismounted, and he suffered himself to be kissed and hugged in like manner to his father. Questions about his being there, his health and his studies were heaped upon his head. Her arm went about his shoulders as she hurried him over to his grandfather.

Louise dismounted unaided, such happiness delighting even as it saddened when she considered how she and Marguerite only had each other. Seeing the groom take the reins of John's horse, she decided that she might as well leave the family alone a moment and lead her mount to the stables. She was barely through the doorway when she collided with Harry.

For a moment neither of them spoke. His eyes, so like John's, were surveying her from her fur-framed face to the mud-splatted hem of the russet houppelande. 'So my brother's arrived,' he said at last. 'But why you, Mam'selle Saulnier? Couldn't he bear to let you go?'

She flushed. 'Marguerite was not where you said she would be,' she murmured, allowing a stableboy, who looked at her curiously, to take the reins from her gloved hands. 'The man Wat has met with the burning death. Marguerite arrived there but Dykemore ordered her to be taken to John's wife's house. But she had died and Marguerite was not there, and now I don't know where she is.' Her voice was rough with unexpected emotion and weariness. 'We need to know the name of the man you gave her to.'

'Dorothy's dead!' His eyebrows almost disappeared beneath his fringe of black hair, and he seemed struck dumb. Then he murmured, 'She's dead, and you're here still clad like a lad. Did the pair of you travel all this way alone?'

'Peter came with us.' She half lifted a hand then dropped it. 'John will explain. But if you could tell me the name of the man who has Marguerite?'

He stared at her. 'I never told you? The pair of you would have been better travelling south, my dear,' he drawled.

'What do you mean?'

He half opened his mouth but footsteps sounded outside and John entered. There was a moment's silence before he said in that silky tone that Louise hadn't heard for a while, 'So you've found each other, then?'

'If you mean Louise and myself—ay, brother,' said Harry, a sudden gleam in his eyes. 'To meet her so suddenly, looking so pretty, is an unexpected pleasure.'

'I'm sure it is,' drawled John. His smile came and went. 'Has she told you about Dorothy and your godson?'

Harry nodded. 'I'll be out to see him in a moment.'

'All right.' John faced Louise. 'Come. I want you to meet Mother and Father.'

'But Harry was just——'

'Now! If you please!'

Her gaze went from one brother to the other. There was something about the way they were staring at each other.

John seized her arm and almost pulled her off her feet. She had no choice but to go with him.

His parents were not where she had last seen them, and her heart raced a little as he led her up the steps and into a large hall. Tapestries hung on whitewashed walls, already smoky with winter's fires. It reminded her of the hall in the manor in Kent because there was the same noise and bustle, and children playing. Peter had already joined a group of lads sitting astride a great log decorated with ribbons and greenery. But coming towards her, accompanied by John's parents, was a man who held a striking resemblance to Master Adam Milburn, only this man was taller and fiercer-looking.

'Our host,' whispered John in her ear. 'His wife, Lady Jane, gave birth a week ago, and is still abed; that's why my mother and my cousin Blanche are here. Mother believes you a lad, so best we stick to that at the moment.'

'But——' began Louise, but he was already speaking.

'M'sieur Louis Saulnier, this is my cousin, Sir Hugh Milburn. My father, Master Guy Milburn, and my mother Mistress Philippa.'

Louise received a stiff nod from the knight and his expression was frosty. She made the slightest of bows. He then excused himself. The hand she had extended was taken by Master Guy and firmly shaken. The blue eyes that smiled into hers wore a slightly questioning, amused expression. '*Enchanté*, M'sieur Saulnier. John has been telling us a little about you, and that you speak some English.'

'*Oui, m'sieur.* God give you a good even.'

'And you, lad. May I introduce my wife?' Guy did not need to usher Philippa forward. She had already taken Louise's hand and her green gaze was inspecting her carefully. She leaned forward and kissed her. 'Harry told us that John had found him but not that it was because you told John you had seen him in Caen. I'm so grateful. My foolish son might never have plucked up the courage to come home if you had not helped John.'

'I—was glad to help,' stammered Louise,.

'John told me also that you lost your home and your father, and you are looking for your sister.' Her expression was warm. 'You have my sympathies and I'm certain that my son will do all he can to help you find her.'

Louise involuntarily flashed a glance at John. He stared at her and there was only the slightest lifting of one corner of his mouth to reveal that he found the situation amusing. She doubted if his mother knew anything about her other son's part in her sister's abduction.

Philippa smiled. 'But come and sit by the fire. You are chilled, which isn't surprising after your journey.' She patted Louise's hand before releasing it. 'It's likely that we will have some snow before the New Year.'

'It is very cold.' Louise followed her, accompanied by John and his father, to the huge fire that blazed on the hearth in the middle of the hall.

'Later you will be shown to your bedchamber,' said Philippa. 'We are a little crowded, and I did think to put you in with Peter, Dan and Nat, but John thought that perhaps, if you don't mind a truckle in one of the turret rooms, that would suit you better. I will have a brazier put in it to warm it.' Her pale brow puckered. 'Perhaps Blanche will see to it.'

'Blanche?' Louise looked up from the fire.

'Blanche is the daughter of one of my father's cousins,' said John idly, staring into the fire. 'She was widowed a couple of years ago.'

'And still mourns,' said his mother, almost apologetically. 'So you will pardon anything that she might say amiss, M'sieur Saulnier.'

'Of course.' Louise gave only fleeting thought to what this Blanche could say to her that would offend, while wondering why nothing was said about Dorothy being dead. But perhaps they did not expect John to mourn a wife who had almost caused his death.

'She and Harry have already struck sparks off each other,' said Guy drily. 'But then, my younger son can always find something to argue about with anyone.'

'Where *is* Harry?' Philippa's gaze ranged the hall. 'Ah! He's just entered and I think he has your baggage.' She turned to Louise. 'Do you wish to wash and change your

clothes? I could have water taken to your room but it
will be cold and there is little time before supper is
served.'

'In the morning will do,' said Louise, unable to resist
a glance at John. She would have liked nothing better
than to put on something clean but knew there were only
women's clothes in her baggage. What was she going to
do? She couldn't wear the same garments for the next
twelve days! What a ridiculous situation to be in!

Harry came up to them and placed the baggage at
John's feet. 'I think you'd best sort this out, brother. I
don't know who's wearing what.'

'I think when we left France you were wearing some
of it,' said John in honeyed tones. 'And very well you
looked in it.'

'I'm sure—er—Louis would look better,' responded
his brother, smiling at Louise, who didn't smile back.
She was tired and fed up, was getting a headache, and
wished nothing more than that she had never started this
mad masquerade.

'What *are* you two talking about?' demanded their
mother. 'Anything that fitted either of you would
certainly be too large for M'sieur Saulnier.'

'It's a private jest, Mother,' said John, his eyes dancing
as he put his hand through her arm. 'Remember when
we used to wear disguises when the mummers came and
how we deceived you?'

Her lovely mouth lifted. 'It doesn't seem so long ago.
Perhaps there'll be opportunity for you to attempt to
trick me again. No doubt Hugh will be having the
mummers perform here during the twelve days of
feasting.'

'Nothing more likely,' murmured Harry, glancing at
Louise. 'It'll be entertaining and folk will get up to all
sorts of japes.'

'No doubt,' said his mother drily, 'but do remember,
boys, that you are not children any more.'

Harry raised both eyebrows. 'I'm not likely to forget it when dearest cousin Blanche is on the scene. Her disgust of me would grow apace.'

'You deliberately set out to annoy her,' said his father. 'She is a devout woman and has lost a husband.'

'Whom she cared for as little as John cared for Dorothy,' said Harry. 'She's a hypocrite.'

'She has a mind to play the part of a grieving widow,' murmured Philippa.

'She always did,' put in John, looking beyond Louise's shoulder. 'And talk of the Devil——'

'Certainly, brother,' said Harry wickedly, his eyes following John's. 'But more like a dove in appearance, don't you think?'

Louise, who had been able to understand much of the conversation, stepped back and turned to see a woman coming towards them. She was dressed in grey and white, and her long fingers toyed with a large gem-studded crucifix on a gold chain about her neck. She was as fair as John and Harry were dark. Her pale blue eyes were large and fringed with barley-coloured lashes in a heart-shaped face. There was no denying she was beautiful, in a madonna fashion.

'Well met, coz.' She held a limp hand out to John. 'You have to be the more sensible twin,' she said in a husky voice.

Louise did not catch what John said because Harry sidled up to her and drew her aside to mutter, 'Sensible! I wonder what she would think if she knew about you. But then she always did have a fancy for my brother, primarily because he's the elder and has more coming to him. Possessions matter to Blanche.'

'You don't like her?' said Louise in a low voice, unable to resist learning something of this woman.

He shrugged and said softly, 'She's devious—and if you have an eye to my brother still setting you up in a house, then I would watch her.'

'I have no intention,' she retorted, her eyes sparkling.

'Perhaps it's marriage you have in mind.' His tone was pensive. 'I doubt if my brother will marry you. He generally behaves in a manner that is sensible.'

'I'm not so foolish as to consider that he would marry me,' she said with dignity. 'I'm only here because I need to know the name of the man who took Marguerite.'

'So you want something from me.' He smiled. 'There could be a price on such information, my dear. What have you to offer?'

Louise felt the heat run up under her skin, and was angry. 'But you took her!' Her voice rose slightly and there was a sudden hush in the conversation between the others, and Blanche's pale eyes rested on Louise.

'Who is this person?' she asked, fluttering a glance at John.

'This is M'sieur Saulnier,' he said, and it was as if a shutter came down over his face as his gaze washed over Louise and Harry. 'Louis, this is our kinswoman, Mistress Blanche Chutterbuck.'

Louise bowed stiffly, feeling frozen by John's expression.

'A *monsieur*?' Blanche clutched at her cruxifix and her mouth tightened. 'But why is he here? Was it Harry's idea? Likely he did not consider that the sight of a Frenchman would bring back my loss to me tenfold.'

'The *monsieur* came with John,' said Harry with obvious enjoyment. 'He is aiding him in his search for his sister, whom the wicked English abducted and brought here to be a servant.'

For a moment anger flashed in Blanche's eyes as she stared at Harry. Then she turned to John, placing a hand on his sleeve. 'Your brother jests, of course,' she said in a slightly amused tone.

'No,' said John shortly. 'The *monsieur* helped me in my search for Harry. I considered that the least I could do was to return the favour. Now if I'm not mistaken

supper is about to be served. Shall we sit down?' He
waved a hand in the direction of the high table, and,
after a reproving stare at him, Blanche slid her hand into
his arm.

'I forgive you. Come, John. You can tell me about
all your adventures.'

'Neatly handled,' murmured Harry, taking Louise's
elbow. 'Her husband perished at the siege of Harfleur—
that's why she was rude to you. Although he wasn't even
killed by the French but died, like many an Englishman
did, from a surfeit of tainted oysters.'

'Then she should not behave the way she does,' said
Louise tersely, determinedly keeping her eyes from
wandering to John and Blanche. 'I'm not overfond of
the English but I wouldn't be so rude to a guest.'

'Of course you wouldn't,' murmured Harry, his face
expressionless. 'Now what did you call my brother when
you met him? And didn't you try to kill him?'

Her eyes glinted. 'I had just cause when I thought him
you.'

'Do you still want to kill me?' He swung a leg over
the bench and eased himself over before sitting down.
'I swear my brother does if the look on his face is anything to go by.'

Louise glanced in John's direction and for a moment
their gazes held before his attention was demanded by
Blanche on his left. 'He's probably relieved that you have
taken me off his hands,' she muttered.

'Probably,' agreed Harry with a grin, holding out his
hands to the boy who was passing along the bench with
a bowl and pitcher of water.

'You're enjoying this,' muttered Louise, hunching her
shoulder at him.

'Relax, my dear,' he said in French as he dried his
hands. 'If you can't have my brother in your bed, why
not try me?' His eyes danced in a way that reminded her

terribly of John and there was an ache in the region of her heart.

She said quietly, 'No, thank you.' And turned to the boy who was holding out the bowl to her. Harry shrugged and turned to the woman on his right hand.

Throughout the meal she avoided looking at John and Blanche, and she and Harry exchanged little conversation. As for the man on her left, he was taken up talking to the woman the other side of him. If she had not begun to feel sleepy then the evening would have proved more of an ordeal. As it was she felt as if she were existing in a dream, and her head nodded.

A tap on the shoulder caused her to look up. 'I think it's time you were in bed.'

'Do you?' Louise tried to focus on the weather-beaten face. The blue eyes seemed to bore into hers and demanded—what of her? 'Perhaps someone can show me my room?' She spoke in French and the words were slurred with weariness.

'I will.' He took hold of her with one hand, the other held her baggage, and she was hoisted into an almost upright position.

She groaned. 'I don't think I want to see another horse for a long time,' she muttered.

'No?' A slight smile eased the grimness about his mouth as he slipped his arm about her waist. She heard him say, 'I'll see Louis to his room, Mother. He's tired out with travelling.' Was he really talking about her? She wasn't sure that it was right that Harry should go with her into her bedchamber, and said so in a sibilant whisper.

'Don't be foolish,' he muttered, frowning down at her as they walked down the hall. 'You're almost asleep on your feet. Someone has to take you up and it's better I do it than anyone else. I know you'd probably prefer my brother but you'll just have to put up with me.'

'Where's your brother?' She blinked up at him.

'Somewhere with Blanche. They probably have more in common than everybody thinks.'

'Ay.' A deep sigh escaped her. 'I know he won't want to marry me. I'm not good enough. It's all right suggesting setting me up as his mistress—but marriage, that's something different.'

He stilled. 'He's really asked you?'

'You know he has.' They had come to a door.

'And what did you answer?' he demanded.

She scowled. 'That would be telling. You ask too many questions, Master Milburn.'

His mouth tightened as he released her and opened the door. 'I won't ask any more.' They came out into a stone passageway lit by torches set in sconces on the wall. She could see the bottom of a curving flight of stone steps at its far end.

Louise had only ascended four steps when she stumbled. Immediately his hand was there lifting her up and helping her up the rest of the twisting steps.

At last they came to her bedchamber. It was partly circular and had only a narrow slit opening for a window, which had fortunately been glazed, shutting out the winds that had once made the room chillier than it was now. True, a brazier was glowing not far from the low truckle-bed, but it threw out little heat.

He placed the baggage on the truckle-bed and leaned against the stone wall, his arms folded across his chest, watching Louise warming her hands by the brazier. 'You can go now,' she said, barely glancing at him.

'It's come to this, has it?' he said angrily, dropping his arms. 'The first time we're really alone for days and you tell me to go. You're going to be cold in here, sleeping on your own.'

'I'll survive,' she said stiffly. 'You forget that I spent two years in the wild in worse conditions than this due to your king and countrymen.'

'Sweet Jesu! Are we back to that subject? It's because of Blanche, I suppose, and my brother.'

'If you know so much about my feelings, Master Milburn,' she muttered crossly, 'then you'll know I don't want you here.'

'Don't you?' he demanded, pushing himself away from the wall and coming to stand behind her. Immediately she made to move away but he seized her shoulder. She gasped. 'What is wrong?' The tone of his voice changed.

'My shoulders are stiff with riding,' she said in a tired voice. 'In truth the whole of me is weary. Now if you don't mind leaving?'

There was a short silence before he murmured, 'Let me ease you.'

'No!' she cried, and would have moved away but his hands gripped her shoulders.

'Be still, woman! I'm not going to rape you.' His fingers began to gently massage the muscles at the back of her neck. 'Be at ease, Louise.' The words were but a thread of sound and presented no threat. A sigh passed through her and after a few minutes she managed to roll her head round.

'Thank you,' she whispered. Lethargy caused her to droop against him.

His arms went round her and his mouth pressed a kiss on the nape of her neck. She jerked herself awake and began to struggle, but his muscles seemed to be made of steel. 'Let me go,' she demanded through gritted teeth.

'No,' he said calmly, turning her round. His lips found hers, forcing them apart with a passion that flamed such a response within her that she was shocked because it could have been John kissing her. But that wasn't possible because he was with Blanche and that thought hurt even as it angered. Perhaps even now he was kissing Blanche just as Harry was kissing her. Maybe Harry could rouse the same feelings within her as John! For several minutes she allowed herself to be swept along by physical desire and only came to an awareness of what they were doing when he tore free her shirt from her hose.

She was so dumbfounded that for a moment she was lost for something to do and say as his hands cupped her breasts, before rubbing his palm back and forth across her nipples, sending sensations darting along her nerves. Her pulses raced crazily. Sweet Jesu! What was she thinking of behaving in such a way? Harry would believe that he could treat her just as he had Clotilde. She tore her mouth from his and struggled, taking him by surprise so that she managed to free an arm to bring it up and slap his face. 'Don't ever kiss me like that again!' she panted. 'Or touch me!'

'What?' he demanded, his chest heaving and his eyes dark with emotion. 'Is this some kind of game you're playing, Louise?'

'I'm not very good at your kind of games,' she cried, pulling her shirt tightly about her. 'Now get out of here. I'm not prepared to pay the price for your help to find Marguerite.'

'What are you talking about?' His amazement was turning to anger. 'Are we really back to you believing that's what my wanting you is all about? A quick romp in payment?'

'Isn't it?' she said, forcing ice into her voice. 'I'll not be your mistress. I've told you before.'

A painful laugh escaped him and he moved over to the door. 'What a fool I am. I'd begun to trust you, to believe that life with a woman like you could be worth trying. Even just now I tricked myself into believing that you really cared and wanted me too.' He paused, riffling a hand through his hair and raising it into a curling crest. 'I don't understand. I could have sworn that you...' He shrugged and his expression hardened. 'You don't have to worry, Louise. I won't bother you again in such fashion. But I'll still keep my promise and help you to find Marguerite.' He closed the door behind him.

His words took moments to sink in. Had she misheard him? Or had he really said that he would keep his promise to find Marguerite? Her heart beat jerkily as she listened to his footsteps ringing on the stone floor and then heard them clatter down the steps. If he had then that meant that he was not Harry but John. Hadn't she thought it was John when he kissed her? She should have trusted her senses.

Her blood felt as if turned to ice and she sank on to the truckle-bed and put her head on her hand. Dear God, she loved him and she had sent him away!

CHAPTER ELEVEN

LOUISE'S instincts were to go after John and explain that she had believed him to be Harry, then she remembered her response to his kisses. She sank on to the truckle-bed and gazed unseeingly at the glowing brazier. How had she come to love him? This Englishman! She had been a fool not keeping her distance, knowing that what he could offer her was not acceptable. Three years ago it would have been her right to marry a man in John's position now that his wife had died—but not now! Tears sparkled on her thick lashes and she brushed them away fiercely. Damn kings and knights who made war!

Kicking off her boots, Louise pulled back the rough blankets and, fully-clothed, got beneath them. This night and all the nights to follow she was going to miss John's warmth, the male smell of him, his shoulder to pillow her head on. The tears started again and this time she let them fall, and cried into her pillow, until exhausted she slept.

The sound of a door closing woke Louise the next morning. She sat up slowly and gazed bleary-eyed about the room. Immediately the memory of what had happened last night was with her and it did not seem to matter that the brazier had gone out and the bed-chamber was cold and dimly lit. Someone had placed a bowl of water and soap on the floor. At the foot of the bed was a towel and some clothing. She leaned forward and saw that they were boy's clothing, sensible and hardwearing. Perhaps it was just as well that they were so plain and would do little to attract a man. But why was she thinking in such a way? John no longer wanted anything to do with her. He had made that clear.

Although she felt no enthusiasm for the coming day, she clambered out of bed and stripped. She washed thoroughly in the cooling water, before, with a frowning countenance, she donned the clean boy's clothes.

In no mood to go down to the hall yet and face John and a group of strangers, who, on the whole, seemed to possess no warmth of feeling towards her, she went over to the window and gazed out at overcast skies. It would have been better if she had never left the forest in Normandy! At least there her expectations of finding love and comfort had been low. Yet if she had stayed it would have meant giving up all hope of ever seeing her sister again, and she could not, would not, do that. Had John really meant what he had said about still helping her to find Marguerite? She thought of Harry and slammed a fist against the wall in angry frustration. Did he tease her when he talked of her paying for the information about Marguerite's captor? She did not think so.

Several minutes longer she stayed by the window, looking out on the unfamiliar landscape, wondering what she was to do, and whether John could make his brother tell him where Marguerite was, then she straightened her shoulders, picked up her cloak, and left the room.

Louise hesitated in the doorway of the hall. It was occupied by scurrying servants, going about their tasks, and there was much calling one to the other. She felt the excitement in the air and suddenly remembered that it was Christmas Eve. Over by the outside door a group of people had gathered, muffled up in fur-trimmed cloaks, ready to brave the cold weather outside. John and Harry were among them, as was Blanche.

Uncertain about what she was expected to be doing that day, Louise did not go over to them, but instead made her way across the rush-strewn floor to a trestle and sat on a bench. There was a loaf in front of her and she picked up a knife and cut a slice of bread, and spread it with honey. Her teeth bit into it, and her hand had just reached out to pour some ale when footsteps stopped the other side of the table.

'We're all waiting for you,' said a male voice that sounded far from patient.

Louise looked up and met the glinting blue eyes. He looked so annoyed that this twin had to be John. Her heart sank but she said politely, 'Pardon?'

'You understood me.' A muscle tightened in his lean cheek, which in daylight she could see still bore evidence of his beating-up in the forest.

'Oui!' She gesticulated. 'But how was I to know that you were waiting? No one told me! Am I supposed to read minds?'

'I've told you now,' he said emphatically, both his hands coming down hard on the table. 'So get moving. Bring your breakfast with you or you'll have it dark before we're done.' He turned and walked away from her.

'But where are we going?' she called, managing to swallow a mouthful of ale before scrambling over the bench and following him, bread in hand.

'Foraying for greenery to decorate the hall,' he shouted over his shoulder.

As soon as John reached the group, people began to move through the doorway, and were down the steps before Louise caught up with them. She found herself in company with Peter and his cousin Nat, who both smiled at her before continuing their conversation. She matched her pace to theirs. John certainly mustn't want her company if he hadn't waited for her. Probably he was with that Blanche woman who didn't like her!

Moodily she kicked a pebble and gazed about her as they came out of the courtyard. A hamlet of grey stone houses and a tiny church huddled in the shelter of a group of trees. From somewhere near came the sound of water rushing over rocks and a few moments later they crossed a bridge and headed towards the dark shape of a forest on a knoll to their right. There were sheep in the fields.

Once beneath the trees most of the group split up and from all directions came the sound of voices.

'I know where there's mistletoe growing,' said the gap-toothed Nat, who had a crop of tawny hair like his father, but possessed a wide, friendly smile. He led the way through a tumble of undergrowth, and they had to stoop to avoid sprays of thorny brambles, narrowly missing getting their clothes torn, and sending a boar crashing away from them. 'That was a near escape,' he said absently, getting back to the subject in hand. 'It's got miraculous powers, has mistletoe, so Mam told me. It can heal almost anything and if you hang it over your doorway then it wards off witchcraft and brings good luck.' He flashed Louise one of his grins. 'As well as that everybody kisses everybody as they come in the house, so that it's getting so that wherever you hang mistletoe people kiss under it.'

'We do not kiss under the mistletoe in France,' said Louise, smiling. 'But we do decorate our houses with holly and that is also said to have healing properties, and to protect the home from fire and storm.'

'Then it'd be good if we got some of both,' said Nat in a determined voice.

'But no ivy,' said Peter, his blue eyes bright as they went from one to the other. 'It's said to have been used by the Roman god Bacchus to decorate his halls when he held his drunken revels.'

'Now I never knew that,' muttered Nat, rubbing at his ear. 'That's what studying learns you. Although I knew 'twas unlucky to have inside.' He came to an abrupt halt in front of an enormous oak tree.

All of them looked up into its black spreading branches to a bole of the tree, where, as if by magic, a bright green clump of mistletoe sprouted. Nat fingered the knife in his girdle. 'I'll go up,' he said, eyeing the lowest branch. 'Lend me your back, Louis.'

'Pardon?' Louise gave him an uncomprehending stare.

'Bend over,' said Peter, arching his back so that his arms dangled and his fingertips touched the ground. She aped him but was not prepared for Nat's foot on her spine as he sprang up and seized a branch. She was sent sprawling on to a carpet of mouldering damp leaves, and came up spitting them out with the sound of the boys' laughter ringing in her ears.

There was a rustling of undergrowth and the twins and Blanche appeared through the trees.

'Is it leaves that they eat in France for Christmas?' said Blanche, her pale eyes passing disdainfully over Louise's sprawling figure. 'I always did consider them beasts.'

Louise's temper ignited and her voice contained a note of anger. 'I'd have you know, *madame*, that France is the most...' She sought for the right word in English and came out with it in French.

'What is he saying?' demanded the other woman.

'That you are uncivilised, coz,' drawled Harry, while John stepped forward to help Louise to her feet.

'Just what I would expect from him,' said the older woman, her eyes sparkling. 'Tell him, John, that I consider him rude and vulgar.'

'You don't have to tell me,' said Louise, her glance passing over John's frowning face as he helped her up. 'And tell her that I did not say exactly what Harry said. I spoke of France and that it is the most...' Again she sought for the English word.

'Civilised is the word I believe you're looking for,' said John coolly, his fingers tightening on her arm.

'Tell him that he is mistaken,' said Blanche in vexed tones. 'England is the more civilised.'

'But don't expect civilised behaviour from our cousin,' said Harry promptly, his expression maliciously amused as he shifted the basket of holly he carried to his other hand. 'She's been spoilt from the cradle because her parents could have no more children. And no doubt if they had lived to have seen how their daughter turned out they'd have been glad that they didn't!'

Blanche gasped. 'How dare you, Harry?' She flew at him. 'Pig! Beast! I hate you!' She managed to catch him a blow on the nose before he seized her wrist and twisted her arm up her back.

'Harry! Blanche!' John's voice was sharp. 'Do you call that civilised behaviour? What will M'sieur Saulnier think of you?'

Harry dropped Blanche's arm and glared at her. 'I should have had the handling of you from early days; you would have been a much nicer person now.'

'I suppose you consider yourself a saint?' flashed Blanche, her expression animated.

'Hardly. But at least there are times when I do think of other people's feelings.'

'Like when you went missing for five years and didn't let anyone know where you were?' she cried.

'John knew I was safe,' he countered tersely.

'He did not know. He only had a feeling!'

'Those feelings count,' hissed Harry. 'Ask John about when he was nearly killed in Normandy and Louise saved him!'

'Enough, brother,' said John, sending him a warning look.

Harry ignored him. 'Ask him! Didn't I know he was hurt?' He whirled round to Louise, who was brushing dead soggy leaves from her surcote. 'You tell her, Louise, how I was trying to get a ship to England.'

'Will you be quiet?' roared John. 'Hasn't your tongue led us into enough trouble in the past as it is?'

Harry went suddenly silent but it was too late. Blanche was gazing at Louise with an arrested expression in her eyes. 'You called him Louise—that's a girl's name.'

'Louis is a girl,' Peter surprised them all by saying as he caught a clump of mistletoe which had been sent hurtling down from the tree. 'But she rides as hard as a man, and never complained of aches and pains and being tired on the journey like Mother used to all the time,' he said with obvious enjoyment of the effect he was creating. 'She's as good as a boy.'

'Thank you, Peter,' murmured Louise, her cheeks burning. 'You're very kind.'

'But—why is she dressed like that?' Blanche asked of John, staring at Louise doubtfully. 'It's unseemly.'

'To save her virtue from the civilised English when they overran her town,' said John quietly, 'her father cut her hair and had her wear boy's clothes.' Louise looked at him with gratitude.

Pink colour slowly washed over Blanche's pale skin. 'But—why does she still wear them?' she said hesitantly. 'Has she no women's clothes at all?'

'I have some,' answered Louise quickly, not wanting her pity. 'Harry gave me several of Clotilde's gowns, and——' She stopped abruptly.

'Who is Clotilde?' asked Blanche in a chilling tone, her gaze passing over Louise to Harry, whose black brows were knit together in a furious scowl. 'It seems that I've not been told everything about your brave deeds in Normandy.'

'Not quite everything,' he said briefly.

Louise put in, 'It's a long story and not what you think.'

'And how would *you* know what I'm thinking if you're such an innocent? Just looking at you speaks of the kind of woman you are!' Blanche whirled round and marched out of the clearing.

John said in a rasping voice, 'I'd best go after her and try and persuade her not to talk of this. You'd have both been better keeping your mouths shut.'

Harry swore softly and Louise felt like swearing. There was a silence as they gazed after him.

It was suddenly broken by the sound of cracking timber and a yell. Bits of twigs and mistletoe came flying down with Nat, who managed at the last minute to save himself from hitting the forest floor by seizing hold of the lower branch of the tree. He swung by his hands several feet from the ground, relief mingling with the fear that lingered in his eyes. Harry moved forward to take his weight and ease him down.

'Thanks,' said Nat in heartfelt tones. 'I was that taken up with listening that I forgot I was up a tree.'

'Big ears,' said Peter, his eyes laughing, despite his sober expression. 'I wager that you can't keep this a secret as I've done for days.'

'How did you know?' demanded Louise.

'I'm not stupid,' said Peter in a scornful tone.

'No,' muttered Louise, frowning. 'But you never said anything.'

Peter shrugged. 'If Father had wanted me to know he'd have told me.'

'Blanche'll tell your grandmother and grandfather,' said Harry moodily, pressing his foot down hard on a fallen twig. 'And cousin Hugh! That's the kind of woman she is.'

'Perhaps she won't,' Nat said, a slight furrow between his brows.

'But most probably she will!' Harry's voice was impatient. 'It's bound to create a scandal. I knew that you should never have come to England with my brother, Louise.'

Her eyes flashed. 'If you hadn't abducted my sister then I wouldn't be here! Anyway, from what I've heard, scandals are not new in your family.'

'And what's that mean?' he said sharply.

'It doesn't matter,' murmured Louise, gaining control of her temper. 'Bickering will get us nowhere.'

'That's true.' Harry stared at her. 'We'll just have to wait and see. And if it does come out that you're a woman, then best put on the dowdiest women's clothes in your possession. There's less likelihood of the family believing the worst of you if you play your charms down.' He smiled unexpectedly. 'Perhaps you can paint a wart on your nose and I could cut your hair shorter.'

Louise swiftly put both hands to her head and stamped her foot. 'You will not touch my hair! You want me to look ugly! *Merci, m'sieur,*' she said sarcastically. 'I was the daughter of the richest clothier in Caen! I wore the finest samite from Venice and the best woollen material that the Flemish weavers could make! Is it not enough that I've been brought so low that it was needful for me to wear the clothes of a prentice? I will not shame myself any more! And besides——' her voice rose on a triumphant note '—Clotilde possessed *nothing* dowdy. She wore clothes that were intended to attract a man's attention.'

Harry grimaced. 'You've made your point. John's reputation will have to carry us through if the worst comes to the worst.'

'His reputation?' She threw back her head and laughed. 'Why his reputation? Anyway, perhaps the fair Blanche will be persuaded by him to remain silent about me.'

'It's possible.' Harry scowled. 'She considers him a paragon in most matters. And if someone is normally honest and upright then it's easier to persuade people that what they say is truth.' He added silkily, 'Now if you'd travelled in *my* company it would have been a different matter.'

'Of course,' she said drily. 'But what are we going to do now?'

He was silent a moment, then shrugged. 'Carry on as if nothing had happened.' He looked at the two boys, who were picking up the mistletoe that littered the ground. 'Nat! Peter! Keep silent about all you've heard, unless it appears obvious that our cousin has blabbed, and there will be an extra present for you on New Year's Day.'

Peter just gave him a look as if to say, I know how to keep quiet, but Nat grinned. 'Haven't heard a thing.'

Harry slapped him on the shoulder. 'Good lad! Now let's be getting back or the hall won't be getting decorated in time.'

They retraced their steps and met up with the rest of the group. John and Blanche were already with them. John's glance met Louise's briefly, and he nodded slightly. She was uncertain whether he meant that Blanche had been persuaded to keep quiet or not, and she thought that maybe Harry would go over to them and find out. But he did not; instead he began to talk in an animated fashion to herself and the boys as if he did not have a care in the world.

When they entered the hall the servants were ready to bring in the food for dinner, and no sooner had the party put down the spoils of their labours and discarded cloaks than it was time to sit and eat. Harry stayed by Louise's side, while John sat next to Blanche. Louise's spirits plummeted, and suddenly she thought longingly of her old home, where life was much simpler.

Yet it was a merry company that set about decorating the hall after dinner, with laurel, bay, rosemary, mistletoe and holly. There was much horseplay, as well as talk of food and drink and entertainment on the morrow—but no mention was made of the French visitor's being a woman. Louise listened to the jests and smiled, although she did not understand everything that was being said, and she could not prevent her gaze wandering at times to the part of the hall where Blanche, in a surcote of pale blue, was handing up bunches of holly to John.

'I think she's going to keep quiet,' muttered Harry in Louise's ear as he caught her watching them. 'I felt sure that John could persuade her that I'm the villain of the piece while he's St George, out to help any damsel in distress.'

Louise's hazel eyes darkened. 'But you *are* the villain of the piece! If you hadn't abducted my sister then I wouldn't be here! But I doubt that John will tell Blanche that you are to be blamed for her being in England.'

'Why?' he said bluntly. 'You think you know him better than I? It would certainly make her not wish to have anything to do with me—and put him in a good light.'

She wrinkled her nose in bewilderment. 'You sound as if you care what she thinks about you. Yet the way you behave towards her is abominable.'

He shrugged. 'Only because I know I don't stand a chance with her now that Dorothy's dead. She'd make a perfect wife for John because she knows the trade.'

'That is true,' said Louise, lowering her head so that he could not see her expression, and twisting stems of laurel together. 'But I still don't believe that he would say things detrimental to your character. Why should he, when you damage your own case?'

His mouth twisted wryly and his blue eyes were amused. 'You certainly know how to rub salt in a wound. But I suppose I've been doing that to you by linking Jack and Blanche together. You're fond of my brother, aren't you, my dear?'

She lifted her head: there was no way that she would let him know how much she cared. 'He's an Englishman and you know how I hate the English,' she murmured.

'So you say.' He laughed suddenly. 'Let's forget them both, Louise. Did you know the mummers come tomorrow? It's great fun and there's much dressing up. We wear masks and costume and often men wear women's clothes and vice versa. Don't you yearn to wear something pretty—to dress up for the festivities? I'd like to see you in that green samite gown that Clotilde was so reluctant to part with—and I'm sure my brother's reaction would be interesting.'

Her hand stilled on the garland. 'You think so?'

Harry smiled. 'It's worth a try. I'll go and find you a mask.'

She watched him dodging between people as he went over to the large chest against the far wall, and suddenly was aware that she was not the only woman watching him. So was Blanche, but her expression was unreadable. How did she really feel towards Harry? It seemed to Louise that she insulted him almost as much as he did her. How fitting it would be if Blanche and Harry... No! She would not pin her hopes on that happening. Besides, as Harry had said, a marriage between John and Blanche would be extremely suitable.

She was not sure if John and his family would go to the Mass that evening, but everybody went to the tiny stone church. Louise determinedly suppressed her guilt— it was not as if she would commit adultery again—and she took the sacrament.

One of the first to leave the church, she walked back to the house alone and was welcomed indoors with a cup of hot spiced ale and a mince pie shaped like a manger with a little figure of a baby, representing Jesus, on its crust. She ate and drank as quickly as she could, not wanting to speak to anyone, tired out as she was by physical activity and emotion. It was well gone midnight when she went to bed, and knowing that the feasting would start at noon and go on all day she planned to sleep as long as she could.

The first act Louise performed when she rose the next morning was to search in her baggage and take out the green houppelande of silky samite and hang it on the hook on the wall. A yellow silk corset and a white chemise joined it. She found a head-dress and veil and put them on the bed next to the mask taken from the chest. Then she started on her toilet.

Just the feel of cotton and silk against her skin gave Louise pleasure, and she hummed as she laced up her corset. Somehow she managed without a mirror to fix her head-dress and veil and adjust the mask. She felt a moment's anxiety before opening the door. What if John was furious with her for dressing up the way she had, and refused to act as her emissary between her and his brother to discover where Marguerite was? Then she considered Blanche and her beauty, and, tilting her chin, she flung the door wide.

She was not the only one wearing a mask and there was a lot of teasing and people trying to guess who was who, and there were several puzzled glances sent in her direction. There was no sign of John or Harry, although their mother was busily directing the servants where to place dishes.

The tables were already covered with white cloths and candle stands set in place, while the servants loaded the tables with dishes containing boiled capons, partridges, larks and roast geese. There were containers of fruit, hot pies, and apple-wood bowls of ale with toasted apples bobbing in them. There were sugary sweets shaped into ships and castles, as well as plum porridge, a mixture of raisins, spices, breadcrumbs and fruit juices that was spooned down with the first course. It was special because somewhere in the mixture there was a silver coin, a ring and a thimble. The place in front of the host and his lady was still empty—reserved for the boar's head, which would be ceremoniously brought in once everybody was in their places.

Quickly the hall began to fill up, not only with members of the family and their friends, but also people from the hamlet who had been invited to sit at the lower tables. Musicians with pipe, drum, harp and trumpet were practising at one end of the hall.

The noise swelled and people began to take their places at table. Louise slipped on to the edge of a bench near

Peter and Nat, and still she could not see either of the twins. She did notice Blanche, clad in a violet-coloured houppelande with scalloped edges to the sleeves, sitting a few places up from the end of the high table. There was a man sitting next to her, but she did not recognise him as either John or Harry. Perhaps they were wearing costumes and masks. Now their host was in his place and a woman whom she took to be his wife, up from her laying-in bed for this special occasion.

Then a fanfare sounded and everybody rose to their feet and gazed at the chief cook who entered carrying a great silver dish containing the boar's head. It had sprigs of rosemary sticking out of its ears and an apple in its mouth. It held all of Louise's attention so that she did not instantly notice the man who quickly took up a stand beside her. She was thinking of how the rosemary represented the returning summer and the fruit the sun. At this darkest time of the year it was good to look forward to the hot days to come. The silver platter was set down in front of Hugh. Grace was said, and then everybody took their seats.

'Why are you dressed like that?' hissed a voice Louise knew well. 'I might as well not have spent all that time in Blanche's company persuading her to keep her mouth shut.'

Louise's head turned swiftly and she stared at the masked man dressed in a damson-coloured surcote trimmed with lambswool. 'How did you know me?' she whispered.

'I didn't at first!' His gaze glinted behind the mask. 'It was my brother who pointed you out because he recognised the gown. Don't you realise that it fits you so snugly that it reveals your shape? Most looking at you would know you for a woman. As well as that your accent, which will give away who you are.'

'I will not speak, then,' she said in a sparkling undertone. 'So why don't you go away and sit with your little dove who's looking this way, and who I think recognises you despite the mask?'

'You'd like me to do that, wouldn't you? So that you can flirt with Harry.' His fingers drummed on the table. 'Well, I'm not going to allow that. You wouldn't suit.'

'How do you know?' Her expression darkened. 'You have only known me in circumstances that have been unusual to say the least. You forget that I was not reared for such a life. I *was* a clothier's daughter!'

'So you have said several times,' he muttered, bidding a maidservant to fill their goblets, while another set slices of capon on their platters, and poured plum porridge in their bowls. 'Do you consider that good enough reason for my parents to give countenance to your marrying Harry?'

Her pulses jerked in a peculiar fashion. 'I don't see why not,' she said boldly.

'I won't allow it,' he said in a tight voice, and, picking up his goblet, he tossed off the contents.

'And how would you stop us?' she said recklessly. 'You aren't your brother's keeper for all your peculiar feelings about one another's safety, and the way you're mirror images.'

He seized her wrist as she made to pick up her spoon. 'This has gone far enough, Louise.'

'This conversation has,' she murmured. 'Let us talk no more on this matter. May I eat in peace now?' Not waiting for his answer, she pulled herself free, and seemingly gave all her attention to the capon and plum porridge.

John made a dissatisfied noise in his throat and began to cut his meat. She watched him out of the corner of her eye as she spooned plum porridge into her mouth. Metal clinked against her teeth and she spat out a ring on to the palm of her hand.

'Tell me if this is lucky?' she asked of John innocently.

He scowled at her. 'I think you know exactly what it symbolises.'

'Tell me.' Her voice was sweet.

'A wedding.' His fingers clenched on his knife.

Her mouth curved into a smile as she wiped the ring on her sleeve before trying to fit it on to her middle finger.

'It's too small.' He could not conceal his satisfaction.

'That doesn't change the good fortune,' she murmured, determined to tease him by placing it on her little finger. 'And to think that I never looked to be married when I came to England. I hated all Englishmen.'

'You hated Harry!' With an impatient gesture he pulled off his mask and her heart lurched in her breast as she looked into his stormy blue eyes. 'Doesn't it matter to you any more that he was responsible for your sister being taken from you?' he asked in French.

'Of course it matters!' She sounded surprised. 'But forgiveness is a Christian virtue.'

He snorted. 'Common sense should be one.'

'I have enough for the two of us,' she said with an assumed calmness. 'We will go back to France and live happily ever after.'

John ground his teeth. 'He won't marry you, woman!'

'So you say.' She shrugged expressively, fingering the pattern in the pewter goblet. 'But he has a fancy for me—so we shall see.'

'We certainly shall,' he said tersely, and, getting up, walked away.

CHAPTER TWELVE

HAD she gone too far? Louise touched the back of the ring with the ball of her thumb as she watched John, carrying platter and goblet, sit next to a masked woman on the other side of Blanche. Instantly he began to talk to her. She experienced a spurt of jealousy because to all appearances they seemed to be having a lively conversation, but she comforted herself with the thought that he was taking little notice of Blanche. She continued to keep her eye on him, the woman, and Blanche, as the afternoon progressed, while wondering where Harry was.

The noise level grew, as people imbibed freely, and the musicians entertained, one singing the carol 'As Joseph was a-walking'. Some children, having had enough to eat, rose to play blind man's buff.

A banging on the door signalled the arrival of the mummers, and there was much hushing as people prepared to watch their performance. It began with a sword dance, which finished with the man dressed up as Robin Hood kneeling in the centre of the ring while the rest of the dancers locked their swords round his neck. There was complete silence from the watchers as the swords were drawn and the victim fell 'dead'. Harry had explained to Louise that it was symbolic of the death of the spirit of life. Now the dancers were carolling round and round. They stopped suddenly and reached for the swords and withdrew them. Robin Hood sprang up and began to caper about with the rest of the dancers. Life had been renewed, just as it was every springtime.

Young people started to get up and dance, and an elderly man dressed as a jester fooled about. Then Louise's shoulders were seized from behind and she was pulled off the bench, only being saved from falling on to the floor by those same hands sliding round her waist. She looked up into the familiar masked face.

'Let's carol,' he muttered, sweeping her into the circle of dancers. One of her hands was held firmly in his grasp, while the other was seized by a complete stranger. She was danced around the hall, so energetically that there was no chance of or breath left for speech. Eventually the circle broke apart and people collapsed on settles or chests, but her partner swung her into his arms and danced her just as vigorously over to the doorway. He brought her to a halt and kissed her under the mistletoe.

There was nothing gentle about his embrace or the kiss. He held her so tightly that she thought her bones would crack, and his mouth bruised hers before it lifted. 'Little witch,' he. whispered unsteadily. 'If you choose to be a wanton then let it be with me.'

'What do you mean?' she stammered in a voice barely above a whisper.

'I mean your giving yourself to Harry for the name of the man who has Marguerite.' His voice was low and harsh.

'But I——'

'Don't make excuses.' John dragged her through the doorway and out on to the top of the steps. It was already dark and Louise felt a snowflake land on her cheek before he planted several small kisses on her mouth. 'It's only fair after all, my sweet,' he murmured between kisses, 'that I should demand payment for my part in helping you find her.'

'But I never said any such thing to Harry,' she cried.

'He says you did—and that what you said about going to France is true—although he has no plans to marry you, dearest Louise.'

Her eyes sparkled with anger. 'He's lying.'

'You mean he did say he'd marry you?'

'No! About my going to France with him.'

'But you said it yourself to me.' His tones were satiny.

She hesitated before saying, 'I didn't mean it. I was teasing you.'

His face tightened. 'Teasing me! After the other night I would have thought you'd think twice about such games. It seems that no woman can be trusted to play fair.'

'I believed you Harry that night.'

'What?'

'I was tired and confused. And you *are* alike!'

'But you kissed me as if—and allowed——'

'I thought you were with Blanche.'

'I see,' he said sarcastically. 'So if I'm with her then it's all right for you to be with my brother. We're that much alike it doesn't matter which one of us beds you. Perhaps we could share you and then you'll be able to compare which of us you like best!'

She felt the colour drain from her face and pulled herself out of his arms. 'That's a terrible thing to say,' she whispered. 'And just what I'd expect from an Englishman. I wish I'd never trusted you and come to England.'

There was a silence, but for the sound of the icy wind that sent snowflakes whirling about them. Then he said savagely, 'You'd test the will-power of a saint! Don't you think I wish I'd never brought you?'

'I never intended...' Her voice, barely audible, broke off, then she resumed again with a strength in her voice that had been lacking. 'I was the innocent so do not lay the blame on me for your lack of control as men have always done with women since Eve! Allow me to go south now! I know enough English to get by on my own!'

A muscle tightened in his cheek. 'That's a damn foolish suggestion! I might have my faults, *mam'selle*, but sending you out into the snow alone isn't one of them. I said that I'd help you find Marguerite before you go back to France and I damn well will! So don't be talking nonsense.'

Her eyes sparkled and she folded her arms tightly across her breast, tensing against the cold. 'You should never have brought me north; I didn't want to——'

'You know we had to come north,' he interrupted ruthlessly. 'I explained!'

'We wouldn't have had to come if you'd have thought of asking Harry the man's name when we were in Kent!' She scrubbed at the dampness on her cheek, and hoped that he did not think that it was tears she was rubbing away.

'Well, I didn't,' he rasped. 'Because I wasn't to know that Dykemore had had Wat burnt alive!' He thumped the wall. 'Think sensibly, woman. How was I to know? Anyhow, as matters worked out I would have come anyway for Peter's sake! I do have a life of my own to live that doesn't involve chasing round looking for your sister, who's probably perfectly safe and happy!'

She gasped. 'Live your own life, then! Don't concern yourself about me and Marguerite any longer. I will do whatever's necessary to find her myself!' She turned and wrenched open the door.

John was quick on her heels but no sooner was he inside than his mother swooped up on him, sending Louise a curious, frowning glance, and Louise heard her say, 'Harry! What have you been up to? Blanche has been looking for John. Do you know if he is with M'sieur Saulnier somewhere? Because they both seem to be missing.'

Louise did not catch his reply because the woman who had been sitting next to John took her arm and spoke in her ear in Harry's voice, startling her so much that she could not think of a sensible answer to his, 'My dear, do you really think it's good for our reputations that you go outside with my brother?'

'Why are you dressed in such a way?' she hissed.

'I thought it would be amusing.' He wiggled both eyebrows. 'And it was for a while, sitting next to Blanche and pretending to be what I'm not.'

'You are as stupid as your brother!' Her eyes sparkled. 'What chance have you with her dressed like that?'

His eyebrows rose. 'Now what has my brother done to rile you?' She scowled at him but said nothing. He shrugged. 'I never believed I had much chance, anyroad. But now I wager I have none. Now that everybody thinks Jack's me!' He pulled a face. 'Not only do they believe that I've been flirting with myself most of the afternoon because Jack came and poured his fury into my ear, but that I've danced completely unabandoned with you!'

'It serves you right,' she retorted tartly, 'making out to John that you and I were——'

'What?' He grinned and his eyes gleamed through the holes in the mask. 'I only went along with what he said that you said.'

'And more, I'll wager,' she said crossly. 'You consider no one but yourself.'

'Now there you're wrong. I was thinking of both of us, especially when I watched the way my brother danced with you, and kissed you, before whisking you outside.' He pulled her down onto a settle, and spread his skirt dextrously. 'What were you doing out there?'

'Getting cold and wet.'

He nodded resignedly. 'You're not going to tell me.'

'It was snowing.' Her voice was stiff.

'Very informative.' He sighed heavily and looked dejected. 'I hope it's not going to spoil the hunting tomorrow.'

'It's not a lot of snow for all he says that I couldn't travel,' she said comfortingly.

'It'll get thicker.' He stared at her. 'You were thinking of going somewhere?'

'It's none of your business.' She rammed her chin into the palm of her hand and stared moodily at him. 'Just tell me the name of the man who has Marguerite and how I can get there.'

Harry smiled. 'My dear, you're willing to pay the price?' He did not wait for an answer but gazed across the hall. 'My brother doesn't like us talking, but Mother's got him in tow and he can't do anything about us. She's taking him over to Blanche. I wonder if he'll pretend to be me to Blanche?' he said softly.

Louise's frowning gaze followed his. 'Why should he pretend?'

He shrugged. 'Once upon a time we used to see how long we could keep people guessing who was really who. Anyway, would he want her to know it was he who was dancing with you?'

A heavy breath escaped her. 'I suppose not. But why don't you go and change and come back as yourself? People will know then that you're you.'

'Most likely they'll believe me to be John.' He gave her a droll look. 'Of course I could pretend to be John to Blanche and that way I might learn what she really thinks of me.'

'It smacks of trickery.'

'My dear innocent,' he said softly, 'there's no better way to pass the time than by indulging oneself in playing such intriguing games. Perhaps you could pretend that I'm John? We could go to a quiet place somewhere and have a pleasant time. Nobody would be any the wiser with me in this garb.'

'That is a scandalous idea.' Her voice was cold.

'I'd give you the name of the man who has Marguerite.'

Her eyes challenged his. 'I've just been thinking about that, and you could give me any name and I wouldn't know if it was the right one or not.'

A smile lurked about his mouth. 'Not so foolish.' He stood. 'Hey ho! I'll out of these skirts and tease the fair Blanche.'

'You could try wooing her,' she muttered. 'Love isn't a game, you know. It hurts.'

'You're telling me?' He smiled grimly and left through the door to her right.

Louise suddenly made up her mind that nothing was to be gained by staying in Yorkshire any longer. Harry would never give her the man's name, and maybe both brothers were right and her sister was happy. Besides, she did not want to ask John to help her ever again. She stood and was about to go through the same door as Harry when she saw Blanche approaching. She had a mind for instant flight but that smacked of cowardice so she stayed as the woman stopped in front of her.

'So you would play the harlot with both brothers, *mam'selle*.' Her voice was low and angry.

Louise's expression hardened. 'I don't know what you are talking about, *madame*. But you insult me.'

'You would deny it, of course,' she said scornfully, her pale blue eyes glinting. 'But I watched the way you danced with Harry, and then came over here with John.'

There was a pause before Louise said in careful tones, 'You really believe that woman was John?'

'Of course!' She threw back her head. 'I know him well enough for such a disguise not to fool me! But that you should resort to wearing women's clothes surprises me when John told me that he was trying to avoid a scandal.'

'I'm certain no one else has any idea who I am, *madame*.' Her voice was cool. 'And if I choose to dress like this, then it's my affair, not yours. Have you given any thought at all to what it has been like for me having to wear a boy's clothes? Before the English took Caen my position in life was similiar to yours. My father was wealthy and I was accustomed to wearing gowns similar to the one I am wearing now. I wonder how you would have fared if you'd been in my place, *madame*? It's Christmastide and I wanted to look my best. Is that so wrong?'

'I'm sure you must have had a terrible time.' Blanche flushed. 'But I didn't say that what you did was wrong. I just question your wisdom in putting on such a gown.'

'You consider it unattractive?' said Louise, her expression grave. 'The colour—you perhaps consider doesn't suit my complexion? And that maybe the gown doesn't fit me so well?'

'No!' Blanche's pale brow knit. 'It's a lovely shade of green and a perfect fit. You look a complete woman! But anyone listening to your voice would know you for M'sieur Saulnier and your secret would be out. No one likes being made a fool of, *mam'selle*—especially my cousin Hugh, whose guest you are. You are too attractive, and I only speak like this because I would avoid a scandal,' she said bluntly.

Louise's mouth twisted. 'Do you? Is it that you consider me a rival? Be assured you have no need. I would never have set foot in England if it weren't for my sister.'

Blanche moistened her mouth. 'You couldn't be a serious rival. I mean, it's hardly likely that either of them would marry you.'

'Of course not. Do you think I'm such a fool that I don't know that?' She forced a smile. 'But perhaps you're right about the clothes. I'll go and change now and no one will be any the wiser.'

'A sensible decision, *mam'selle*.' Blanche gave her the smallest of smiles and walked away.

Louise left the hall, feeling unexpectedly exhausted. Once in her bedchamber she seriously considered undressing and going to bed. It would save the emotional

strain on her nerves of having to face the twins and
Blanche again. But it would be a long night up here in
this cold room on her own, because she was not fool
enough to consider leaving in the dark on such a night.
The cloak which was spread over the bed felt slightly
damp and she decided that she would take it into the
hall and warm it by the fire. She changed quickly and
went downstairs, taking up a place by the fire, where
she was almost immediately spotted by John's father.

'We missed you at the feast, lad,' he murmured, his
keen gaze scrutinising her delicately boned face, which
was flushed from the fire's heat. 'Where have you been?
My son's been seeking you.'

'Oh!' She sought quickly for an answer and stuck to
the truth. 'I was—at the feast, *m'sieur*,' she responded
hurriedly. 'I was clad differently and wearing a mask.'

'You were in costume perhaps?' His blue eyes twinkled
slightly.

'You—could say that.' She cleared her throat. 'Was
it for anything in particular that your son wanted me?'

'He didn't say. But he seemed vexed when he could
not find you or Harry. It might be best if you sorted
out whatever it is that you've disagreed about as soon
as possible.'

'I was not aware that we had quarrelled, *m'sieur*,' she
said brightly.

'Perhaps I misjudged the matter.' Guy smiled. 'But
he's gone to the stables to check on the horses. A quieter
place than this rowdy hall, I deem, where you wouldn't
be disturbed.'

'*Merci, m'sieur.*' She returned his smile despite the
tightening of the muscles of her stomach. 'You can tell
the difference between your sons?'

'I have been known to mistake them one for the other,'
he said frankly. 'But that is not often. There is something about their expressions, as I'm certain you'll have
noticed, having been in John's company for some weeks.'

He paused, and his eyes held hers. 'How did you meet exactly?'

Her heart bumped. 'Didn't he tell you?'

'Calais—down by the waterfront—you were looking for your sister. You saw his likeness to Harry and told him of it, and in return he promised to help you find your sister. It seems unlikely behaviour for a youth whose sister had been taken from him by the enemy.'

'I was desperate to find Marguerite,' she said gruffly, swirling the cloak about her shoulders.

'So you were prepared to take any risk to your person?'

'*Oui!*' She lowered her eyes, seemingly giving all her attention to fastening her cloak. It would not be a bad idea to check that her horse was all right, although her heart pounded at the thought of seeing John so soon after their quarrel. 'I will go and seek out John now, *m'sieur.*'

'Of course.' He laid a hand on her shoulder and pressed it gently. 'Perhaps we can have another talk some time. I would know you better, Louis. After all, we do owe you much for helping bring Harry back to us.'

'*Oui, m'sieur.*' Her voice was soft, devoid of artifice. He took his hand from her shoulder and she walked away, thinking that there was much she could like about John's father.

A few snowflakes swirled in the air, but the night sky had a peculiar cast to it that hinted at more to come. There was a thin white layer on the steps, broken by footmarks. She trod carefully and came to the bottom safely. Huddling inside her cloak she put her feet into John's footprints and followed them across the courtyard to the stables.

A candle was set on a niche in the wall, casting wavering shadows about the building, as she opened the door to let in a freezing wind that caused the horses to shift restlessly.

'Shut that door!' John's irritated voice came at her from a dark corner. 'Who is it?'

'It's Louise. Your father said that you were looking for me,' she said with an assumed calmness, thinking suddenly that maybe he was sorry for what he had said and would apologise to her. There was a brief silence.

'So you came to find me.' There was a hint of surprise in his words. 'I'd have thought being alone with me would be enough to prevent your seeking me out here.'

'What did you want me for?' she said wearily, disappointed. She leaned against a wall.

There was a hesitant note in his voice. 'I just wondered if you wanted to be included in the hunt tomorrow. Our host and cousins are presuming that you will. If you don't wish to go, then I can make up some excuse for you.'

She thought quickly. 'I'd like to hunt. It is something to do—unless you would rather I didn't?'

'I'm honoured that you should defer to me,' he mocked. 'But I agree with you that it's something to do.'

There was another silence, before hesitantly she said, 'Did you explain to your mother that you weren't Harry?'

He glanced at her, then looked away again, caressing his horse's neck. 'She knew it once we started talking, and she asked who you were.'

'What did you tell her?'

'That I had no idea. That I'd imbibed a little too freely of the wine and got carried away by the sight of a fair stranger. She scolded and teased me a little, but accepted my story. It's feasible. There is the occasional traveller who passes this way even at this time of year. The laws of hospitality being what they are, all are welcome.'

'Blanche thought that Harry dressed as a woman was you,' she said, infusing amusement into the words. 'That she knows you well enough to tell the difference.'

'Did you tell her that you made the same mistake the other night?' he rasped. 'Except that it was the other way round?'

'We're not on those sort of speaking terms. But she'd guessed who I was—and warned me of the dangers of being unmasked and almost ordered me to change out of my skirts and into my doublet and hose. She has a dread of me creating a scandal.'

'So you changed.' He eyed her up and down. 'I prefer the skirts.'

'You should not say that,' she murmured, her fingers trembling slightly as she rested her arms against the wall. 'Look upon me as one of the lads. Blanche doesn't like it at all that I'm a woman.'

There was a silence, not an unfriendly one, but when he burst into speech she jumped. 'Louise! The other night! Did you believe I was Harry all the time?'

'Didn't I explain that I was confused? When you said that your brother was with Blanche, I presumed the brother was you because I'd last seen you with her.'

'But when I kissed you——?'

'That's when I became really confused, because——' She stopped abruptly.

'Because what?' he insisted, seizing her arm.

'What does it matter?' she murmured. 'You'll marry Blanche because she's a suitable wife for you.'

He drew her close and touched her cheek with a gentle hand. 'I'm not looking for a wife, Louise. I mightn't mourn Dorothy, but it's not long since she died, and I can't forget what life was like with her. I'm in no mood to rush into another such alliance.'

'But *you'll* marry her one day! Harry said——'

'Forget what Harry says. He enjoys making life complicated. Being unhappily married once, I might never marry again.'

She was shocked by his reply, but did not want him to realise that, so sought for something else to say. 'Harry was going to change and pretend to be you because Blanche was certain to believe you were him.'

John grinned reluctantly. 'See what I mean?'

She nodded and realised that she could not leave the way she had planned now if what he said about Blanche was true. 'Do you think that you can find out where Marguerite is from him? He's got me so that I don't feel that he'll tell me the truth because he teases me so.'

'He's amusing himself at your expense.' He sounded resigned. 'So much more interesting than telling you the name straight away. It's like fishing. Get your fish on a hook, and then play him awhile before reeling in.'

'He's impossible!' She shook her head. 'So you reckon that he'll tell me sooner or later?'

'If he doesn't tell you, he'll tell me,' he said grimly, pulling her hand through his arm. 'Now let's get you out of here and in by the fire. Your hand's cold.'

Louise unexpectedly remembered how he had saved her from the freezing sea at Calais. Suddenly she turned to him. 'John! Your father doesn't know the truth about me, does he? Only he questioned me about our first meeting.'

He flashed her a glance as they made their way across the courtyard. 'He's extremely perceptive. I should have warned you that I had to skirt around the truth about that meeting. What did you tell him?'

'I didn't tell him anything—he told me that we made a pact to help each other find your brother, my sister.' She gnawed at her lower lip. 'He thought it unlikely behaviour for enemies.'

'He didn't say anything else?'

'He seemed to believe that we'd quarrelled and that I should find you and make peace,' she said shyly.

John stopped and stared at her, an odd expression in his eyes. 'So you obeyed him—and we've made our peace.'

'I suppose we have.' She smiled. 'Till the next time we disagree.'

'Then we'll just have to make peace again.' He kissed her lightly, and led her up the steps and into the warmth. And Louise wondered if she had been a fool to make peace with him, knowing that she loved him. What kind of future could there be for such a love as hers for him?

Louise had to drag herself out of bed the next morning. She looked out of the window and saw a white world. There was no water to wash in this morning and she presumed that the water supply must have iced over and there was a shortage. She dressed quickly before going downstairs.

The hall was occupied with only a sprinkling of people, who were mainly men. John and Harry sat together, and one of them lifted a hand and signalled her over. She went, glad that it looked as if the brothers had also made up any quarrel they'd had. John asked her could she use a bow, as she slid into a place next to him. She nodded, accepting the one offered and a quiver of arrows. A few minutes later a platter of bacon and egg was set before her. She ate hungrily, listening with half an ear to the conversation between the brothers. It seemed that their father was considering bringing the visit to an end sooner than planned if the snow worsened, before the journey became impossible.

The hunting group gathered and mounted. Several hounds, yelping excitedly, milled around, leaving paw prints in the snow, which was a few inches deep. There was a sharpness in the air that caused breath to come out as steam, and flushed the cheeks. A few snowflakes twisted their lazy way to the earth.

Soon they set off. Some of the men carried spears, but John and Harry both had bows on their backs, and knives in their girdles. They headed for the forest. Bows were strung as they rode slowly beneath the trees. There were plenty of tracks in the snow—deer, boar, rabbits, foxes, weasels, as well as bird marks. Harry was after a couple of squirrels, not only for food but for stomach fur to trim a houppelande for his mother. They talked little, knowing that sound travelled the swifter in the snowy landscape, and kept their eyes and ears open.

A sudden movement in the undergrowth sent Louise reaching for an arrow, as it did John and the cousins, who accompanied them closely. Two rabbits. They moved on, the party splitting up. A flurry overhead and a couple of arrows winged their way into trees, bringing down a blackbird and a thrush. A couple of hounds went after them, and they were placed in a saddlebag. They went further in with one of the dogs, nose to the ground, zigzagging a trail ahead of them. It disappeared behind a bush and the next moment there was a terrific outburst of barking and grunting. Both cousins reached for spears while the others sought their arrows.

A boar came charging out from behind the bush with the hound yapping at its hoofs. It headed straight for Louise's horse, which whinnied and reared. One of her feet slipped from the stirrup and she dropped her bow but managed to seize the horse's mane. The next moment the horse was in flight, and she was desperately trying to get a hold on the reins. Despite the snowy conditions underfoot, branches whizzed past and, but for her being crouched low over the horse's neck as her hand sought blindly for the reins, she could have been knocked from the horse.

Louise was aware of hoofs beating behind her, but had no time to look behind to see who it was. She was aware of snow falling more thickly, but was intent on catching the reins that were being tossed about as much as she was. After what seemed an age she caught them and looped a length around her hand and pulled. The horse began to slither and slide, as it slackened speed, twisting this way and that to avoid the trees, but partially blinded by the snow it blundered sideways into a tree trunk. All down one side of her, from shoulder to knee, received the full impact of the collision, and her head caught a glancing blow from a branch. She swayed dizzily in the saddle as the horse continued to stagger round and round. The reins slipped from her fingers and she slid from the saddle.

CHAPTER THIRTEEN

JOHN reached where Louise was slumped on the ground. She forced her head up as he dismounted, groaning and blinking snowflakes off her eyelashes. He looked anxious as he knelt on the ground, and lifted her so that her head rested against his knee. Brushing the sodden copper tendrils from one side of her face, his unsteady hand touched the lump there and she winced. 'Poor Louise. That was some knock you took.'

'It hurts,' she said dolefully.

'I wager it does.' Gently he kissed the swelling and she was moved by his gesture. 'How does the rest of you feel?'

'Crushed!' She smiled faintly. 'But help me up and I'll get back on my horse. I'm getting covered in snow.'

The side of his mouth lifted and he slipped an arm about her shoulders. 'Do you think you can stand?'

'Of course.'

'Good girl.' He smiled encouragingly but despite her brave words she began to tremble so much with the effort that he had to hoist her up and keep his arm round her once she was on her feet.

'I don't think I will be able to ride after all,' she said in a shaky voice.

'Of course you can,' he said with a confidence he was far from feeling. 'But not alone, sweeting. We'll both ride my horse, but I don't think that we'll be able to make the return journey to cousin Hugh's. We've travelled some distance and the best action to take would be to go on to my father's house, which is nearer.'

'I'll do whatever you say,' she returned wearily, having faith in his capabilities to look after her. 'But won't they be worried about us?'

'Most likely,' he said, sounding cheerful. 'But there's nothing I can do about that.' He lifted her up on to the horse and she clung to its neck while he swung up behind her. Then his arm went round her and he took the reins. 'We'll take it slow and easy,' he murmured against her ear as the horse began to move.

'What about my mount?'

'It'll either follow us or go back home. I'm not worrying about it now.'

'No.' She rested against him and closed her eyes, attempting to block out the pain in her shoulder and hip, and left it to him to take care of getting them out of the weather, which had worsened so that their hats and hair and fronts were smothered in snow.

It seemed an age before John tapped her on the shoulder. 'We're here, and not surprisingly everywhere looks deserted. Although, thank God, there's a wisp of smoke coming from the roof.'

Louise raised her head and pushed back the rim of the fur hat, wiping her face with a wet sleeve in an attempt to see the better the sprawling building created from grey stone. The roof wore a mantle of white and the wind had swept snow into the crevices between stones and sills. There was a well and outbuildings, and from somewhere came the forlorn sound of sheep bleating.

'The house was built by my great-grandfather,' said John, 'and is somewhat old-fashioned.' He dismounted and lifted a shivering Louise down from the horse. With his arm steadying her, they trudged their way over to the front entrance. The door opened beneath his hand and he ushered her inside.

It was a relief to be out of the blizzard and her eyes swept the low-pitched room with its dark-beamed ceiling, and the ladder leading upwards in one corner under

which there were shelves. She thought that there were
several books there and baskets and pots. There were a
couple of armed oak chairs, stools, and a small table.
Trestles and tops were placed near a far wall, and a
beautifully carved settle covered with tapestry cushions
was set close to the fire which glowed in the middle of
the room. A tabby cat, which lay warming itself, opened
both eyes and stared at them. 'There's nobody here,' she
whispered, finding the cat's green stare combined with
the unearthly silence unnerving.

'Agnes must have gone to visit her family,' said John,
his voice sounding loud in the empty room. He led her
over to the fire, took the saturated cloak from her
shoulders and lowered her on to the settle, before easing
off her boots. He ordered her to lie down before going
over to a basket of wood. He soon had the fire burning
more brightly so that the copper warming-pan and
cooking-pots winked dully. He went and fetched a pot
from the wall and picked up a jug from the floor near
the fire.

Louise, stretched on the settle with her head resting
on several cushions, still shivered slightly as she watched
him pour ale into the pot and set it on the grill over the
fire. Then he vanished through a door at the far end of
the room and came back with a small jar and a nutmeg.
His clothes steamed as he spooned honey into the ale
and then grated in some nutmeg. She gazed at his profile
lit up by the flames and experienced pleasure. A moment
later he brought her a wooden cup.

'Drink it up as hot as you can,' he commanded, 'while
I go and find us some dry clothes and some blankets.'

'What of yourself?' she said quickly. 'Will you not
have a drink first?'

'I'll have one soon enough,' he replied, stripping off
his wet houppelande. 'But I want to make certain that
you don't catch a chill.' He placed the garment he had
discarded, and her cloak, on one of the chairs near the

fire, and vanished up the ladder in the corner of the room.

Louise sipped at the ale, finding the feeling of warmth that it sent trickling through her blissful. The cat rose from its place by the fire and settled a little further away. It gave a perfunctory lick at one of its hind legs then tucked its nose into its tail again. She envied its *savoir-faire* because now she was a little more comfortable and warmer it occurred to her that there was need for her to do some thinking. If the snow continued to fall then she and John would have to spend some time in this house and she knew that was not good if she was to get him out of her heart. Yet she soon came to the conclusion that there was nothing to be done and that she might as well make the most of his company because sooner or later they would part.

A moment later Louise heard the thud of feet on the ladder and John reappeared with a couple of blankets flung over his shoulder and clothes clutched in one hand. 'You can change in front of the fire. I'll have to go and see to the horse,' he muttered with a frown. 'I'd forgotten about it with worrying about you.'

'I'm sorry to be of trouble,' she said quietly. 'But there's really no need for you to worry. I'll be fine soon.'

'I believe you'd say that even if it wasn't true.' His voice had softened. 'I admire your courage, Louise Saulnier. There are not many women around like you.' His words warmed her as much as the ale and she could not take her eyes from him, watching him place the clothes over the back of the settle and drop the blankets on her feet before sitting down on the edge of the settle. 'Are you hungry?'

'Ay,' she replied, grimacing. 'Is there any food?'

'I've got some of the game we shot in my saddlebag. I could skin a rabbit and Agnes can cook it if she's able to get back here.'

'You think she mightn't?'

'It's still snowing.' His expression was serious. 'And, although she's likely to have only gone to the hamlet, if the snow continues to fall for the rest of the afternoon it wouldn't make sense for her to try and get back tonight.'

She nodded. 'I understand that. But what if the weather doesn't let up and we're stuck here for days? We'll need more food than two rabbits.'

He smiled. 'There's plenty of flour and salted meat in the store-room, as well as fruit and sheep's cheese, and other provisions. Also the chickens are probably in the barn out of the weather. And if we can get to the shepherd's house on the hill there's mutton to be had. Not that that's possible right now. But we won't starve. So you mustn't worry but rest.'

Her mouth firmed determinedly. 'I feel that I've rested long enough. Could I not help you? I could skin the rabbits.'

Both his dark brows elevated. 'You really know how?'

'It was something useful I learnt living in the wild,' she said with a grin, pushing herself up into a sitting position. 'Now you go and bring me the rabbits and then see to the horse.'

He hesitated. 'Are you sure you shouldn't be resting?'

'Go and fetch the rabbits before you do anything else,' she said imperiously.

He went, and she flopped back against the cushions and closed her eyes briefly, feeling her aches, but she only lay there a minute before sitting up and searching for the clothes he had spoken about. Those which were his were obvious as were the ones he intended for her. Women's clothes! His mother's, perhaps? She began to peel off her damp surcote.

Louise was just fastening up a cream undergown when John entered the house, looking like a snowman. He stopped abruptly and there was a look of appreciation on his face. 'That fits all right? There are more clothes upstairs, which belonged to my half-sister. Mother never gave them away, hoping one day that she might have a daughter of her own.'

'This is lovely and warm and the wool is really soft.'

'It's Cotswold wool.' He came towards her, the rabbits swinging in his hand, and he placed them on the table. 'You must know that English sheep produce the finest wool there is. Some of the best comes from the Cotswolds.'

'Around Burford?'

He nodded. 'As soon as it's possible to travel I'll have to return there and sort matters out with Dykemore.'

'You'll take me with you?' she said quickly. 'I've been thinking that if the man that Harry gave Marguerite to is a wool merchant, then maybe she's living in that area.'

Again he nodded. 'It's possible that I could know him with his being in the trade. We must get his name from Harry.'

She barely hesitated before saying lightly, 'The sooner the better. It seems an age since I set out to find my sister.'

There was a silence before he said, 'I know Harry and I have said that your sister is better off in England, but have you thought that she might consider it so?'

Louise quashed any qualms she might have on that score and shook her head vigorously, picking up a saffron surcote from the settle. 'You think Marguerite will be content to be a servant in England?' She forced a laugh. 'My sister will be as ready to return to France as . . . I am.'

'You're so sure?' he said quietly. 'Perhaps she's not so unhappy as you make her—or yourself—out to be.' The tone of his voice changed suddenly, 'Let's talk sense, Louise! We'll find your sister by all means, but if she's well fed, well clothed, and well treated—as she may well be if she knows something of the clothier's trade—then be prepared for her not to be so willing to go back to Normandy.'

Louise had listened in growing dismay. 'You believe that she'll be swayed by material advantages,' she said hotly.

'If she's got any sense she will be.' His voice was dispassionate. 'How long do you think the pair of you will last in that forest winter after winter? Swallow that pride of yours, and accept that you and I could have some kind of future together.'

She stared at him and a line of scarlet ran under her skin. 'You made me an offer something like that before and I said no,' she whispered.

He nodded. 'Ay! We didn't know each other that well. Even now I'm not asking you to give me an answer immediately. Shall we see how well we bear with each other's company while we're here?' His blue eyes were intent as he gazed at her. 'It'll be a good testing ground.'

'I—you and me—here. Will we—sleep together?' she stammered.

His dark lashes swept down, concealing his thoughts from her. 'If it's not what you want—no.' He went over to the fire, removed the ale that still simmered there, and poured himself a measure into a tankard. 'Of course it does get extremely cold here at night, but if you wrap up well you should sleep all right.' He darted a glance at her. 'I'm sure you managed to keep warm the last couple of nights without me.'

'Ay!' Her hands moved agitatedly over the surface of the gown. 'Let's leave it for now. Shouldn't you go and see to the horse? I'll start on the rabbits. Where's a knife?'

He took the one from his girdle and held it out to her. 'Don't cut yourself.'

'I'm not that much of a fool,' she said pettishly, snatching it from him. 'Now leave me be, John.'

'There's no need to be anxious, my sweet.' He kissed the tip of her nose and she felt tears start in her eyes. 'Everything could be worse.' He downed the rest of his ale and picked up his wet houppelande. 'I won't be too long.'

'Be as long as you like,' she flung at him, before shuffling painfully over to the table. She removed the cat, which was sniffing at one of the rabbits.

'Sweet Jesus! You're walking like an old woman!' He followed her over. 'Leave them for me and lie down.'

'I don't want to lie down,' she flashed, rubbing at her cheeks. 'I'm bruised, that's all, and there's nothing you can do about that.'

His brows knit. 'I'll find you some salve later. But are you sure you're all right?'

'We have to eat,' she said fiercely. 'And you've got to see to the horse. And if there are chickens then you'd better feed them. Is there any water to stew the rabbits?'

'Use ale.' He scowled at her. 'The well doesn't generally freeze but it's something extra to think about and I'd rather not worry about it now.'

She glanced at him, hating the thought of his having to go outside in the blizzard again but knowing it was necessary. 'Very well, then I'll cook them in ale as you suggest. Have we any onions and turnips and herbs? Salt? I know you've got nutmegs.'

'I'll see what's in the store-room.' He left her to the task of skinning and cleaning the rabbits and was only a few moments fetching the vegetables, which he left on the table near to hand, before disappearing outside again.

Louise tried to give all her concentration to her task but while her hands busied themselves her thoughts were chaotic. The more she tried not to think about how comfortable and pleasurable it would be sleeping with him the more it filled her mind. She forced herself to hope that the missing Agnes would turn up, and as soon as the cut rabbits and vegetables were simmering over the fire she went slowly over to the window to see if there was any sign of her. The glass was cold to her touch and it was almost impossible to see out because the snow was banked up on the sill and the daylight was already fading, and the only sign of movement was the falling snow.

Louise went back over to the fire and stirred the stew before limping through the door that John had used. Her eyes searched shelves. There were jars of honey and wine, and bottled pears and blackberries and dried fruit, flagons of wine and ale. There were sacks of cereals, dried beans and peas, as well as salted hams and onions hanging from the ceiling. She found a bowl and ladled some flour into it, and took down a jar of honey, then she remembered that there was no water.

Frustrated, Louise went back into the hall just as John entered it. 'I was going to make some griddle cakes,' she called, 'but I don't think they'll taste quite the same with ale.'

'We could melt some snow for swiftness's sake,' he replied, wiping his hand across his wet face.

'I won't need much,' she said quickly. 'And I'd rather not have to send you out again, but if you're really hungry...?'

'I'm really hungry,' he said emphatically. 'Just get me a bowl. I don't want to come further in and drip all over everywhere.'

She hurried as much as she could and it was only seconds before she was placing a small pot of snow on the griddle and she had turned back to him.

'Could you help me off with my gloves?' He was slumped against the wall by the door, having removed his hat, and she realised how tired and wet he must be.

She went over to him and eased the sodden cold leather from each finger. 'You must come by the fire. You look exhausted.'

He nodded and forced himself away from the wall, saying unevenly, 'It's been quite a day and I'll probably be all right soon, but could you do the honours with my houppelande as well? My hands are frozen.'

'You'll have to bend,' she said, concealing her concern as she undid his buttons and felt him shivering under her hand. 'More ale for you, and into warm clothing.'

'It sounds good.' He smiled faintly. 'I'd like to lean on your shoulder but I suspect it would hurt.'

She returned his smile, and said brightly, 'Arms round waists and we'll manage that way. It's not far to the fire.'

They crossed the room and she was reminded of how many times they had needed to help and support the other in the short time that they had known each other, and could not prevent herself from thinking that must mean that their relationship was perhaps more than just sensuous.

John refused to sit on the settle in his wet state, swaying close to the fire as he ordered Louise to bring a chair closer. He sank into it, and shut his eyes. She took a cushion from the settle and dropped it on the floor before kneeling awkwardly to rid him of his boots. It was not an easy task but she managed it. He did stir himself to help and opened his eyes. Relieved that he showed some signs of life but worried about his staying any longer in the wet clothes, she chided him to get up and undress while she poured him some ale, turning her back on him.

John roused himself and did as he was told, albeit slowly, but he did not bother dressing, just took a blanket and wrapped himself in it before settling in the chair again.

Louise turned when she heard the wood creak and their eyes met. 'That's better, is it?' she said jocularly.

'Wonderful.' He smiled. 'Where's that ale? And how's the food coming on? It smells good.'

'The food will be a little while.' She handed him a tankard and he took it with a murmur of thanks. 'Perhaps you'd like a handful of dried fruit to eat with it while you're waiting? I can get some for you before I start on the scones.'

'It's me who should be taking care of you,' he said softly. 'You're hurt.'

'You took care of me before.' Her tone was warm. 'I'll rest soon.'

'Good.' He stretched out his bare feet towards the heat as she went over to the store-room. 'How are you feeling now, lass?' he shouted. 'Your head not giving you too much pain?'

'It aches a bit,' she called, her voice slightly muffled. 'But nothing to worry about, and I suppose my other aches and pains will take a few days to be gone but at least I haven't broken any bones.' She came back into the hall.

'You did well keeping in the saddle so long.'

She laughed. 'Don't you think I've had plenty of practice in the last weeks? I've never spent so long on a horse before in winter.' Sitting on the corner of the settle, she poured some raisins from a jar into a small bowl and held them out to him.

He took a few and tossed them in his mouth, chewing as he glanced up at her in the saffron gown. Her copper hair had grown a little and was curling about her head like a burnished halo. 'We seem to have spent most of our time together travelling and being tired and dirty,' he said quietly. 'It'll be good if the snow does last and we can stay here and rest.'

'You—might find it tedious with just me for company,' she said hesitantly.

'I never did before.' His eyes held hers and the expression in them caused her to catch her breath.

'You mustn't look at me like that,' she whispered, getting up quickly and taking the melted snow from the griddle.

'Like what?' His voice was deep and low. 'As if I was thinking how beautiful you look and how I never want to see you in a boy's clothes again? You're too womanly for such garb.'

'I'm not beautiful,' she murmured, delight at his words rippling through her. 'My hair's too short and my skin's not pale enough.'

'Your hair will grow and I like it as it is anyroad, lass. As for your skin, it's soft beneath my caress and glowing and healthy to my eye. As for your shape, I consider that quite perfect. Your breasts and your waist fit my hands' span beautifully. As for——'

'That's enough!' She was blushing.

'Come here.'

'No. I'm making cakes.'

'The scones can wait. I want to kiss you.'

'But I didn't say that I wanted to kiss you,' she said, trying to steady her breathing as she poured honey and water into the flour, which she combined with nutmeg and cinnamon.

He rose and came to stand at her shoulder. 'You do, though, don't you, dearest Louise?' The uncertainty in his voice caused her to twist her neck and look at him.

Suddenly it was only he and she that was important. 'Ay.' Turning completely round, she held up her face to his and their lips met in a kiss that was gentle at first but deepened and demanded before they drew apart for breath. 'I've started the cakes so I must finish them,' she said in a flurried voice, moving away from him. 'You go back and sit by the fire.'

'Don't be too long.' John lipped her finger before leaving her.

Louise's hands worked with a swiftness that revealed her agitation. When she went over to place the flat cakes on the griddle he was not sitting but standing over the fire, with the blanket wrapped about him like a toga while he stirred the stew. Their eyes met and she could not stop her mouth from smiling as she gazed at him.

'I never thought of your being able to cook,' he said, moving the pot of stewing rabbit to the right so that there was room for her to place the scones on the griddle.

'My aunt—the sister of my mother—taught me,' said Louise. 'She died when I was fourteen and father hired a cook, considering that I had enough to do taking over the running of the household and looking after Marguerite.'

'I suppose you've missed being the mistress of your own household since the fall of Caen?' He put down the wooden spoon and sat on the settle.

'I stopped thinking about it an age ago.' She placed the last scone and sat a few inches away from him. 'Staying alive was more important than wishing to turn time back,' she added with a lack of rancour.

'I wish that you hadn't suffered the way you had,' he said vehemently, 'and yet you wouldn't be the Louise you are now if you hadn't.' He put his arm round her.

'No.' Hesitantly she rested her head on his shoulder. 'There are some things I would have been terribly afraid of doing.' There was a shy note in her voice.

'If you refer to what I think you do,' he said softly, 'then that would have been a pity because it was good between us despite what the priests say about such pleasures.'

She lifted her head and looked at him. 'Don't let's talk about priests and sin!' Her tone was urgent.

'I don't want to talk about them, sweeting,' he said tenderly, his mouth covering hers with a passion that instantly roused an overwhelming response within her.

'We mustn't forget about the cakes,' she said unsteadily against his lips. 'It would be a shame for them to burn.'

'No, we mustn't,' he agreed, and nuzzled her ears and then her throat. 'Later—we'll save this for later. We have all the night before us.'

She did not dispute his assumption that they would sleep together. It was cold in the hall beyond the fire's circle. Later—in some future that she could not imagine now—she would have to accept that a time would come when he might no longer want her, just as his brother had not wanted Clotilde.

Their kisses grew more fervent despite their talk of cakes, and it was only the smell of burning that brought Louise to an awareness that there would be no supper if they didn't control themselves. She struggled out of his arms, telling him just that, and he sat back, his eyes smouldering as he watched her not only save the singeing scones from utter ruin but the stew from drying up completely and sticking to the pan.

As they ate their food on their knees, John said, 'It might be best if I brought the mattress down here on the floor near the fire. I'll pile on more wood and we'll be as snug as any fox in its hole.'

'What if Agnes returns?' asked Louise with an air of anxiety, licking a crispy slice of onion from her spoon.

'She won't,' said John confidently. 'We're marooned, sweeting, and I can only be glad that it's you I'm with.' He cleared his bowl and leaned back with a satisfied sigh. 'That was the best meal I've ever tasted.'

'Burnt scones and singed rabbit!' she exclaimed, unable to prevent a laugh. 'You're easily satisfied, my lord. You were hungry.'

'Don't decry yourself, Louise. You're a good cook!' He grinned, rising to his feet. 'While you finish I'll go and get the mattress.'

'Can you manage getting it down the ladder?' She rose hurriedly. 'You could trip.'

'I'll slide it down.' He whistled as he left the fireside and went upstairs. Louise started to feel nervous and wondered what his feelings towards her really were, hoping that he loved her a little. There was a thumping and a bumping, a slithering, sliding sound, and she turned to see the mattress lying at the foot of the ladder. Her nervousness grew as she watched him climb down and drag the mattress towards her. Perhaps she would not be able to please him this time and he would turn from her. She chided herself for so cold-bloodedly planning to have carnal pleasure with a man who was not her husband.

'Stop worrying, Louise.' John's quiet voice, a foot from her, took her by surprise. 'If you don't want to do this, you don't have to. We can just sleep.'

'Sleep?' She stared at him. 'But I...' She almost said love, but changed it to, 'Want you.'

He smiled faintly and drew her into his arms. 'I want you too,' he murmured against her chin. 'So much that it's an ache inside me.'

'Almost a pain,' she said, adding hesitantly, 'But I also have a different hurt, John, all down one side. I don't know if——'

'You mustn't worry so much.' He rocked her gently before his mouth searched for hers.

There was after all nothing much for her to be anxious about because once he started undressing her and laying kisses on her throat and breast, and the dark shadows on shoulder and hip, her aches diminished in proportion to her growing desire for him. Her passion matched his and she smothered his shoulders and chest with biting kisses as his hands stroked her thighs and buttocks. Yet he delayed entering her, caressing and nuzzling, licking and nibbling so that he roused her to a fever pitch of impatience and longing, until she forced herself with such urgency against him that he entered her immediately, to her relief. Joined, they became a single pulsating unit giving and giving until both received intense physical pleasure.

Afterwards she cried against his shoulder and he took her chin in his hand. 'Regrets, sweetheart?' he questioned, concern a faint gleam in his blue eyes.

She blinked away her tears. 'You must consider me a wanton, but I have never known any other man.'

'You've told me so before and I believed you then.' He kissed her. 'Why should I change my mind now? Go to sleep, lass. You've had a long day.'

She wanted to believe him, and so, although plagued by self-doubt, she relaxed and slept dreamlessly.

The next morning Louise woke first and bit back a groan, before managing to rise and put on her chemise. She built up the fire and went to look out of the window but could see little, although she had a feeling that it had stopped snowing. She went back over to the mattress and slid beneath the blankets alongside John. She leaned on one elbow, gazing into his slumbering face, willing him to wake. Gently she ran a finger along his unshaven chin and kissed his mouth. He took her by surprise when he responded and pulled her on top of him. He entered her without any preliminaries. She would never have thought of getting into such a position and was shy at first about moving on top of him, but discovered that she had more control over the pace of their lovemaking and it was very enjoyable.

But there were other urgent matters to see to as well as their physical need for each other—such as food and drink and the means of keeping warm. 'We'll need more logs,' said John, after he had managed to force the back door open. The front had refused to budge because the snow had drifted against it.

'Will we have to go to the forest?' Louise uneasily surveyed the white expanse that stretched as far as the eye could see. The snow had stopped falling but what lay on the ground was deep and the air felt colder.

'No.' His eyes narrowed as he gazed ahead. 'My father always makes sure there's a good supply of dried kindling and logs in the barn. I'll have to dig out a path that far.'

'Perhaps I should help you?'

He kissed her lightly. 'Digging is men's work. I'll need feeding, woman. You get a meal cooking. And the hose I took off yesterday have holes in the toes. Mother's sewing basket is on the floor in the far right corner under the stairs.'

'Do you think Agnes will return today?'

John looked towards the nearest hill. 'No. If the snow stays off, perhaps tomorrow—or the day after next. It depends how it's drifted and how deep it is.' He glanced at Louise, and said seriously, 'It doesn't bother you being so alone with me?'

'No.' She lowered her eyes, suddenly shy of him. He was so masculine and she found herself wanting him again. 'I'll soak peas and cut some ham. If I had some leaven I'd make bread.'

He grimaced. 'We'll have to live without it. Yeast is something I don't know about. I just took it for granted when bread arrived on the table. But there's a sack of oats in the store-room. You can mix them in much the same way as you do flour with water and make oat-cakes. They're good with cheese or honey.'

She nodded. 'I'll try.' And reluctantly left him to his digging.

The oatcakes were not perfect but they filled their stomachs later that day when John came in, ruddy-cheeked and famished. The pottage, though, was good, thick with onions and peas and chunks of ham.

Half an hour later he drew her into his arms again and made love to her. Afterwards she lay contentedly drowsing in front of the fire beside him, before he stirred and asked her did she want some fresh air and to stretch her legs? They made their way along the slippery path to the barn, where Louise found a couple of eggs while John split logs.

There was still plenty of pottage over for supper and they had some bottled blackberries on griddle scones after it. Then they lay on the mattress and made love again, and she wondered if it would have been like this if their parents had arranged a match between them and they'd married. She longed to belong to him in name but did not voice such a hope.

Afterwards they talked of their childhoods, of the cloth trade, of Antwerp and Venice, and John told her about the Knaresborough Fair and how beautiful England could be in the spring. That night it snowed again and Louise was glad.

Their days settled into a pattern, one that she would have been content to have go on and on, although sometimes her eyes longed for relief from looking out on the snow and she wondered about Marguerite. Some nights John would read to her from the few precious handwritten books on the shelf—tales of chivalry or stories from the Scriptures. He also talked of his concern for the shepherds and his father's sheep on the fells. 'He'll lose some—bound to in this weather,' he fretted, pacing the room. 'He must be worrying, too.'

'Do you think he'll have guessed where we've gone?' Louise looked up from shortening one of the undergowns she had found upstairs. The mattress had been moved back on to the bed, which was aired and made welcoming with a warming-pan each night.

His dark brows drew together. 'Harry'll tell them I'm all right.'

'You really believe he knows?'

He nodded. 'As soon as a thaw sets in, Agnes will arrive first—and then they'll come,' he said positively.

'And this life will end,' she said sadly, and so quietly that he only just caught the words.

John stopped pacing and knelt on the floor in front of the settle. His blue eyes were intent as he stared into her rosy face. 'You've been so content, Louise? You don't hanker after your own country? Or towns? You haven't fretted to seek out Marguerite?'

'Occasionally I have thought of these things, but...' She fell silent and lowered her eyes to her sewing again.

He did not press her to finish what she was saying, only removing her sewing and drawing her into the circle of his arms and holding her tightly.

That night when they made love he raised her to heights of ecstasy that were new to her and she wondered how she would live without him when eventually he tired of her. Perhaps people really did die from lack of love? But when the time came that he no longer wanted her then she would go out of his life rather than live off his goodwill.

Two days later the thaw came, and the sound of dripping and rushing water seemed to be heard on all sides. Patches of green showed in the valley and on the fells, and John and Louise squelched their way around the hill to the hamlet, only to meet on the way a woman of middle years, scrawny and dark-haired, who surveyed them both with keen interest.

The conversation that followed between Agnes and John was so rapid and accented that Louise, whose English was almost fluent, had trouble understanding it. The outcome was that Agnes, with a toss of her head and a sniff, went back to the hamlet.

'What did you tell her? asked Louise, her hazel eyes surprised as she clutched at his arm. 'She seems displeased.'

'I told her to come tomorrow, that likely my parents would be here then—that we were managing alone,' he said unemotionally.

'But she'll believe——'

He raised both eyebrows. 'Not necessarily.'

She was left wondering what that meant when his arm went about her waist and he sounded reasonably cheerful when next he spoke. 'At least she was able to tell me that there's only been a few ewes in lamb lost.'

She slanted a sidelong glance at him. 'Your father will be pleased?'

'Ay. It could have been much worse.' He took his arm from about her and seized her hand. 'Let's get back and have something to eat, and then...' His eyes met hers and he lifted her chin and kissed her with a great deal of deliberation. It was as if he had set a seal on her, she thought dazedly.

It was later when John was reading to Louise that he stopped in mid-sentence and did not resume reading, but rather placed the book carefully on the shelf.

'What is it?' she said slowly, putting down the shirt, which he had torn on a nail in the barn. He did not answer immediately but stood, staring at the wall and drumming his fingers on the shelf. 'John?'

'Hmm?'

She rose and went over to him, putting a hand on his arm. 'What's wrong?'

He looked at her but his eyes did not quite focus on her face. 'It's Harry,' he said in a vague voice. 'There's something...' His hand curled into a fist.

'He—he's not dead?' she stammered, pressing her fingers into his arm.

'Not dead.' He shook his head. 'We won't wait for Father to come in the morning. We'll set out as soon as it's light.'

She nodded, her heart sinking as he began to pace the floor again. The idyll was over. Hadn't she known it would come to an end sooner or later? John's mind was already reaching out to tomorrow, worrying about his brother.

And suddenly she was concerned because he was. What could be wrong with Harry?

CHAPTER FOURTEEN

NEITHER John nor Louise needed to wake the other the following morning. Both had lain silently, staring into the darkness for a while, before the first shafts of light outlined the shuttered window. As soon as he slid out of bed, she followed him.

Louise suddenly paused for thought, her hand stilling on the white chemise, and she looked at John. 'Do I wear women's clothes or...?'

He was silent for a second and then he freed a long breath. 'The need for pretending you are a youth is over.' His fingers fastened buttons swiftly as his eyes met hers. 'My parents might as well know about you sooner rather than later. What they think will make no difference to my plans, so there is no need for you to look so apprehensive.'

'But I like your parents,' she said fiercely. 'I don't want them thinking——'

'It's too late to worry about that now!' His voice was sharp. 'Let's not talk about it. Harry's too much on my mind.'

'Of course! I'm sorry! Worrying about Harry is much more important than talking about my worries,' she said jerkily, dragging the chemise over her hips with a violence that revealed how distraught she was. 'It was the same when we first met. Finding Harry was the be-all and end-all of everything!'

He stared at her. 'What's wrong with you? Wasn't it your need to find your sister that led you to me? You of all people should understand family feeling.'

'I do,' she cried, running a hand through her hair. 'But you talk as if your—your *mistress* meeting your parents is an everyday occurrence.'

'Do I?' A slight laugh escaped him. 'I assure you it isn't. How the mighty are fallen! I wouldn't even consider such a meeting if it weren't that you and Harry are both in my thoughts.' He finished fastening the points of his hose to an overshirt and reached for his doublet. 'And have you thought that since we've been missing Blanche has probably told Mother and Father that you're a woman?'

She stilled and her hazel eyes widened. 'No, I hadn't!'

'And have you considered that they might trust me not to take advantage of you?'

'I never gave it any thought,' she murmured. 'But even if they did, won't they think it strange that you haven't told them that I'm a woman?' There was the slightest hint of mockery in her voice.

He rubbed his nose and screwed up his face. 'Let's not talk about this now. If Harry's in trouble, as I believe him to be, then their concern will all be for him. Agreed?'

She hesitated. 'Agreed.'

'Right! You cook up something hot, while I go and saddle up the horse.' He pulled on his houppelande and left her to it.

An hour later they were on their way.

They met up with Guy and Nat in the middle of the forest. 'So it's true,' said John's father, shifting his calm, estimating glance from Louise in the russet gown to his son. 'Louis is a Louise.'

John nodded briefly. 'Where's Harry? What's happened to him?'

Guy shook his head, almost in disbelief. 'It never fails to amaze me these feelings you have. You're both so different and yet——'

'Father! What's wrong with Harry?' demanded John.

It was Nat who answered, unable to keep quiet any longer. 'He's vanished. Him and Peter!'

'What?'

Louise glanced at John. Some of the colour ebbed from his face and a muscle in his neck twitched. 'When? Where?' he said harshly.

'Knaresborough. Yesterday,' replied his father quietly. 'The thaw came the day before last at Hugh's place. Harry has been restless ever since you went thundering off in the snowstorm after Louise. He said that you were all right, but you know Harry. He doesn't seem able to stay in one place too long. So when I said that I had some business that needed seeing to in Knaresborough, he jumped at the opportunity and offered to go. Blanche, Nat and Peter asked to go with him.'

'But how did they disappear? Someone must have seen something! Nat?' John's gaze moved swiftly to the boy.

'Didn't see nothing,' said Nat dolefully. 'Peter and me had wandered away from cousin Blanche and Harry, and were some way along the riverbank when I was hit on the back of the head. When I woke up, cousin Blanche was slapping me face and I was all wet and cold with lying in the slush. There was no sign of Peter and she said that Harry had gone into some wool merchant's house while she was buying some gloves, but on knocking at the door to ask after him she was told he'd already left. We looked everywhere we could think but couldn't find them.'

There was a silence but for the jingle of a harness as one of the horses moved its head.

'Dykemore,' said John in a hard voice. 'It has to have something to do with him.'

'But how?' cried Louise, her brow creasing. 'The weather's been terrible. And how could he know that Peter and Harry were to be in Knaresborough that day? He just couldn't!'

'Chance,' replied John. 'Dorothy must have had more money than I realised. We could have been seen leaving Burford and Dykemore's guessed we'd go to Yorkshire. It won't be he who's abducted them. He's too indolent to make the journey. It'll be a couple of his henchmen. They'll have arrived up here after us and been stranded in Knaresborough because of the snow.'

'But why Harry?' Louise paused. 'Of course, they thought he was you,' she said slowly.

There was a whiteness about John's mouth. 'He doesn't know that Harry's in England. Dorothy knew of his being missing, of course, and would have told her uncle.'

'What'll—he do with them?' said Louise huskily. Her throat had gone tight.

'He won't kill them,' said John, his brows drawn together in thought. 'Not yet, anyhow. A quick death isn't his way.' He kicked their horse into action. 'They'll be taken south. Peter will be held to get me—Harry—to sign some papers that'll probably give Dykemore authority over Dorothy's estate, and Peter. Knowing him, he'll indulge in a little torture as well.'

'And when Dykemore does that he'll discover that Harry's Harry,' said his father, gazing at him.

John nodded. 'And I don't give a farthing for Harry's chances then. He won't need two hostages to bring me running.'

'We'll have to leave right away, then,' said Louise. 'They've already got a day's start on us.'

'Us! We?' John look was incredulous. 'You don't think you're going with me?'

'Naturally I am.' She frowned. 'You weren't considering leaving me behind?'

'Of course I was. Do you think I'd take you into danger? I've told you the kind of man we're dealing with!'

'Exactly! So I'm not staying up here, wondering what's happening to you,' she said calmly.

Guy shot her a glance. 'I know someone, *mam'selle*, who said the same thing once during the great rebellion.'

John scowled at him. 'Yours and Mother's affairs have got nothing to do with this, Father. Louise is staying here.'

Her temper flared. 'You can't make me! You're not my husband that you can command my obedience. You'd have to drag me, screaming and kicking, and lock me in somewhere!'

'That can be arranged,' he snapped.

'You wouldn't!'

'Wouldn't I? Try me.'

Louise pressed her lips tightly together and her eyes smouldered. She would argue with him no more but pretend to be amenable.

There was a long silence before John said quietly, 'I'll go alone. I don't want to chance him getting his hands on any more hostages, and I have friends in Burford if I need help.'

'You believe that's where Harry and Peter will be taken?' said his father.

'Either there or the house in Oxford.' John ducked a dripping branch. 'Now let's not delay talking but ride.'

They arrived at Hugh's manor a short while later and had no sooner clattered into the courtyard than Blanche, and John's mother, came out of the door at the top of the steps. 'You are safe,' cried the older woman in a trembling voice. 'Thank God one of you is! But where can Harry and Peter be?'

'John has a fair notion, Philippa,' called Guy, giving the reins of his horse to Nat and going up to meet her.

'Go and find me a change of clothing, Mother, and pack me some food,' said John, dismounting. 'I'll be leaving within the hour.'

'So soon!' Blanche, her face seeming paler than ever, came carefully down the slippery steps. 'Could I not go with you, John?'

'What?' He stared at her disbelievingly.

'I'm worrying myself sick about Harry.'

'That's a change,' he said frankly. 'But you're not coming with me. You can keep Louise company.' He brushed past her and went up the steps to his mother.

Louise and Blanche exchanged glances and neither looked pleased with what he said, but it was Louise who said dispassionately, on dismounting, 'It's a woman's place to wait while the men go off to fight the dragons. Surely you know that, Blanche?'

'It's not easy,' she said tearfully, pulling at a handkerchief.

'Of course it isn't,' replied Louise with assumed cheerfulness. 'But men will not believe that some of us would rather fight alongside them, chancing death, than live without them.'

'You feel like that about John?' said Blanche with a touch of amazement.

Louise nodded. 'That's why I'm not going to be left behind. Can you find me some boy's clothes?'

Blanche's pale eyes rounded. 'You mean it? But how? Why? Where is Harry? What is all this talk of fighting?'

Louise told her, believing that it was her right to know about John's suspicions if she truly cared for Harry. And she finished generously with the offer that if she wished to come with her then she was welcome to find two lots of boys' clothes.

'No, I don't think so,' said Blanche wistfully. 'I would fear John's anger—and besides I have no mind to cut off my hair.'

Louise shrugged. 'You could tuck it inside a hat. But no matter. You bring the clothes to the stables. I will hide in the loft till you come, and if anybody asks after me tell them I'm sulking and have gone for a walk.'

Blanche nodded. 'You can trust me. I only wish I had your courage.'

'I'm not brave,' said Louise honestly. 'I'm quaking inside. But I have to go.'

The other woman shook her head and left her.

Louise took the horse to the stable, talking softly in its ear till Nat left, and then she climbed the ladder to the hayloft and made herself comfortable. It seemed a long time before she heard Blanche's voice below. She took the clothes handed to her and whispered a goodbye. A 'God keep you!' floated up to her, and then she was alone.

The clothes, she presumed, were another set of Nat's because they fitted just as well, and were warm and comfortable. Silently she praised Blanche for remembering a cloak, hat and gloves. Then she eyed up the horses in the stable and picked out a nice grey palfrey and saddled up.

Louise mounted outside and was soon beyond the walls of the courtyard, and cantering along the road towards Knaresborough. She took it for granted that John would travel south the way they had come and determined not to stop until she was beyond the town. There she would wait for him.

Louise was anxious. There was the glimmering of a pale moon in the afternoon sky and soon darkness would fall. What if John did not come this way after all? Yet within the hour she heard again the sound of hoofs on the muddy road and to her relief recognised John's outline. With a heavily beating heart she urged her horse from behind the rock to meet him.

Before Louise had a chance to speak she had to duck the cudgel he swung at her. 'John! 'Tis me,' she cried frantically.

He swore loudly, adding, 'By all that's holy, woman, what are you thinking of coming at me like that?'

'You're not surprised to see me?' she asked in a faltering voice, bringing her horse alongside his.

A grim smile played about his mouth. 'I'm annoyed to see you, but I suspected you had tried a trick like this when you weren't there to wave me off. I didn't quite believe that you'd go for a walk and not be back in time to wish me God speed. You've been crafty enough to have travelled this far as well, knowing that I wouldn't have the time to delay and take you back.' His eyes narrowed. 'I could send you back, of course.'

'But you won't, John? I thought if we're going south then we might as well look for Marguerite as well.' She clutched at a fold of his houppelande and gazed up into his face. 'Please let me come.'

'I should tan your hide,' he said crossly. 'Marguerite's the last person I have on my mind right now. Hasn't it sunk into your head that trying to get Harry and Peter out of Dykemore's clutches could be dangerous? He has the ear of the King!'

'But the King's in France,' she said eagerly.

'He comes home occasionally.'

'Not yet, though. He'll delay till he's married the princess Catherine.'

He had to agree with her. 'But I'm going to travel through the nights sometimes. It'll be a hard ride,' he warned. 'You'll suffer.'

She smiled. 'That should please you.'

A reluctant grin eased his face. 'Let's ride.'

It was like old times travelling together and Louise did get sore and weary; not that she admitted it to John. But he was not impervious to her suffering and he made sure that they stopped often enough for them both to sleep and rest the horses. He asked after his brother and son in towns and inns whenever he could, and never once did he receive an answer to his liking. It was as if they had vanished utterly. He had not really expected anything different but it filled him with self-doubt. Perhaps he was mistaken about Dykemore.

They came to Burford at dusk one day and John knew that he would have to go carefully. If Dykemore was in the town and it got back to him that he had been seen then his advantage would be lost. It would be best if he went to Master Fulcombe who had had Peter in his care. He lived further down the street in one of the old timber and thatch houses, although he had spoken last time John had met him of building a new one of stone. He huddled inside his collar and pulled his hat down over his face as they passed down the high street, barely glancing in the direction of his own house.

Master Fulcombe was a man of enormous height with a mop of grey hair, a large nose and a ready smile. He was surprised to see John but made him and Louise welcome. 'Surely you can stay here,' he said, leading them into a stone-flagged kitchen where a merry fire sent shadows dancing round whitewashed walls and a round, dark-headed woman sat sewing. 'And I reckon I know why you're asking me. That barrel of lard of a priest is firmly ensconced with a neat little guard around him. There was a rumour going the rounds that you'd been and taken the lad off, but I said to the wife that you'd be back.' He waved a hand in the direction of a settle. 'Sit you down and I'll have my good wife bring you some supper.' The woman had risen and was smiling at them.

'That's kind of you, mistress,' said John, and Louise murmured agreement as she sank wearily on a seat. 'Dykemore's there now, you say?' He addressed the master of the house as its mistress bustled over to the fire.

Master Fulcombe nodded. 'Been busy about your business,' he said bluntly. 'Had several familiar faces from round about visiting him. Fetterstone of Newsbury, the clothier, and his mistress, are staying with him right now.'

'You haven't seen anything of my brother or my son?'

Master Fulcombe's eyes widened and he rested one of his great hams of an arm across his knee. 'Peter isn't with you?'

John shook his head and began to tell him what had brought him to Burford. The older man nodded his grizzled head several times. 'He was always trying to take the lad out of my charge but, give your wife her due, she wouldn't let him. I could have the boys keep a watch out for you. Send them up on a couple of errands—spy out the land, like. See if there's anything suspicious going on. Although if he's got guests, can't see how——'

'Neither can I,' said John ruefully. 'But I can only think of here or Oxford.'

'Reckon if your brother and Peter were captives then they wouldn't be travelling on horseback,' said Master Fulcombe. 'Come by waggon—which would take longer.'

'Dammit! Of course,' groaned John, slapping a hand against his head. 'That means we've arrived before them.'

'Which could be a good thing,' put in Louise, yawning. 'We could take them by surprise.'

'Ay! That's right, young master.' Fulcombe's eyes twinkled warmly. 'I reckon the best thing to do is for you to have supper and put your head down. And in the morning we'll get the lads to have a look around. If you take Old Lardy by surprise before he can whistle up reinforcements, then you'll do the job nicely if matters lie the way you reckon.'

John nodded agreement, and the next minute Mistress Fulcombe was setting food before them. The talk became more general. Louise dozed off without finishing her supper.

The next morning she woke to a wintry sun streaming through a window and she was lying on a pallet in the kitchen covered with a blanket. John blew on her face gently and she blinked at him sleepily. 'What is it?'

'You've slept late but that doesn't matter. A waggon's just gone up the alley to the house.'

Louise was fully awake immediately. 'You think it's the one?'

'Could be. Fulcombe's sent one of his prentices to have a look.'

'What do we do?'

'Wait.' John's eyes were bright. 'I don't want Dykemore having an inkling that I'm here. If the lad comes back with the answer we want then we act.'

'What will you do?'

'Get in and get Peter and Harry out.'

'How, if the place is guarded?'

'We've got in before.'

'Ay, but...' Her worried gaze held his. 'There were only a few of them that time.'

He leaned towards her and kissed the tip of her nose. 'Stop worrying. We've got surprise on our side—and I'm not alone.'

'No.' She forced a smile. 'Why do you think he's got so many guards?'

'He's not liked in the area. He's greedy and cruel— one of those churchmen who don't live up to their calling.'

'Is Master Fulcombe a Lollard?' she asked curiously. 'Is that why he's so willing to help you?'

John shook his head. 'No, but he'd like to see changes in the Church and he's a thinking man. He hates the burnings.' He stood, picking up his hat and pulling it down as far as he could over his eyes. 'I'm going to walk up the hill and have a word with the shepherd. Fulcombe's not far away, and the mistress of the house has gone marketing. She left word for you to help yourself to something to eat. And there's water in a pail in the corner for you to wash. If the lad returns before I'm back, Fulcombe will know where to find me.'

Louise nodded and he left her. She yawned widely but did not dally any longer, rising and going to the privy before washing and breaking her fast. Afterwards she planned to go for a walk herself.

Burford was a pleasant little town but not very busy that January morning. Louise found herself the target of several pairs of eyes as she strolled up the steep high street. She paused at the entrance to the passage that led to John's house, and on impulse walked up to it and into the courtyard.

There was no sign of a waggon, but there was a man leaning against the wall of the house by its entrance, and two more, wearing padded and studded jupons, stood as if on guard outside the door of an outbuilding. She began to stroll over to them but one of them began to make his way towards her. 'That's far enough. State your business, lad!'

'I'm new to the town,' she said, smiling. 'I was just finding my way around.'

He glowered at her. 'Then find your way out again. A very important man lives here. A witch-hunter!' he said with relish. 'So you don't want to be hanging about round here.'

'A witch-hunter!' Louise looked suitably scared. 'It's a good house. Fine stabling and storehouses as well.'

'You're a furriner?' The man jerked his head in the direction of the house and his eyes narrowed. 'There's a maid visiting with those from Newbury inside, who speaks like you.'

'Speaks like me?' Louise's pulses jumped.

'Ay. A Frenchy. It's getting that way that there's too many of you around these parts. Now get back to your master before I haul you up before his eminence. He's planning a bit of entertainment tonight, and you could be part of it.' He laughed raucously. 'I wager you won't like it, lad.'

'No.' Louise's smile flashed briefly as she backed away. Then she turned and ran. Her thoughts were chaotic but her hopes were high.

She tore down the street and was sent sprawling when she collided with Master Fulcombe. He seized her by her upper arms. 'What's the rush, lad? You look as if you've found a fortune.'

'Something like it,' she said. 'Where's Jo—Master Milburn? Is he down from the hill yet?'

'No.' He dropped his hands. 'And my prentice was sent packing from yon house,' he muttered with a hint of anger.

'So was I.' Her voice was slightly breathless. 'But there were only three of them outside. We must get inside.'

'Ay, lad. We know that,' he said drily.

She closed her eyes briefly, took a deep breath, and opened them again. 'Not for the reason you are thinking. In my opinion Peter and Harry are not in the house but in an outbuilding that two of the men seem to be guarding.'

His look was keen. 'If he's got guests inside then he'd want to keep them well away from them. But we'd have to be sure about it.'

She nodded. 'Let's find John and work out a plan.'

'Ay, lad.' He gave her a curious glance as they strolled down the street.

John had just got back so Master Fulcombe told him what had happened. As soon as he had finished Louise burst out in her own tongue. 'John, there's a French girl in the house. One of the men told me.'

'What?' John stared at her. 'You think it's Marguerite?'

'Don't you? She was supposed to have come here.'

'Ay! Weeks ago! But it mightn't be her,' he said gently. 'Don't get your hopes too high. Marguerite wasn't the only French child brought to England.'

Some of the excitement faded from her eyes. 'But you'll try and find out if it is her?'

He hesitated. 'We must get Peter and Harry out first.'

'I understand that. But Master Fulcombe seems to think we need to have a look in the house,' she said earnestly, leaning forward across the table. 'Surely there's a chance *then* to see if Marguerite is there?'

'I'm for leaving the house out of the reckoning for now.' He glanced at Master Fulcombe. 'It doesn't make sense to guard an empty outbuilding.'

The older man said gruffly, 'You've got to consider that they could be minding valuables. Confiscated property.'

'Stolen, you mean,' said John, frowning. 'It's doubtful. You'd stow it in the house. We'll go for the outbuilding. Tonight! Hopefully there'll be no moon.'

Louise wanted to mention Marguerite again, but realised that John's thoughts were for his son and brother. She understood, but she felt dissatisfied as she half listened to them making plans for Harry's and Peter's rescue. Knowing John she felt certain that they would not include her. Which was perhaps just as well, she decided suddenly. Convinced that the French girl was her sister, she decided to make her own plan and put it into action that evening.

CHAPTER FIFTEEN

LOUISE darted into the next patch of shadow as she followed John, Master Fulcombe and a group of men up the street. It had been as she had suspected and John had told her that she was staying behind—that a fight was no place for a woman. Considering it wiser to feign anger and sulk rather than behave amenably, she had pretended to be furious with him, speaking of how she had fought in the forest against King Henry's men, but that had not swayed his judgement. He did not want her getting hurt and she was to behave like a sensible woman.

A sigh escaped Louise. He would be furious with her if he found out what she was doing and for a moment she wondered whether to return to the house. Then she squared her shoulders and looked to see where the men were. They were out of sight and she presumed they were already up the passageway that led to the courtyard. Which meant that any second now battle could be joined. Fingering the dagger at her belt, she pulled it out and a few seconds later she entered the pitch-dark alley.

Immediately she could hear scuffling, a shout and a muffled yelp, but she did not hesitate, running to where a lighter shade of darkness could be seen at the end of the alley. It was necessary to act swiftly if she was to take advantage of the disturbance.

The noise of the mêlée taking place seemed much louder once inside the courtyard, and she spared an anxious glance towards the struggle going on around the outhouse but she was only able to make out dark shapes and was unable to tell who was who. She prayed not only for John's safety but that her suspicions were correct about Harry and Peter being there.

Skirting the edge of the courtyard, Louise came to the corner of the house and moved into deeper darkness until she came to the buttery door. No light showed beneath it but only now did she consider that it might be locked. She held her breath as she lifted the latch. The door gave and she slipped inside.

Careful not to trip over any of the jars or flagons on the floor, she made her way to the door and opened it a crack's width on to a lamplit passage. Instantly she heard the sound of hurrying footsteps going past and she froze. A door further along opened. There was a babble of conversation which was soon silenced by a sharp querulous voice, telling someone to be quiet and asking what all the noise was about outside. A man answered that there seemed to be some kind of fight going on and he was sending out more men to deal with the matter. He was told to report back immediately he discovered what it was all about—some other words were added at a lower pitch that Louise did not catch. Doors slammed and footsteps echoed along the passage till they faded away. She presumed that he had gone outside and she waited a few moments, considering carefully, before opening the door and slipping out. The door was left a little ajar.

Louise moved soft-footedly along to the next door and listened. The voices were muffled as they came to her but she stayed, trying to pinpoint one particular one in growing excitement until she was certain that it was not just wishful thinking on her part, but that it really did belong to Marguerite. Then, controlling her spiralling excitement, she made her way back to the buttery and slipped inside to consider her next move.

It was precipitated when a few moments later the kitchen door opened and the sound of light footsteps came along the passageway in her direction. She put an eye to the crack between the door and the jamb and saw her sister carrying a warming-pan. Louise's first instinct was to greet her immediately but common sense asserted itself and she waited until her sister had gone past and was making her way upstairs. She placed her dagger back in her girdle and quietly followed her.

'Marguerite!' The name came out as a husky whisper but the girl on the upper landing started and nearly dropped the warming-pan.

'Sweet Mary, mother of God!' said her sister in French. 'Is it really you, Louise?'

Louise nodded, her throat suddenly tight with emotion. 'Did you think that I would not try and find you?' she said unsteadily, taking the warming-pan from her sister's slack fingers and placing it on the floor.

They hugged each other fervently. 'I never thought that you'd be able to find me and yet here you are!' Her tone marvelled over the fact. 'How did you do it?'

'It's a long story.' Louise held her off from her to gaze at her properly. She wore a simple gown of brown homespun and a linen apron. Her golden hair was almost completely concealed by the white head-dress and veil that surrounded her rosy freckled face, which had filled out in the months since last Louise had seen her, and she felt certain that she had grown. 'You've been treated well?'

'I was unhappy at first. But once I got to know Ned better everything was fine,' she said eagerly. 'He was an archer at Agincourt and can speak some French. He wishes us to wed and——'

'Wed!' Louise's face was a mask of disbelief. 'How? You're far too young! Who is this Ned? You can't possibly marry him!'

Marguerite's full pink lips set in a straight line. 'I can and I am. Not yet, naturally, but when I am fourteen. Ned's father is Master Fetterstone's best weaver and Ned is a skilled craftsman already!'

'But what about going back home?'

Marguerite smiled. 'I will be going back home eventually. Ned has spoken to me of taking up King Henry's offer of monetary help and a home, and he plans for us to settle in Caen.'

Louise was almost speechless, but not quite. 'You'd be happy to do that?'

Marguerite's eyes widened. 'Why not? I'm not going back to the forest. I'd be crazed to want to.' She clutched at her sister's arm. 'You can come with us, Lou. I've told Ned all about you knowing about the clothier's business in Caen. We could find a little house and all be happy together.'

Louise felt as if her world had been turned on its heels. How could she tell her sister that she did not want to go back to France? She moistened her mouth. 'We'll talk about it later. But now you can come with me.'

'I can't do that,' said Marguerite, her mouth setting stubbornly again, as she bent to pick up the warming-pan. 'The mistress has been kind to me. I couldn't leave her just like that. And what about Ned? He got me this job. And besides, where are you going to take me?'

'Only down the street for now. I came here specially to rescue you,' said Louise, getting a little bit angry.

'I don't need rescuing,' retorted Marguerite promptly. 'You tell me where you're staying and I'll come and see you in the morning. Perhaps the mistress can find you some work so that we can be together.'

Louise stared at her, not knowing whether to laugh or cry, or how to reply, feeling let down after being so keyed up about finding her sister. 'You'll find me at Master Fulcombe's down the street on the right,' she said quietly. 'I'd better go. I daren't be late or John will be vexed with me.'

'Who's John?'

Louise took a deep breath. 'He's my lover.'

Her sister's eyes rounded. 'Is he English?'

'Of course he's English,' snapped Louise, flushing.

'But you hate the English!' exclaimed Marguerite.

Louise shifted uncomfortably. 'I don't hate John, and if it weren't for him I wouldn't have found you. Although now I'm wondering why I bothered looking for you.'

'Don't feel like that,' said her sister in an anxious voice. 'You should be glad that I'm happy.'

There was a silence then Louise hugged her. 'I am glad but I don't know what to do now.'

'You must do what you want.' Her sister pulled away from her. 'I'm quite happy with Ned and what he plans. You try and find happiness, Lou. And if it's with this John—well, God bless you. But if you want to come with us to Caen then you're welcome.'

Louise could not help thinking that her sister had grown up since they had parted. They hugged each other again and promised to see other on the morrow and then she made for the stairs, while Marguerite cheerfully carried on with her task.

Louise was halfway down the stairs when a door below opened and she heard a heavy tread on the stone flags. She froze but it was too late.

'You there on the stairs! Come down here immediately!'

Recognising the scarlet-clad Dykemore from John's description when they had been in Kent, she did not move for a moment, remembering the cruelties he had inflicted on her lover.

'Do you think I don't see you?' said the high-pitched voice. 'I'll call out the guard if you don't come down now.'

Louise came to a decision and she ran down the last few stairs. *'Pardon! Je ne comprend pas.'*

A look of annoyance crossed his plump face, and he answered in the same language, 'Who are you, boy?'

She looked gratified, 'Ah, you speak our tongue. I am Mistress Fetterstone's French maid's brother.' She halted outside the buttery door, and knew exactly what John had meant by saying that he looked like a cherub—although she had never seen one so richly clad in velvet and ermine, and his expression at that moment was far from cherubic.

He stared at her from eyes that had the unblinking cold stare of a reptile. 'I've not seen you before and maybe you're connected with that rabble outside. You'd best come in to the parlour and I'll check this with your master.'

'But he's not my master,' she said quickly. 'My sister and I were parted after we were taken by the English and I've been searching for her. We've arranged to meet tomorrow. I was just leaving.' She put her hand to the buttery door and pushed, but it did not give. As she tried to open it he moved forward and seized her arm in a pincer-like grip that caused her to cry out.

'Why such haste?' He smiled unexpectedly as he gazed down at her. 'You're a pretty boy and I could be lenient with you.' He ran his free hand over her left hip and patted her buttock.

Her fear spiralled and she struggled. 'Let me go, you dog,' she demanded in a voice that trembled despite her efforts to control it.

The grip on her arm tightened painfully. 'Come, boy,' he whispered. 'There's no need for you to be frightened of me, but I'll have to lock you up and ask you some questions later. It'll be up to you whether that involves inflicting more pain. But if you please me—then it won't.' His free hand wandered to her buttocks again and he pinched her.

She bit back a cry but she realised suddenly what kind of perversion he might have in mind and she tried to inflict steel into her quivering nerves. She continued struggling but his grip did not shift as he began to force her along the passage.

Louise remembered the dagger in her belt and reached for it. As she brought her arm up, the torchlight flashed on the blade, and he cursed, and tried to turn her so that she would injure herself. She only just averted doing so but instead of plunging the knife into his arm she slashed across his wrist and the blade cut deep into his flesh. A frightened yell escaped him as blood spurted out. She was shocked by the speed with which it gushed, but with a final effort she freed herself and ran in the direction of the front entrance. Just as she reached the door, it opened and two men entered.

The three of them stared at each other and both men swore, before one of them relieved her of the blood-stained dagger.

'Oh, John, thank God!' She flung herself at him. 'I think you'd better come and see,' she stammered. 'I think I might have killed him!'

'What are you doing here?' he demanded, holding her tightly. 'Killed who?'

'The fat cherub.' Her voice shook.

The two brothers exchanged glances. 'Dear Lord,' said John. 'What did he do to you—to make you act in such a way?'

'He captured me and thought me a boy and made a lewd suggestion. I was frightened.'

'We'd best look,' said Harry in a low voice.

John nodded. 'You wait here,' and he would have let go of her but she hung on to his arm.

'I don't want to be alone,' she whispered. 'Please, John.'

He put his arm round her and together the three of them crept along the passage until they came to Dykemore.

He was slumped at the foot of the wall in an ever-increasing pool of blood. His eyes flickered over the twins and for a moment showed astonishment, then pure hatred. Then they closed.

A white-faced Louise whispered, 'I didn't mean to kill him.'

'It's all right,' John said, his brow creasing. 'What to do about it, that's the question.'

'Let's get rid of this,' murmured Harry, calmly wiping Louise's dagger on a fold of Dykemore's robe and hiding it inside his doublet, before taking a jewelled-hilted blade from the dead body, dipping it in the blood and folding Dykemore's fingers about it. 'He tried to defend himself from some revengeful vagabonds, who entered through the front door,' he said quietly.

'Who'll believe that?' whispered Louise. 'Surely someone would have heard them?'

'You'll be surprised at how many will be prepared to take it as true,' said John, under his breath. 'And we've entered and nobody came out to see who we are. Where are the Fetterstones?'

'In that room where you saw Dykemore the last time, I think,' she said softly. 'The servants are in the room next to the buttery.'

He nodded and looked at Harry. 'I want Louise out of here. Best if nobody knows she's been in the house.'

Harry nodded. 'What do you want me to do?'

'Take her into the stables. I'll meet you there. I'll try and get rid of the Fetterstones.'

'John!' Louise clung to his arm. 'Marguerite's here. I've spoken to her.'

He swore softly. 'Do you think she'll mention you to the Fetterstones?'

'I don't know. She talked about getting me a job with them,' she said quietly. 'She doesn't want to come with me and I don't know what to do.'

He stared at her, his expression grim. 'Get yourself out of here. I'll have a talk with her. Didn't you have some female garb in your saddlebag? Get it and change—and Harry, get us a room at the inn. If Louise's sister mentions her to the Fetterstones, she'll refer to her as her sister. But don't leave Louise on her own. She can't be trusted.'

Harry grinned and agreed, and at any other time Louise might have argued with John but she was still in a state of shock and she went with Harry peaceably.

John waited till they were out of sight and then he banged on doors and shouted, 'Thieves, murder!'

Both doors opened and the Fetterstones and the servants came out. 'I've just come home,' John said in shocked and bewildered tones, 'to discover that there's been some kind of fight going on outside and now here's Dykemore dead.'

'Heaven preserve us,' cried Mistress Fetterstone, her mouth gaping open. 'Thieves must have got in!' She clung to her husband's arm, swaying and averting her gaze from the body on the floor.

'Probably thought the house would be empty with my being away,' John said, his expression grave.

'We heard noises and fighting,' said Mr Fetterstone in a strangled tone, 'but he told us to ignore it—that his men would see to all.'

'They probably tried their best,' said John, shaking his head. 'There's several dead men outside, wearing Dykemore's livery. But whoever's responsible has gone now.' He turned to a couple of the menservants. 'Do you think that you could do something about removing your master's body? It's upsetting for Mistress Fetterstone to see it lying here—and if one of you could clear up the mess on the floor...' They murmured agreement. 'In the morning we'll have to inform the sheriff. But it looks clear enough to me what took place here.'

While the servants did as John ordered he gave his attention to the Fetterstones. 'I suggest, sir, that you take your good wife upstairs and make her lie down. Perhaps in the morning you can tell me what business you were transacting here in my house.'

Mr Fetterstone cleared his throat. 'He said that you wouldn't be coming back, Master Milburn. Said there were fears of your being lost at sea.'

'Rumours of my death have been exaggerated before,' said John softly, and he held the other man's gaze steady till it dropped.

'I think we'd best pack and leave this minute,' said Mr Fetterstone. 'We'll find an inn.'

'There's no need for that,' said John, relenting, and considering that he would not want them staying in the inn where Louise was. 'You'll be needed as witnesses. You're welcome to stay. I have some matters to attend to myself with Master Fulcombe down the street.' He paused. 'Is there anybody else in the house?'

'My wife's maid. French girl,' said Mr Fetterstone. 'She's upstairs.'

'Can you send her down without telling her anything about this? It might upset her. I'll wait at the bottom of the stairs.'

The man nodded and hurried his wife upstairs. As soon as they were out of sight the servants set about their gruesome task, and John walked along the passageway. A few moments later Marguerite came down the stairs.

She stared in astonishment at John. 'We've met before. You're the man who abducted me.'

He said gravely, 'Your sister made the same mistake. I'm his brother. I'm John Milburn and I've been helping your sister find you.'

'She mentioned a John.' She frowned. 'I don't understand all this. She said that you were her lover.'

'I love your sister, and if you love her then you won't mention to anyone that she's been in this house this night.'

'But why? I don't understand!'

He took her hand and smiled, and she understood why her sister had set aside all her principles. 'Louise will explain in the morning.' He kissed her cheek. 'Now I have to go. Don't forget what I said. You haven't seen your sister.'

Before Marguerite could ask any questions he had gone striding up the passageway.

Louise had been more than a little anxious as she entered the Fulcombes' stables with Harry. Her saddlebag still hung on a peg on the wall and she took it down. He had left her to go and book a room at the inn and explain to Master Fulcombe and Peter what had happened to Dykemore. Now she changed swiftly into the russet gown she had been wearing when she had left John's father's house.

She was adjusting her veil when John entered the stables.

She turned to him hurriedly. 'Is everything all right?'

'I think so. The Fetterstones believe thieves broke in and killed him. I've had word with your sister and she will keep quiet about you. I told her that you'll speak with her in the morning.'

'Thank you,' she said unsteadily. 'Was she surprised to see you?'

'A little, I fancy—but I explained who I was.' He paused. 'You told her that we were lovers. Why did you do that?'

She flushed. 'I thought she should know.' There was a silence and she licked her lips. 'Are you very angry with me?'

'I was—but you were so frightened. I couldn't be angry for long.' He took a deep breath. 'Louise! There are things we have to decide. Although I don't want to upset you—you're still looking terribly pale.'

A slightly hysterical laugh escaped her. 'It's not every day you kill a man. As if my sins weren't enough as it is!'

'But you didn't mean to do it—and having done so you've done me and a lot of other people a great service,' he said soothingly. 'But you took a damn stupid risk going there.'

'I know. I'm sorry. But at least I did find Marguerite and had a few words with her.'

'What did you discuss?' His eyes were intent as they stared into hers.

Louise toyed with her fingers. 'She has plans to return to Normandy and wants me to go with her.'

'What?' he exclaimed, seizing her hands and squeezing them tightly.

She moistened her mouth and stared down at their joined hands. 'There's a weaver who wants to marry her—take up your king's offer and settle in France! She's told him about me and how much I know about the clothing business. I could live with them.' She paused. 'I could go home and not have to live in the forest. It's a better plan than I ever thought of,' she said slowly. 'And if it's what Marguerite wants—I did after all come to England to find her and go back to France with her.'

He swore softly. 'You can't tell me it's what you want, Louise?'

Slowly she lifted her head. 'It's not the future I dreamed of exactly. But you're forgetting how little I have. Beggars can't be choosers.'

'But you do have a choice,' he said roughly. 'I thought we lived quite amicably when we were snowed up. I made you an offer once and now is the time to choose, Louise.'

'Ay,' she murmured, wishing he had stayed a few feet further away. Having him so close filled her with a longing to bury herself against him and find comfort in his arms. 'I don't doubt that we could be happy for a while. But maybe it would not always be like that. I could make you angry—we would quarrel, and you might consider yourself better rid of me. I love you and I don't think I could bear living with that uncertainty. Better to part now.'

'You've made me angry often, sweetheart.' His voice was soft. 'But never so angry that I wanted to be rid of you. Rather I've enjoyed the making up. I don't want to live without you, Louise.' He paused and his eyes held hers. 'I love you. I want to marry you.'

For an instant Louise could not speak—could not believe him. 'You can't mean it,' she stammered at last. 'You're not thinking straight. I'm a nobody.'

John laughed. 'You've never been a nobody even when dressed in rags.'

'But I've got no dowry. I can't bring you anything.'

'Tonight I wouldn't be surprised if your actions have returned Cobtree to us. Dykemore only had Dorothy and Peter for kin—and she's dead. It'll come to Peter. So you see—you have brought us something.'

He pulled her into his arms and kissed her hungrily and she responded instantly. Their passion for each other rose, carrying them along on its tide, and she was convinced he would take her there and then in the stables, but he stopped abruptly. 'No, we won't. Not yet,' he whispered unevenly. 'We'll wed this night and damn what anyone thinks.' He rose to his feet. 'Button up, my love. We'll go and wake the priest.'

'This is madness,' she whispered, trying to control the excitement inside her. 'What will the Fulcombes think? What will your parents think?'

'They can think what they like.' He seized her hand, pulled her out of the stables and ran her down the street and along a lane till they came to the priest's house.

They did not have to wake the young priest up after all. But when John stated his reasons for coming, he was a little taken aback. 'I understand that you don't want Peter left motherless while you're away, Master Milburn,' he said in a flustered voice. 'But what about the banns?'

'You can marry us without them,' said John promptly. 'I'll pay for the inconvenience, and provide you with some good woollen cloth for winter vestments.'

The priest hesitated. 'I'm not saying it's inconvenient but it's rather unusual.'

'We love each other, man,' said John quietly. 'Isn't that a good enough reason to marry us?'

The priest looked at him and then at Louise, and almost drowned in the depths of her beautiful luminous hazel eyes which pleaded with him. He subdued a sudden longing and married them.

'Do we go and tell the others?' said Louise as they walked hand in hand up the street.

'Tomorrow,' he said. 'You'll be able to tell Marguerite—and you don't have to be worrying that if she goes back to France you'll never see her again. We can do business with her and her Ned. As for Harry, he'll have guessed we've gone to the inn, no doubt. To-night I want you to myself—to love away all your fears, and to talk about the future.'

'I never considered I had much of a future when I first set eyes on you. Especially when you threw me in the sea.'

He smiled and drew her into the shadows and into his arms. 'O thou of little faith. Didn't I tell you that I believed that God had sent you to me?'

'To give us both a little happiness,' she whispered, pressing against him.

'A load of happiness,' he retorted, kissing her passionately, before taking her hand and leading her to the inn and their marriage bed.

The other exciting

MASQUERADE
Historical

available this month is:

OUTRAGEOUS FORTUNE
Marion Carr

Lady Caraddon was a persistent matchmaker for her grandson, Sir James, but he really thought she had gone too far when he had to accompany her to Cornwall to meet Miss Charlotte Forbes. Ambitious, James was intent on carving out a political career in Pitt's government, and he certainly didn't want a wife just yet.

First impressions were not favourable, and James was even more perturbed when he discovered that Charlotte's background held a scandal that could rebound even now in 1786! On her eighteenth birthday, Charlotte was to be told the truth of her parentage, and that she was an heiress — but delegated to break the news, James had no idea of the turmoil that would ensue, or that he would be so thoroughly embroiled in trying to keep Charlotte safe!

TWO HISTORICAL ROMANCES

Masquerade historical romances bring the past alive with splendour, excitement and romance. We will send you a cuddly teddy bear and a special MYSTERY GIFT. Then, if you choose, you can go on to enjoy 4 more exciting Masquerades every two months, for just £1.99 each! Send the coupon below at once to – Reader Service, FREEPOST, PO Box 236, Croydon, Surrey CR9 9EL.

& TWO FREE GIFTS!

- - - - - - - - - - - | **NO STAMP REQUIRED** | - - - - - - - - ✂

Yes! Please rush me my 2 Free Masquerade Romances and 2 Free Gifts! Please also reserve me a Reader Service Subscription. If I decide to subscribe, I can look forward to receiving 4 Masquerade Romances every two months for just £7.96, delivered direct to my door. Post and packing is free, and there's a free Newsletter. If I choose not to subscribe I shall write to you within 10 days - I can keep the books and gifts whatever I decide. I can cancel or suspend my subscription at any time. I am over 18.

Mrs/Miss/Ms/Mr _____ EP04M

Address _____

_____ Postcode _____

Signature _____